Ever alert to the slightest sound, sometimes the Ranger and Tonto carried things a bit too far. This was the *third* time the masked man and Indian woke me for what turned out to be a roadrunner. "Hey, guys, back off on the French Roast!"

The Lone Ranger's
Code of the West

An action–packed adventure in
values and ethics with the
legendary champion of justice.

—◆—◆—◆—

As told to
JIM LICHTMAN

Scribbler's Ink

Library of Congress Catalog Card Number: 95-92728

ISBN: 0–9648591–0–6

FIRST EDITION

To
Francis Hamilton Striker

And

B.B. Mahoney

ACKNOWLEDGEMENTS

Of course, none of this could have been even remotely possible without the help, advice and careful review by several people. My thanks to Mike Jones, Michael Josephson, Dr. James Melton, Deborah Nesset, and Randy Schultz.

I am, of course, deeply indebted to a few key personnel. *(The Ranger and Tonto have their own "people" who had to be consulted. After all, this is the real world.)*

To Dave Holland, the Ranger's Senior Staff Advisor.

Dave Parker, the Ranger's Analyst.

Terry Salomonson, the Ranger's Chief Archivist

Fran Striker, Jr. who held the keys to it all.

and finally... my sincere thanks to the Lone Ranger and Tonto not only for their assistance and active participation but for making this country of ours a better place to live.

CONTENTS

FOREWORD

The Lone Ranger has been—both figuratively and literally—a member of my family since before I was born. In 1932, my dad was writing and successfully syndicating dramatic radio scripts. When one of his customer–stations requested a western, he created a character and submitted a few sample scripts. Some suggestions were returned, Dad made some changes, and on January 31, 1933 The Lone Ranger was launched—the rest is history.

As the author of thousands of radio dramas, numerous novels, comic strips and many of the television episodes, Dad quickly became aware of the impact his characterizations had on the audience. As the popularity of the radio program grew, so did the ethical constitution of the hero. Dad, along with the broadcast executives, the actors and virtually everyone affiliated with the Lone Ranger, recognized the faith and trust bestowed on the character—from both children and adults alike. The public's faith was carefully nurtured and protected through the age of radio on into television, prompting Dad to observe, "The Lone Ranger is no ordinary man. He is a composite of all strong men—he's a legend. He is Americana."

Since my dad's death in 1962, I have been honored many times by accepting awards on his behalf or giving talks about his life and of his Lone Ranger. It has been my pleasure to meet thousands of interesting people, yet I've never met anybody who disliked the Lone Ranger—or felt the character presented a negative image or role model. So when Jim told me of his idea for a book about the Lone Ranger's Code, it immediately captured my interest.

Codes of the West have been written about frequently, but the Lone Ranger's Code has never been fully explained. Codes of the West attempted to define—and perhaps rationalize—law and order, but the Ranger's Code was intended to mold individual character. Codes of the West were territory–wide justifications *of* action, but the Ranger's Code was a set of personal dictates *for* action.

Early on, my dad defined the Lone Ranger's character so other writers could understand the personality of the crimefighter. Surely, bringing the bad guys to justice was a result of the Ranger's code, but it wasn't the code itself. In more than 3,000 radio adventures the Lone Ranger and Tonto's Code is never specifically explained. Rather, it was simply taught by example... by how they lived their lives... by the manner in which they conducted themselves.

The Lone Ranger's Code was one that young fans could admire, emulate, strive to achieve and not only take with them into their adult lives but apply in order to become responsible citizens of a great nation. Many of the people I've met—who were childhood fans—have matured with full possession of those traits of character that the Ranger demonstrated.

Unlike any other country on earth, the Constitution of the United States—along with our Declaration of Independence—focuses, almost exclusively, on the rights of the individual. As a society, we are left to our own devices and intellect to grow our Nation to it's manifest destiny. The Lone Ranger's Code is a vehicle that can contribute to the development of our intellect and our country.

I won't tell you about the years of research Jim invested in this book, or of his proficiency on a vast range of topics. I'll just say that as I read the drafts and the final manuscript I knew that he had fully captured my dad's values and acquired his unique style of writing. I love what Jim has done. My dad would be honored by what Jim has done.

Reading Jim's book will present some challenges to a lot of people. Some will be surprised to find they are rethinking, evaluating and perhaps even changing the way they perceive themselves and others. I'm confident that everyone who reads this book will be surprised at the rewards they find. All can benefit or be refreshed from what Jim has done with the Lone Ranger's Code. There's just one thing that bothers me...

Why didn't I write it?

Fran Striker, Jr.
Runnemede, New Jersey
September 1995

OVERTURE

A fiery horse with the speed of light, a cloud of dust and a hearty, 'Hi–Yo Silver! The Lone Ranger...

With his faithful Indian companion Tonto, the daring and resourceful masked rider of the plains led the fight for law and order in the early western United States. Nowhere in the pages of history can one find a greater champion of justice.

Return with us now to those thrilling days of yesteryear. From out of the past come the thundering hoofbeats of the great horse Silver. The Lone Ranger rides again!

PROLOGUE

What do we care about? What do we stand for? If we all want to do the right thing, then what is the right thing, and can we stand by our beliefs in the face of those who may not agree?

These are a few of the questions I asked myself when I was invited to help write a seminar on values. After researching everyone from Aristotle to Zeno and taking pages of notes, I resolved the following: that the study would be as thorough as possible, that its purpose would be clear and concise, and that it would be the most stunningly enlightening lecture on values in the history of modern American seminars.

This was, of course, all before the dream.

Actually, it was more like a nap. Nevertheless, something, the likes of which I had never seen before, happened. Something shocking. Something inconceivable. It began like this—

Silence, intense and oppressive, gripped the desolate landscape as two lone figures rode toward the town ahead. The taller of the two sat astride a magnificent white stallion and although his face was masked, all who had known him knew that he was as legendary for his remarkable sense of justice and fair play as for his skill with six–gun, rope and horse. His faithful Indian friend was his only companion.

A few miles more and they'd arrive at Pine Needle, a small mining town on the other side of Flint Ridge. It had been a long ride, harder than most but a satisfying one, nonetheless. The Lone Ranger and Tonto had successfully captured Buck Bledsoe and his gang. They retrieved the payroll money stolen from Dave Collins and saved the Lucky Strike mine from imminent bankruptcy, not to mention the jobs of many of the town's small population. All that remained was to ride to the other side of that ridge and they could call it another job well done. But first they stopped to water their horses.

As they do, the Ranger goes to his saddle bags and removes the money. Counting the gold coins by hand, he starts to figure. "Bullets, $10.00; food while tracking the bandits, $3.00 a day for five days, that's $15.00; health insurance, $10; laundry, $2..."

"Don't forget–um horse doctor for Scout shot in gun battle," Tonto says.

"Thanks, Tonto," the masked man said. "That takes care of expenses. Now, our 30% finder's fee should complete the total. Here's your share, Kemo Sabay." The Ranger handed a portion of the proceeds to his trusted friend, then repacked the balance. A moment later, the masked man leaped onto his sturdy horse.

The Indian eyed his share skeptically as he returned to his saddle without a word.

"Let's go, big fella," the masked man said.

"Get–um up, Scout," grumbled Tonto.

"Hi–Yo Silver, Awaaaaay!"

Later, in Pine Needle, after the Lone Ranger and Tonto delivered the money to Dave Collins and left town in their usual uncelebrated manner, a few more facts came to light, disturbing facts. For one thing the Ranger never mentioned anything about expenses or a finder's fee. For another, he told Tonto that they would always split fifty–fifty, but the sharp eyes of the Indian recognized that his take had been reduced by a whopping 15%!

And what about the payroll money? How is Dave going to pay all the people in the town he supports without the right amount? Who's going to "eat" the difference?

After deducting for expenses plus a little "put–by" for himself, Dave tells his workers that he'll divide the money in a fair–shared sacrifice.

"Now, hold on, Dave."

"Yeah, we got families to feed, too!"

"Why not just file for the in'surance?"

Dave explains that his "liability coverage will skyrocket if Big Rock Insurance gets wind of the robbery and that'll kill any possibility of raises in the fall."

Quickly, the townspeople agree.

"Okay."

"That's fair."

"Don't want to lose our raises!"

However, one disgruntled worker, Foreman Ed, decides that Dave's offer isn't good enough and begins to pocket a few extra nuggets from the mine when no one is looking. "After all," he rationalizes, "Dave owes it to me. I work hard and I need every bit I can get."

Back on the prairie, after a hearty meal, Tonto's tethering the horses for the night when he notices that the masked man has fallen asleep. Quietly, the Indian walks over to his companion's saddle bags and retrieves his missing share. After a second thought, he "bags" a few silver bullets for himself. "Besides," he reasons, "Ranger never start retirement I.R.A. him promise Tonto last year."

HOLD IT!

What's going on here? Lying, cheating, stealing? Where is the honesty, the respect and has anyone seen fairness lately?

The nap provided more than a colorful dream, it proved to be a provocative opening to the seminar. The audience not only sat in astonishment at all the inequities but were appalled to learn of the many committed by the Lone Ranger and Tonto, the two people dedicated most to upholding law, order and justice in the early western United States.

BUT...

However unusual the dream was, you might have trouble believing what happened next. I mean, the story I'm about to tell you is so strange and incredible, you'll never forget it, but every single word is true!

EPISODE ONE

Ambush at Virtual Pass

Sand swirled and eddied behind my back as I trail–surfed my bike near Gopher Creek trail. The ride was harder than most. I usually hit the torture run whenever I was angry or confused about something. Today was a real medal winner; angry AND confused. I must have hit most every rut and chuck hole in a two–square mile area. How could I be so stupid as to be caught in a lie? Well, how could I lie in the first place!? Not that I'm some pillar of virtue or anything but... I screwed up!

"Turning down a narrow pass, I wondered, "what would the Lone Ranger have done?" With *Blues Traveler* on my portable CD, I never noticed the dust devil that swept over me from behind. I pulled my headphones off and jerked to a stop as it passed. That's when I first heard the voice.

"Over here, Jim."

I turned and there, silhouetted against a crimson sunset, stood the tall figure of... the Lone Ranger. I recognized the big, snow–white stallion conveniently tied to a Joshua tree.

"You," I said, with a dumb look on my face.

He just smiled. "You sounded like you needed me."

"I did? For what?"

"You tell me. It's your moral dilemma."

Walking into the sun, I kept my eyes fixed in a squint to study the form more closely. Remarkable though it was, it just had to be him. I mean, how many people go around wearing a brace of forty–fives strapped low on either side, a black mask and a white Stetson? *(Outside L.A., of course.)*

Instinctively, he talked the language of a cowboy on the trail. "Do you have something cool to drink?"

"Sure." I parked my bike by a clump of brush near Silver, pulled a well–iced Snapple from my pack and offered it to him. Despite his easy manner, he remained ever alert and watchful as he took a long swallow. Then, he gave me one of those "knowing" smiles of his.

(This is one of those hard–to–describe, had–to–be–there kind of things. But it was like he could anticipate what I was thinking.)

"Why don't you sit down?" he said, pointing to a blanket spread near the campfire. "You'll find it easier to talk."

As I dropped my pack, a thousand questions came to mind. After all, how many times do you get to talk to a genuine champion of justice? Of course, most of his answers turned out to be not too surprising.

Both he and Tonto shared laundry chores. Yes, they did pack an extra change of clothes including, what he called, his "cowpoke" and "dude" outfits. These were clothes that he'd use to disguise himself whenever it became necessary to go into town to dig up more information. It went on like this for maybe half an hour or so when he sensed I was leading up to something.

"Do you ever...naaa."

"Go ahead, Jim," he said. "Ask anything you like."

"Well," I hesitated, "...ever wear the mask to bed?"

It was the first time I heard him chuckle. "Why don't

you tell me why you are angry and confused?"

I felt a little embarrassed. "Oh, that." I mean, who wants to go around confessing to the Lone Ranger about... Jeez, I forgot! He can read my......

He smiled back at me.

I stared into the campfire thinking of how to begin this thing when it all sort of spilled out. "Damn it, I'm mad! I'm mad because I thought I was trying to help, but all I did was screw up!"

"Why don't you tell me what happened."

"It's too late! It won't change anything."

"Perhaps by talking about it, you can open yourself to view things from a new and higher perspective."

Oh, that's cute. "LOOK, I'M FACING A MORAL CRISIS, HERE, AND I DON'T KNOW WHAT TO DO ABOUT IT!"

After the echo died down, he just looked at me quietly.

I shrugged an apology. After all, he wasn't the cause of my problem. I was. I could tell him what happened, but what would he think? What would he say?

I watched as he leaned back and took another swallow of his drink. I can't explain why, but somehow I trusted him.

"It began a few weeks ago," I started. "I was with a friend and his nine–year–old daughter in their backyard. He was in the process of cutting down a tree when it snapped unexpectedly and caught his arm, nearly ripping it off. Of course, we all jumped into my truck and drove to the emergency room.

"At the hospital, the emergency team immediately got to work on him. He had lost a good deal of blood and for awhile, things didn't look good.

"In the meantime, while trying to calm his daughter, and reach his wife at work, the nurse asked me about medical insurance. I took the forms back to the waiting room with me along with John's wallet. That's when I discovered that he had absolutely no insurance. I remembered he was between construction jobs and for whatever reason, he just didn't have any in—between coverage.

"The nurse came back and asked if I knew my friend's insurance carrier as it was the policy of the hospital to have this information. It seemed that John would need a transfusion and additional care. Without the insurance, he would have to be moved to another facility that dealt with uninsured patients.

"Faced with the idea of postponing treatment, I gave the nurse *my* insurance card. I figured, until we could sort things out later, John would just be me. It was much simpler and besides, he needed treatment now.

"In the waiting room, little Becky looked at me and knew something wasn't right when I started to tell the nurse that the man in the emergency room was me instead of her dad. I explained the situation as best I could."

"But that's a lie," she said.

"Yes, I know, but right now, your dad needs treatment and I want him to get the best possible care right here."

She gave me a puzzled look.

"Sometimes," I explained, "it's okay to lie for really important things."

"Of course, at the time, I thought I was doing the right thing. I mean, when you're faced with the welfare of a friend, you do everything you can to help, don't you?"

The Ranger just listened without making any kind of judgment.

"Later," I continued. "I sorted things out with the insurance company and John had an uncle who offered to pay the hospital bills. So, nobody was hurt in the deal."

"Well, then," he asked, "what's your problem?"

"The problem," I said, "happened yesterday. Becky came home with a note from the school principal. It seems she let a friend copy the answers from her page on a test they were both taking, then lied to cover it up. Her teacher was surprised at her behavior, but more shocked when she told the principal that a friend of her daddy's told her that it was all right to lie for really important things.

"Because she cheated and lied, Becky was suspended from school for several days and her grade in class was lowered one point. And all because she had seen me lie to the nurse at the hospital."

"I see."

"Although John understands and was grateful I helped him, Becky's mother was not happy about my teaching her daughter that it's okay to lie.

"The whole incident with Becky made me realize the many ways I rationalize and justify lots of things, all for the sake of helping others or myself. So, that's it," I said. "I'm angry about what happened and confused about where I go from here."

He didn't say anything right away and the silence felt awkward. "How would you have handled it?" I asked.

"Jim," he began, "the Lone Ranger is truthful."

I stood there for awhile, waiting for the rest of it when I realized from his expression that he'd finished!

"That's it? That's your great advice?" I pour out my guts to the Lone Ranger for a little helpful advice and... "Didn't you ever face a crisis? Oh, of course not. You're the Lone Ranger. The good guy. Mr. Hero who always does what's right."

A strange look came to his eyes that suggested there was more there than perhaps I knew. "Do you really believe that, Jim?"

"Well, everyone knows the story of the Lone Ranger. How you and your brother and those other Texas Rangers were ambushed by the Cavendish gang, and everyone was killed except you. And how Tonto came along and nursed you back to life in that cave."

He stared out at the mountains. "I remember when I was as angry and confused as you. I remember how helpless I felt."

"You... helpless? Get–outta–town!"

"You didn't think I just walked out of that cave with all these values and a mission of justice without going through some serious changes, did you?"

"Well... I guess... I never thought about it much."

"That's just not how it happened, Jim." He got up and began to walk around the campfire. It was a moment or two before he began again. "I was full of rage and vengeance. And I had every good reason to be. My friends were dead. My brother was dead. And it wasn't even a fair fight." The emotion showed in his face as he recalled the events. "It was lucky for me that I was wounded so badly that I couldn't move for several days.

"All I wanted to do was to recover so I could spend as long as it took to track down each of the killers and..." he broke off here, from the intensity of the memory.

He sat down and stared into the fire. "I must have passed out because the next thing I remember is hearing my brother's voice. During those first angry hours in that cave he seemed to speak to me. 'The best way of avenging yourself,' I heard him say, 'is not become like the wrong–

doer.'

"Many times I tried to ignore his voice. Several times I even argued with it, quoting from the Bible our mother used to read to us: 'An eye for an eye, do unto them, as thou has done unto you.'

But Dan's voice remained as clear and strong as ever.

"When I felt helpless, he would reassure me: 'A person of strong character nurtures that character through fruitful action.' When I would despair, he would inspire hope: 'a person of character strengthens himself constantly.'

"Throughout the many painful days I spent in that cave, Tonto's expert aid and Dan's words are what restored me. 'The Lord is my shepherd; I shall not want. He leadeth me in the paths of righteousness for His name's sake.' It was then that I focused on justice instead of vengeance, on truth instead of justification.

"Every action we take, Jim, no matter how trivial, sends out ripples of effects, many times unknown to us. At least you understand what effect your momentary lapse in truth had on Becky." He stopped and looked at me thoughtfully. He poured what was left of his drink over the dying fire. "We better turn in. We're pulling stakes at dawn."

"*We?*" I asked.

"Sure," he smiled. "This place is a little exposed and I thought you might like to ride with me to a more secluded camp a few hours from here where we can talk more."

Leaning back on my roll I realized there was much I had to learn about what he called, 'qualities of character.' I yawned a good night as I pulled my blanket over me.

(But I kept one eye cracked to see about this mask thing. Unfortunately, the steam from the fire blocked my view and when I finally could see, he had rolled over.)

EPISODE TWO

The Secret of Red Rock Canyon

The moon was still high, just before daybreak, when the masked man nudged me awake.

"Where are we heading?" I said, throwing the last of my stuff together.

"Where it's a little safer." He finished tying his gear to Silver then mounted the horse in one swift move.

I quickly pulled up alongside him on my bike. "Alright, let's rock 'n roll!"

Instantly, Silver did 0–45 in about ten seconds. I was eatin' dust for the better part of twenty minutes when the masked man circled back and slowed to a more manageable pace.

The ride to the campsite gave me a chance to mull over more questions. Who better to explain how to recognize the right thing and how to stick by it? Who better to ask about values and ethics than a legendary figure of justice? And what about that silver mine he's reported to own?

(This is the part of the story where you follow the meandering red line across a topo map as the Ranger and I travel over all kinds of desert terrain until, finally, we reach our destination in the middle of, where else? "Uncharted territory.")

Silver slowed to a walk as we approached a tall, seemingly impenetrable stretch of rocks. The masked man moved toward a spot where two gigantic slabs of red sandstone came together, then he disappeared.

I jumped off my bike and followed him through a gap in the rocks that opened up about fifty feet inside. Red Rock Canyon was perfect. No matter what time of day, the deep walls offered plenty of protection from the scorching sun and the maze of rock corridors made it virtually impossible for anyone without expert knowledge to follow.

After maneuvering through a series of passages, he dismounted and slipped through another narrower slit in the wall. Hugging one side of the rock, I barely squeezed through with my pack and took my first look at what was obviously his base camp.

Carved out of the rocks and well hidden near one side flowed a small, clear stream. On the other, a cool overhang protected a cache of supplies: stores of food, blankets, saddle equipment, along with plenty of sacks of *Purina Horse Chow*. On the far side hung two sets of perfectly unwrinkled pants and shirts.

"Drip–Dry," he said in reply to my unvoiced question.

Something else caught my attention now. Molds, used in making the Ranger's famous silver bullets, sat on a couple of boxes of cartridges, along with a keg of gunpowder.

He finished tying a feed bag to Silver. "That was quite a story you told back there."

"Excuse me?"

"The story for that seminar, really very amusing."

I stretched out my roll feeling a little embarrassed.

"No need to feel uneasy, Jim," he said. "You told a good tale and helped a lot of folks understand just what it's like when people act without a strong code of values in their lives. Tonto and I found the whole thing quite enjoyable. Tonto especially liked the part about the I.R.A."

"By the way, where is Tonto?" I asked.

"He went for supplies. He should be back soon." He gave me another one of those "knowing" smile things as he sat down on his bed roll. "So," he asked, "what shall we talk about?"

I began by asking him many of the same questions I had been asking myself. "What's most important to you? What are your values? And how do you know you're doing the right thing even when it doesn't involve breaking the law?"

"Jim," he said, in that stirring baritone voice, "the Lone Ranger is a doer, not a talker."

(You just have to admire the way a legendary figure is able to talk about himself in the third person like that. And he does it with great humility, I might add.)

"Nevertheless," he continued, "if what I share with you can help you and others understand what it means to live by a code of honor, it can only make this country of ours stronger."

(The Ranger is very big on patriotism, I discovered, although I had absolutely no luck in determining his party affiliation. What with all the traveling he does, it must be hard to register.)

The air grew thick with an impending storm, as he started a small campfire. I pulled a couple more drinks from my pack and offered him one as I grabbed my notepad.

The Ranger stared pensively at the rain starting to fall. "I remember a storm similar to this," he began. "Tonto and I were riding to a town in the northwest part of the Utah territory. We were on a mission for the Governor." He leaned back and spoke slowly, telling his story as if he were reading from some journal in the back of his mind.

~

The town of Rock Stone had grown prosperous over the last several years due to the hard work and persistence of many of the local ranchers. Lately, though, times were tough. Several valuable pieces of land had been lost to foreclosure and even accidental death. However, the one man who seemed to prosper through it all was Jeremy Hargrave.

Having moved from the East several years earlier, Hargrave had risen to become President of the Bank of Rock Stone and had done quite well for himself... too well, in fact. While ranchers in the area were taking it on the chin, the banker was making money from high interest loans to speculators. He used the money to buy a variety of risky investments called secondaries, for himself. Lately, the market had begun to sour. As a result, he kept appropriating larger sums to cover his losses.

Late one afternoon, a grim–faced man who also knew the secret of Hargrave's success stepped from behind the shadows in his office. Although no one recognized him, he was known to the law as the Black Hood.

The Hood had been absent from the territory for awhile, or so that's what most lawmen thought. What they didn't know was that for the last six months he had become Hargrave's business partner. And judging from his manner, it was easy to see that the outlaw was not the type of partner who liked to be kept waiting.

"I told you, Hood, after that bank examiner comes, you'll get your share of the Mason ranch."

"And I told you when you hired me that I'd have to be movin' on," the Hood said with a firm look. "I done your accident. Now, I want my money."

"These things take time. You knew that when I got you that job out at the Mason ranch. The executor of the estate has to complete a thorough search for the last living heir. Joe and Rita only had the one son and he left here ten years ago and hasn't been seen since. The papers'll clear any day. And when they do, you'll get your split. In the meantime, you continue cowpokin' out at the ranch liked we planned and keep clear of the streets. I don't want anybody seeing you hang around here."

"Relax, Hargrave, most people only recognize me like this." With that, the oily outlaw pulled his well–known black hood over his head.

The banker jumped from his chair. "Take that thing off, you fool." He yanked the black bag off the man's head. "You want someone to recognize you?"

The big man laughed as he moved toward the back door. "You better wrap things up soon, Hargrave."

A few miles outside of town, a lean man in a horseman's duster tried hard to ignore the driving rain as he rode his horse down one side of the river. Looking for a place to cross, the man noticed a pony carrying a small girl just ahead of him on the trail. Separated from her parents, she was not only lost but scared. She was almost jolted out of her saddle by sharp flashes of lightning. Snake River had become a raging torrent.

Suddenly, a bolt struck a large pine sending the shattered pieces of the tree in all directions. The man watched as a piece struck the girl's pony throwing her into the brutal river water.

Without a thought to his own safety and through tremendous effort, the man on the black horse managed to pull the girl from the river. He wrapped her in his blanket, and set her on his horse. Then, he slowly continued making his way through the storm. Just then, a broken limb caught the side of his head throwing him into the water. The horse bolted into the night with the girl clinging tightly to it's back.

It was long past midnight but a pale light still burned in the private office of Jeremy Hargrave. Poring over his books, he was desperately looking for an opportunity, any opportunity that could take him out from under the burden of his own dire consequences. That opportunity was about to find its way to his door.

Hargrave was startled by a heavy knock at his back door. The banker pulled a six–gun from a drawer and cautiously moved to the door. "Who's there?" All at once, the wet and battered shape of the man from the river collapsed as soon as the door was opened.

Dragging him inside, the banker began to look him over. "Don't quite recognize you from these parts, stranger," he said, as he propped him up against a wall, "but from the size of that lump on your head I'd..." Hargrave stopped when he felt a large bulge in the man's jacket. "Why there's over $1,600 dollars in this wallet! How'd someone the likes of you come by so much cash money?" The banker reasoned that the man had to be an outlaw on the run. Quickly, his mind raced with a scheme.

"Looks like this is your lucky day, stranger," Hargrave said. "Lucky for you and me, both," he added as he blew out the oil lamp. The silence of the night was shattered by a loud crash and a gun shot.

Moments later, Sheriff Eddie Edwards burst into the back office. "Who's there?" Edwards said, pointing his rifle into the dark pile on the floor. "Okay, stand up slow, the two of yuh's." Edwards recognized Jeremy Hargrave in the dim light, then turned his rifle to the remaining figure on the floor. "All right, fella, no tricks. I got my gun pointed straight at yuh..."

Hargrave lit a lamp as Edwards pressed closer to make an astonishing discovery. "Why, looky there! It's... the *Black Hood!*"

The following morning, Tonto, in town for supplies, found many of the townspeople talking about the attempted robbery and the capture of the Black Hood. He was tying Scout to the hitchrack when he overheard Hargrave and the sheriff.

"And if you hadn't come along when you did, Sheriff, he would have gotten away with over $1,600 dollars. And me with the bank's examiner in my office this very minute."

"Don't you go worryin' about it, Jeremy. I got him safely locked up. Reckon, though that conk on the head you gave him was pretty good. The varmint can't remember a blame thing 'bout last night, much less his own name."

Their conversation was cut short as Edwards caught sight of Manuel Gonzales, a local farmer, riding into town screaming for the sheriff. The frantic man jumped off his horse and charged the burly sheriff.

"Now, hold your hosses, Manuel. You know I can't understand a thing you're saying."

"Him say, need help, quick," Tonto said, interpreting the distraught man.

"You understand what he's saying, Indian?"

Tonto translated as Gonzales continued. "Him say, need help, find daughter. Little one lost in storm. Look all over. No find–um. You help Manuel?"

"Of course we will, Manuel," the sheriff said as he walked the worried farmer into his office. "I'll round up some of the boys, pronto!"

No one noticed as Tonto mounted his horse and rode out of town.

Later, that afternoon, a man with a thick mustache in a gray three–piece suit closed the last of the bank's ledgers. "Well, Mr. Hargrave, I don't think I need to see anything else."

Hargrave felt safe for the moment. "Everything meet with your satisfaction?"

"I think so." The gray haired man headed for the door, then stopped a moment. "Oh, one more thing," he said.

"Yes?"

"I was wonderin' when you intend to fix that leaky roof?"

"Leaky roof?" the banker asked.

"Much of that cash I counted was pretty wet." said Greenfield.

A look of relief crossed the banker's face as he explained. "We don't have a leaky roof, Mr. Greenfield. The bank was almost held up last night during the storm. The thief was just about to leave with the money, when I was lucky enough to overtake him. Happened, almost on the very spot where you're standing! The sheriff has the man safely locked up for trial."

"Really?" Greenfield said, folding his glasses neatly into their case. The elderly examiner moved toward the front door. "I'll be filing my report in the next few days. I'll see you get a copy."

"Thanks," nodded Hargrave as he watched the man leave the bank and move down the street. He was too busy with other work to notice Greenfield enter the Post Office.

(At this point in his story I started to fidget. I'm sorry, but I was beginning to wonder whether the masked man loved the sound of his own words, liked a lot of windy detail, or both! While I knew this thing wouldn't have a prayer of making it to Short Attention Span Theater, I also knew there had to be something important in all that he said. So, I listened

patiently. Sometimes I would stop him to get my bearings, like, "where were you when all this was happening?, where did Tonto ride off to in such a hurry and excuse me for asking, but what has this got to do with values?" "I was just getting to that, Jim," he smiled.)

Tonto hurried out of town to search for the girl lost along the Snake River. He continued long after the sheriff and his men had returned to town. The force of the storm had practically wiped out any sign of a trail.

However, Tonto was like no other tracker. It wasn't long before the sharp eyes of the Indian found something. "Look like horse scared, here. Tracks move in many direction until..." Suddenly, the Indian caught sight of something in the distance. It was the black horse whose tracks he spotted near the river. He was in the process of untangling the horse's reins from the brush, when he heard soft moans.

Later that night, at their campsite outside of town, Tonto told the Lone Ranger about his success in finding the little girl.

"Tonto, I'm proud of you. But it's nothing less than I'd expect from you."

(Whooooa, could this be a tip–off about some value, here? Oh, forget it. I haven't got a clue as to where he's going with this yet.)

The masked man and Indian finished their dinner as they continued their conversation.

"What did you find out at bank?" Tonto asked.

"The disguise worked perfectly, along with my letter of identification. It's been a long time since I've studied bookkeeping, Tonto, but I don't think things have changed much."

"What do you mean?" the Indian asked.

The Ranger added another stick to the fire. "I mean, Jeremy Hargrave has done some pretty fancy footwork to keep things afloat for so long."

"Do you think he's a crook?"

"The Territorial Governor wouldn't have sent us down here, Tonto, if he didn't already have serious questions about Hargrave. The banking system in this country is new and growing. For the economy to prosper, people have got to be able to trust that their money is safe when they put it in the bank. It's our job to see that it stays safe. Unfortunately, I couldn't find enough hard evidence to prove anything, yet. But..," he added, "Postmaster Grigsby is checking something for me. I may know more, tomorrow."

"Hargrave sounds a little more insidious than we may have first believed."

("WHOA! Time out. Stop the story, masked man."

"Yes, Jim?"

"I'm a little hazy on the Tonto thing."

"What do you mean?"

"How come Tonto's talking like that?"

"Like what?"

"You know. He talks... normal."

"Of course he talks normal. He's always talked normal."

"Huh?"

"Work with me, Jim. Tonto has not changed, you have, society has. In my time, people heard what they expected to hear and they expected anyone from Tonto's background to sound different. So, in the stories, that's exactly how he sounded."

"Hmm."

"Shall we continue?")

"Do you have a plan, Kemo Sabay?" Tonto asked.

"I'm not sure, Tonto. Jeremy Hargrave is a smart man. He foreclosed on one ranch about three months ago and is now in the process of acquiring the Mason spread and he's done it all in a perfectly legal way."

The masked man stared silently into the fire for awhile. The Indian was always able to recognize when he was working things over in his mind. After a moment, the Lone Ranger continued. "Hargrave mentioned something about a hold–up attempt. Did you hear anything?"

Tonto told of what he overheard between Edwards and Hargrave. "The sheriff said that the man who tried to rob the bank last night was the Black Hood."

"The Black Hood." The Lone Ranger thought this a curious added development. "The law has been looking for him for some time."

"But," the Indian continued, "the man in jail doesn't remember. Edwards said he must've been hurt bad in the fight because he can't remember a thing."

"Strange." The masked man turned back to the warm fire. "The Black Hood is an outlaw of extraordinary strength. It's not like him to lose a fight with a man who works in a bank all day. You said he was positively identified as the Black Hood?"

"Well, he was caught wearing a black hood," Tonto said. "And no one has ever seen the face of the Black Hood."

"Yes, that's true. However, our friend, Marshal Jim Briggs, was almost killed by the Black Hood six months ago. He is the only man who has ever been close enough to notice one telltale piece of identification." The masked man began to extinguish the fire and pack his gear. "I think we should pay a visit to this man in jail, Tonto. But there is something else I would like to look at first."

Later, out at the Mason ranch, Jeremy Hargrave and the

real Black Hood were finalizing their plans.

"I tell you, Hood, things couldn't get any better. First that drunken cowpoke wanders into my office with more than enough money to balance the books. Then, that bonehead sheriff thinks he's captured the Black Hood."

The two men shared a laugh of delight at their good fortune.

"And to top it off," the banker added, "the man was injured so badly in the storm he can't even remember his own name."

"Nice," the Hood said calmly. "Now, when do I get my split so's I can get outta here?"

"You can come down to the bank tomorrow and pick it up. $1,500, just like we agreed," Hargrave said with a smile. "Meet me there at eight. That's an hour before we open. That way, I can give you the cash without anyone nosin' around."

A short time later, two figures on horses raced across the moonlit expanse toward the town of Rock Stone.

(One guess as to who the racing figures in the moonlight are.. Bingo!

This, of course, signified that we were fast approaching what was well known in Ranger lore as the "Showdown" scene. That's the scene where the masked man's keen mind is pitted against that of the bad guy. Then, through a careful combination of acquired knowledge and some slick action, the Lone Ranger triumphs in the end. Now, back to our story.)

"But Sheriff," the man in the cell pleaded, "I've never been mixed up in anything like a robbery before."

"We've been over this a huner'd times, boy," Edwards said as he blew on his hot morning coffee.

"Maybe Mister Hargrave is mistaken."

"Maybe, nuthin'!" Edwards leaned back, his chair squeaking with the strain. "I may not know much about you mister but I do know Jeremy Hargrave, and, in this town his word's as good as gold."

At that moment, the Lone Ranger walked through the back door. Edwards froze. "Why, you're masked!"

"Easy, Sheriff, I mean you no harm."

"I don't cotton to masked owl–hoots walkin' in and..." suddenly, the burly lawman recognized Tonto walking in behind his companion.

"Tonto," Edwards cracked. "Say, what is this?"

"You remember Tonto?"

"I remember you done me a good turn by finding Manuel's daughter and I'm willin' to be partial tuh ya, but..."

The Lone Ranger removed a small object from his gun belt. "Maybe this will help," he said as he placed the shiny object in the sheriff's hand.

"You know what this mean?" the Indian said.

Edwards examined the silver cartridge closely. "Leapin' catfish!" Edwards almost fell out of his chair. "...then yore the..."

"Sorry to have startled you, Sheriff. "

"Never mind about that. Just tell me what I can do for you and Tonto?"

The masked man relaxed, realizing that he could always count on people of character like Edwards. "Sheriff, as hard as it may be for you to believe, the man you're holding is NOT the Black Hood."

"NOT THE?... why, I caught this man myself. And he was wearin' a black hood, carnsarn it!" barked Edwards.

"Six months ago," the Ranger explained, "Marshal Jim

Briggs was shot in Abilene by the Black Hood. He got a close look at the man's hands and noticed a small, crescent–shaped scar on his left hand."

Edwards checked the prisoner's hands himself, then threw his own hands up in disgust. "Well, dad blame it, then who in tarnation is this feller?"

"I'm not sure just yet, but I think I know of a way you can capture the real Black Hood," said the Ranger, "but, I'm going to need your help."

At exactly 8:05, Jeremy Hargrave's expert fingers counted out fifteen one–hundred dollar bills into the hands of the Black Hood. "It's been a pleasure doing business with you, mister Hood."

The Hood just stuffed the cash in his pocket.

At that moment, an unexpected visitor entered through the back office.

"Mister Greenfield!" Hargrave said. "You surprised me."

The Hood started to go for his gun but Hargrave checked him with a small hand gesture. He was too close to the end for any mistakes.

"Excuse me, Hargrave, but I thought I would..." the examiner stopped as soon as he noticed the two men in conversation. "Sorry. I thought the bank didn't open 'till nine."

"Mr. Peterson is a special customer of the bank and, well, he's leaving on the nine o'clock stage and needed some additional cash for his trip."

"No need to explain Hargrave," Greenfield said. "I just need one more thing before I finish my report."

"Silly, really," Greenfield blushed, "but I lost my tally sheets on the cash totals. Just need to draw up a new sheet is all." Greenfield quickly brushed past the nervous banker, pulled the drawer open and began counting the cash. "So, you just go on with your conversation, there."

Hargrave escorted the Black Hood to the front door. "As I was saying, mister Peterson, this should see you through your cattle buy, but if you should need more, just let me know." They were almost to the door.

The Hood nodded. "I think I've got everything I need." His hand rested on the door knob.

"Just a second, mister Hargrave," the examiner called out. "I can't seem to find the withdrawal slip for mister Peterson's transaction, here."

"Now how do you like that!" Hargrave said, trying to mask his apprehension.

The Lone Ranger wasn't sure just how long he could maintain his disguise. As he walked around toward the two men he kept one hand close to the silver–plated forty–five he had hidden in his coat pocket, just in case. "That's funny," he said perusing a journal. "According to these ledgers, the only record I find of a mister Peterson shows the account closed last year."

The Black Hood pushed Hargrave to one side. His gun cleared leather faster than the Lone Ranger expected.

"EEE–OWWW!" The bandit shuddered from the sting of a silver bullet that came from Tonto's gun. The Hood's six–gun flew from his hand, hitting the floor as Tonto moved inside through the rear door.

Instantly, Sheriff Edwards walked in the front door and held his gun square in the back of the Black Hood. "Move agin' and my aim won't be as partickl'r."

The Lone Ranger eased his gun back inside his coat pocket before anyone noticed.

"Sheriff, I'm glad you showed up," Hargrave said. "This Indian was trying to..."

"Relax, Hargrave. That Indian is working with me." Edwards turned the outlaw toward him. "Hold out yore left hand," Edwards commanded.

"What for?" the outlaw growled.

Edwards jabbed the Hood's side with his gun muzzle. "Mister, yore in no position to argue."

The big man obliged as the sheriff found the scar the Lone Ranger spoke of earlier. "Dog gone, if it ain't so!"

"Sheriff, what's going on here?" Jeremy asked.

"Looks like you were almost hoodwinked agin'. This time by the real Black Hood."

"Hold your guns on him, boys." The nervous banker quickly backed away from the outlaw. "Sheriff, this man posed as a cattleman from Texas."

"He's lyin' through his teeth," snapped the Hood.

Hargrave didn't notice the Lone Ranger, still disguised, silently nod to the sheriff.

"Reckon, you all better come down to the office," Edwards said, "so's we can get this down right." He pushed the Hood out the door as the others followed.

A short time later, the Ranger, still posing as Greenfield, was handed a list of names by Grigsby. It was the same list he had given the Postmaster the day before. "You're quite sure of this, Mr. Grigsby?"

"Mister," the old Postmaster said, as he pointed down the street, "you just take a gander down at the cemetery there and see fer yerself."

Meanwhile, back at the jail.

"Sheriff, you're making a mistake!"

"Don't listen to him!"

"Fresh coffee, Sheriff?"

"SHUT—UUUUPPP! all of yuhs!" The room fell silent under the sheriff's roar as he pulled a cup of coffee from his deputy's hands. He took a long swallow before he sat comfortably behind his desk. "Now, then," he said taking his time, "first things first." He glanced in Tonto's direction.

The Black Hood stood at the bars to his cell. "Sheriff, I can tell ya' what really happened here."

Edwards laughed so hard he almost spilled his coffee. "The day I take the word of a thievin' polecat like the Black Hood is the day they take me to the loony bin!"

Hargrave moved closer to the cell holding the Hood. "Don't believe him, Sheriff. I've heard the Black Hood is plenty smart."

"Not as smart as you, Hargrave." The Lone Ranger walked through the back door.

Hargrave stammered in surprise. "It's... it's another one of the gang, Sheriff!"

Suddenly, the Black Hood's hand shot out and grabbed a fistful of the banker's shirt. "You schemin' skunk. Sheriff, ask him how he hired me to work out at the Mason ranch."

That's a lie!" the banker screamed.

"Ask how he planned it so's Joe and Rita would get caught in the barn during that fire."

"NO!" the banker pleaded.

"Yer not only a crook but a coward tuh boot, Hargrave!" the Hood cried as he pulled the banker closer to the bars.

"Take it easy," the Ranger said in a calm voice. "He'll get all that's coming to him."

"Who is this man, Sheriff?" Hargrave demanded.

"Relax, Jeremy," Edwards said. "The masked man and Tonto work on the side of the law."

The Ranger stepped closer. "Sheriff, Hargrave is the real crook here."

"This is outrageous!" the banker shouted.

"Let the masked man have his say, Jeremy." Edwards turned to the Lone Ranger. "Hope you've got some powerful evidence to back that up, my friend."

"Hargrave has been robbing the good citizens of Rock Stone out of thousands of dollars. Over a period of months, he's been investing the bank's money in several highly risky stocks back east."

"There's nothing illegal about that," the banker interrupted. "The purpose of any bank is to invest the money of its depositors."

"That's true," the masked man said, "providing it's done honestly. But Hargrave was using money that was not his, Sheriff." The Lone Ranger held out one of the bank's ledgers.

"Where did you get those?" Hargrave demanded.

"If you will look in here, Sheriff," the masked man continued, "you'll find the names of fourteen loans that Hargrave made during the last ten months. All of them fell delinquent."

"It's not my fault those people didn't meet their payments," the banker shot back. "Times have been tough on all of us."

"Not for you," the masked man glared. "Hargrave knew these loans would never be paid, Sheriff, because the names on these notes came from fourteen citizens of Rock Stone who died years ago."

Edwards studied the book. "Denny Harris, Jack Kelly. Why, dad blame it, Pete Peterson was deputy sheriff here four years ago!"

"And that was the name Hargrave used to mask the

identity of the Black Hood." The Ranger handed the sheriff another book. "According to these payroll records, that Hargrave prepared for the Masons, a cowpoke by the name of P. Peterson was paid every month for the last six months."

"Sheriff, I can explain!" the banker said.

Edwards scanned the page the masked man indicated. "It'll take a heap o' that."

"Sheriff," Hargrave pleaded. "You caught the Black Hood yourself in my bank just the other night, remember?" Hargrave continued.

"Where exactly did you find that man, Sheriff?" the Lone Ranger asked.

"Why, he was on the floor of the back office."

"That's right," Hargrave added. "He never got past me."

"If he never made it past you that night," the Ranger continued, "Then, how do you explain the fact that the money you found on him was already soaked from the storm outside?"

"Got an answer for that one, Jeremy?" Edwards asked.

Just then, the group heard horses approach outside. Manuel Gonzales and his daughter walked into the Sheriff's office and launched into another conversation with the lawman.

"Here we go agin'." Edwards looked to Tonto for help.

They all turned their attention outside as the farmer pointed to the black horse at the hitchrack. No one noticed the small girl walk to the edge of the bars and extend a hand to the man in the cell who had forgotten his own name.

"Hmm," the Indian remarked, "him say, bring back horse. Not belong to him."

At that moment, Manuel was distracted by something his little girl was saying to the man behind bars.

The Lone Ranger looked at the face of the small child as she stared at the prisoner, then stepped outside, briefly.

Surprise washed over Tonto's face as he heard the girl turn and ask her father a question. "Girl ask why you put friend in jail?"

"What's she talkin' about?" Edwards asked.

The Indian listened as the little girl continued. "She say that this man, man who save her from water."

Just then, the Lone Ranger carried in some papers from the horse's saddle bags. "You better have a look at this, Sheriff," the Lone Ranger said. He held up a page and read aloud. "The last will and testament of Rita and Joe Mason."

"Those... are my parents," the lean man stammered, as he slowly began to remember.

"Can't be," snapped Hargrave.

The Ranger continued. "We hereby leave the sum of $1,600 dollars and the deed to our ranch to our only son, Tom."

Edwards unlocked the cell holding Tom Mason. At once, the little girl put her arms around the tall man's legs.

"So, you're the Mason boy," Edwards said. "Should'a know'd. Ya got yore ma's eyes."

With everyone's attention focused on young Tom Mason, Jeremy Hargrave tried to quietly slip out the back but Tonto blocked his way.

"Where do you think yore goin', Hargrave?" Edwards bellowed.

"Sheriff, I can explain."

"Save it for Judge Skinner," Edwards barked as he walked the banker back to a waiting cell. "Well Mister, looks like you called it straight." He turned and could find no sign of the two men.

"What happened to that masked man, Sheriff?" Tom said. "I never got to thank him and the Indian."

A slow smile crossed Edwards' face. "That's the way he and Tonto do business, son. Ride off before you can even thank 'em."

"Sheriff," cried Hargrave. "I can't believe you're takin' the word of a masked outlaw over mine."

"That's because he ain't no outlaw, Hargrave!"

"Then, who is he, Sheriff?" Tom asked.

A wistful expression appeared in the lawman's blue eyes as he heard the sound of receding hoofbeats from out back. "Why I thought everyone knew, son. He's the... Lone Ranger.

From outside, his ringing voice carried far across the plains. "Hi–Yo Silver, Away–y–y!"

(The Ranger always did have that great signature line. So, it's a little dramatic, but hey, he's the Lone Ranger!)

~

The rain gave way to a cool, gray mist as the clouds began to dissipate. I glanced down at my notebook to find all kinds of neat stuff, like, "thiefin' polecat, schemin' skunk," and when was the last time you heard someone say, "I don't cotton to masked owl–hoots walkin' in here?"

Looking at the Ranger sitting across from me, somehow, I got the feeling this might not be the stuff he was intending me to get.

"Was I able to help you with this story, Jim?"

"Help? Oh, quite a bit," I nodded back. *(Who wants to be rude to the Lone Ranger?)* "Just one thing." I flipped through my notes, looking immersed in valuable subtext. "I'm sure you mentioned it somewhere, but, for purposes of accuracy, could you tell me, ahh... in *your* words, just what the key value was, here?"

He smiled back. "Why don't you tell me what you think the story was about?"

(I always hated it when teachers did that to me. You know, answer a question with a question?)

"Well, this guy Hargrave seemed to be a little... morally dysfunctional."

The Ranger leaned forward. "Excuse me?"

"You know, ethically dissimilar."

He scratched his head. "I thought he was dishonest, Jim."

Suddenly, I realized I had to back up and explain about '90's "social sensitivity".

"What's that?" he asked.

(Biiig self–esteem boost here. Finally, I knew something the Ranger didn't.)

"Social sensitivity," I said slowly removing my glasses, "is an awareness that certain words can insult certain individuals or groups in a multicultural society such as ours." I searched for a suitable example. "For instance," I continued, "people aren't fat, they're... *metabolically* challenged. Someone who's had too much beer isn't drunk, we say they are chemically *inconvenienced*."

I could see his mind working this over. "Are you saying that you don't want to hurt his feelings?"

"Well, yeah. And bankers in general. Isn't that nice?"

A puzzled look crossed his face. "Why should you care about hurting the feelings of someone who was proven to be dishonest, Jim?"

I stared straight ahead for about three days. "Maybe this isn't the best example, here."

"So," he continued, "tell me what you think the story was about."

"All right," I said. "So Hargrave was dishonest. He allowed his greed to overtake him when he borrowed money that wasn't his, and..." I hesitated, trying to remember more. "This caused him to lie and cheat people."

I think he sensed that I was groping around here. "What do you think it means to be honest?"

"Well," I stopped a moment to think. "It means telling the truth and... not cheating and..." I couldn't think of anything else.

"Honesty, Jim, is one of the most essential values in which I believe. To be honest means to tell the truth, be sincere and straightforward. A person of character does not lie, cheat or steal. Such a person demonstrates honesty through his talk and his actions." He paused a moment, allowing me to catch up as I was writing this down.

"A commitment to honesty requires a good faith intention to be accurate, so that people are not misled or deceived. Being honest is like keeping all your accounts balanced, Jim. What do you think happens as a result of being truthful with others?"

(Uh, oh! I lost it on this part.)

"What about Tonto's actions?"

"Well, he rescued the little girl."

"Do you remember what happened as a result?"

"The sheriff trusted him!"

"Exactly. Tonto's actions spoke loud and clear," he said. "As a result, Sheriff Edwards trusted him. Who else was honest?" he asked.

My mind shifted to speed–search. "Manuel returned the horse that didn't belong to him."

"Yes," he said. "Honesty creates a level of trust between people."

"So, Hargrave wasn't thinking of anyone's interests except his own. He didn't have balanced books," I added.

"Yes. In the beginning, Hargrave worked honestly for others and achieved a level of trust. Later, however, greed got in the way of his sense of right and wrong. Soon he began to lie and cheat."

"Wait a minute," I said, remembering a small detail. "What about your disguise in order to spy on Hargrave? That wasn't truthful!"

"I felt it necessary to deceive Hargrave in order to obtain the truth."

I didn't want to say anything, but...

"Go ahead, Jim. Say what you're thinking."

"Well," I said. "It's just that it sounds like a convenient rationalization."

He placed another stick on the fire, then sat back down. "When I talk about being honest, that is not to say that one must be honest in all circumstances, Jim. When moral truths conflict, and they sometimes do, choices and trade–offs have to be made."

"Oh?"

"There was more information behind this story than I had time to detail for you. People in Rock Stone were having their money stolen. Because of the strong background information supplied to me by the governor's office, I had to get in there to look at the books myself. I had to get the proof necessary."

"So the end justifies the means. Is that what you're saying?"

"In this case, yes. But you have to be careful that you do not sacrifice integrity for the sake of expediency, Jim. Each set of circumstances must be studied and options explored. The ethical decisions that Tonto and I made were not always as simple as they may have seemed."

Evidently, ethical choices in the early West weren't any easier for masked law dogs than for some of us today.

This, then is what I distilled from the Lone Ranger's story on honesty.

MY NOTES:
- The Lone Ranger is **Honest**.
- Honesty is telling the truth, being sincere and straightforward.
- An honest person is worthy of trust.

EPISODE THREE

The Weasel

"**S**o, what do you think?" I asked, continuing to unpack the saddle–bag panniers I pulled from my bike.

The Lone Ranger rolled the warm cup back and forth between his hands. "Winy. Regal. Everything's in perfect balance here."

I turned back to find him reading from my *Starbucks* catalog. "You always carry this much with you when you travel, Jim?"

"I like to be comfortable," I shrugged.

He watched as I went through an inventory of C.D.'s, books and gadgets, not to mention a variety of tasty freeze–dried entrees, one of which I started to prepare.

"What's this?" he asked, holding up a small black case.

"Careful, that's my *Watchman*." He looked puzzled. "You know, TV?"

He unzipped it from its case. "Of course," he said. "I just didn't know they made them this small."

"Keeps me in touch with real life."

He snapped it on to find a big, purple dinosaur singing

and jumping around with a bunch of kids. "*This* is real life?" he said. "I'm afraid I've been away from television for awhile." He *surfed* a few channels, then stopped on a manic crowd in boots and fringed shirts. "What are these people doing?"

I glanced over his shoulder at a group of line dancers. "Oh, that. In the '90's," I said, "some people are forced to wear these oversize hats and move around in a ritualistic form of punishment, sometimes for hours at a time."

He lingered a moment longer. "Awful."

"Tell me something," I asked. How is it that you never settled down? You know, hung up the mask, became a rancher or worked that silver mine of yours?"

He helped himself to another cup of my coffee. "After Tonto and I put an end to the Cavendish gang, we realized that there were others who needed our help. That's when we decided to continue the mission we started."

I offered him a slice of my freeze–dried meatloaf. "What, exactly, is your mission?"

"Jim," the masked man said squarely.

(This is another "hard–to–describe" and frankly, I gave up despite repeated attempts. Believe me when I say that when the Lone Ranger talks to you "squarely" he gets your attention.)

"The Lone Ranger is motivated by love of country," he continued, "a desire to help those who are building the West. There are plenty of good citizens in this country and from time to time they need a special kind of assistance in preserving those things for which our ancestors fought and died. After the death of Butch Cavendish, Tonto and I pledged to continue to help people anyway we could."

"So, what about that silver mine?"

He smiled. "The silver from the mine provides for our

expenses as well as the bullets Tonto and I use." He pulled out a bar and placed it in my hands.

"Whoa, it's heavier than it looks." It also looked like a giant piece of Ex–Lax, crosscut so it could be divided into smaller, more manageable chunks.

He looked over my supplies as he finished the last bite of meatloaf. "Have anything for dessert?"

I moved the shiny bar back and forth between my hands. "Cost–you–a–bar–of–silver! Just kidding." I started digging through my pack for just the right thing. "Let's see, are we watching our carb's?" *(Forget it! The Ranger was in better shape than me.)* "Perfect! New York Cheesecake."

"What's that?" he asked.

"You've never had..."

He just shook his head.

"You really have been ridin' the range awhile. Trust me," I winked. "You're gonna like it." I poured the ingredients into a pan and got to work mixing. "This'll take awhile to set up. How about another story?"

"All right." The way he looked into the distance, you could watch him thinking, turning the pages of that journal in his head and even though he hadn't started, I could already visualize the beginning–

A vista of plains broken only by a few well–sculpted rocks in the foreground; the sun, low and majestic in the west; a stirring John Barry score against the background.

"Two men rode slowly across the horizon," the narrator's voice would say, "saving their strength and the strength of their two big stallions, the snow–white one called Silver and the slightly smaller paint horse that Tonto had named Scout."

"He was an astonishing man, this Lone Ranger. He had

become an almost legendary character throughout the length and breadth of seven states in the early West. Some folks regarded him as a myth, but countless others who had seen him in action told amazing stories of his skill, his courage, and his uncanny judgment."

(I like this part. I can't help it! I mean, how many people do you know who are truly astonishing and legendary? And when was the last time you heard any of your friends sitting around the barbecue telling amazing stories of someone's skill, courage and uncanny judgment? —not counting getting sideline seats for the Super Bowl.)

I poured the mixture over a graham cracker crust, as he began.

~

Riff Dening stepped into the office of Sprague Engineering with another batch of material. As on previous occasions, he was turning in soil samples for oil analysis for his boss Blaine Moreland.

"I can have these samples done in short order, if you want to wait?" the engineer said.

"Sure, take your time. I gotta wait on the printer anyway." The rangy Dening grabbed the local paper and sat down in a corner of Sprague's office. He didn't notice that the man who just entered wore a mask.

"Howdy, Mr. Sprague, remember me?" the masked man asked.

The elderly engineer looked up from his work to recognize a familiar friend. "Well, I'll be! It's been a long time, mister, but I shore am glad to see yuh!"

"I'm looking for the man responsible for the information on these handbills."

"Hmm," Sprague said, "let me see that."

"The man behind these flyers has been swindling a lot of innocent people with the idea that there's oil on the property," the masked man explained.

By now the conversation began to interest Dening as he peeked over his paper.

"Each agreement was accompanied by a test certificate," the Ranger continued, "a certificate bearing your name, Mr. Sprague."

The engineer took his time carefully looking over the certificate. "That's one of mine, alright. Say, you don't think I had anything to do with this, do you, mister?"

"I don't believe that you would consciously help anyone in such a scheme, Ed. But I'd like to know if anyone suspicious has been in your office in the past month or so? Anyone, say, bringing a lot of samples to you lately?"

"Nothing outta the ordinary, 'cept..." the engineer hesitated a moment as he looked around his office.

"What?"

"He's gone!"

"Who?"

"Riff Dening. He was just settin' over in that corner a minute ago. Dening works for a man name Moreland, Blaine Moreland in Mesa City."

"Go on," the masked man urged.

"Well, Moreland's done quite a lot of business with us the last several months. In fact, I've got several samples of his in for evaluation right now."

"Moreland could be our man," the Ranger said, thinking outloud.

"If that's so, he could ruin my reputation," Sprague snapped. "I don't hold with any swindler using my good name as part of some phony deal. I better notify the sheriff."

"I don't think that would be wise, Ed."

"Oh?"

"I've got no real evidence yet. If Moreland is the man I'm looking for, anything you say might cause him and his men to just pull stakes and move their operation elsewhere."

Continuing their conversation, the Lone Ranger listened for a way he might catch the cagey con man. Then, the engineer told him about a young couple who bought a piece of land from Moreland. "...they're about five miles outside of Mesa City. But the land don't have a drop of oil on it," Ed continued. "Jim injured himself drilling for water on the property. In fact, he's got a sample in here for analysis right now. Normally, I don't do water tests but, these folks are friends of Doc Melton's and I owe Doc plenty for pulling Millie through that winter fever last year."

"Hmm." Quickly, the masked man began to formulate a plan.

Meanwhile, Riff Dening entered the print shop of Eustace Adams. The stoop–shouldered printer was not only responsible for producing the many handbills of Moreland's but was in the process of printing some wanted posters for the sheriff's office.

"I'll have those handbills ready for you as soon as I finish this run for Sheriff Winslow."

"Yeah, sure," Dening said as he walked around the side of the machinery and picked up a sheet coming off the press. "Wanted posters, huh?" Suddenly, an idea crossed his mind.

A few days later, at the ranch of Jim and Karen McKenna outside Mesa City, Jim was still hobbling around from his injury.

"Jim, you heard Doc Melton," Karen said. "You've got to stay in bed."

"Doggone it, woman, there are chores to be done and..."

Suddenly, they were interrupted by a knock. Karen drew back when she opened the door. "A masked man and an Indian!"

Jim McKenna quickly leveled the Sharps rifle he kept handy at the two strangers. "Who are you and what do you want?"

"Easy, Mr. McKenna. We mean you no harm."

"Then why the mask, mister?"

"And how do you know our name?" Karen asked.

"We're friends of Ed Sprague, Mrs. McKenna. And if you'll let us come in, I'll explain why we're here."

It didn't take long for the Lone Ranger to go through his story about the handbills and the many people victimized by Blaine Moreland.

"Moreland!" Jim thundered. "That's the slimy varmint that sold us this worthless property. Said there was a good chance of oil on it. Even had a certificate that showed it so."

"Tonto and I are here to try and gather evidence against Moreland."

"Just how do you intend to do that?" Jim asked.

"With the help of some friends in town and, hopefully, you and Karen."

Karen stared at the strong, masked face. "I don't know why but somehow I trust you." She nodded approval to her husband.

"I hope you know what you're getting yourself into, mister. Blaine Moreland's as slick as they come. Why, he could sell snake oil to a medicine man."

"That's just what I am counting on, Jim." the Ranger

said.

"Afraid I don't get yuh, mister."

"I have a plan to give Moreland a dose of his own snake oil," the masked man said, "but first, I think we better let Sheriff Grant know what's going on."

(Excuse me for interrupting, but doesn't this sound like a possible case of entrapment, here? And what about Jim? Is it me, or does he sound a little slow?)

At that moment, in Mesa City, Sheriff Grant was going through his mail as his deputy, Harve Dunlap, entered the office.

"Any news, Sheriff?"

"Just re–ward notices, Harve." Suddenly, the stocky sheriff stopped in mid–sentence. "What the... !" Grant couldn't believe his eyes as he read the notice out loud. "Five–thousand dollars wanted for information leading to the arrest of a tall, well–spoken, masked man riding a white horse."

"Masked man!" A flash of recognition crossed Harve's face, "Sheriff, isn't that... ?"

"Can't be anyone else." Grant said.

"What in tarnation did he do to get a price on his head?"

Grant peered through his spectacles more closely. "Doesn't say. Just says, 'The masked man could be headed your way. So, keep on the look out. Signed, H. Winslow.'"

"$5,000 dollars for the Lone Ranger!" Dunlap repeated in amazement.

"Hank Winslow's crazy if he thinks that man's an outlaw." Grant hastily scribbled out a message.

"Are you gonna post the notice, Sheriff?"

"No, Harve," he said finishing the note. "Here, send this

wire to Sheriff Winslow, pronto. I wanna find out just what's goin' on."

Dunlap didn't waste any time. He raced down the street and entered the telegraph office just as Trig Collins was heading out in the direction of the Mesa City Land office and his boss, Blaine Moreland.

The oversized cowboy headed straight for the rear office. "Boss," Trig said, walking through the door. "Take a look at this message from Riff. Something about the McKennas and to be on the alert for a tall masked man askin' questions."

"Lemme see that." Blaine Moreland leaned back in a leather chair behind a big mahogany desk. The crafty con man had a high forehead and narrow–set eyes. But what distinguished him most was a remarkably superficial grin that showed a set of tiny, baby–like teeth. "Says here that he happened to see a report for some analysis work done for the McKennas. Hmm, according to this note, Sprague says he'll have a full report in a couple of days but that things look favorable. So," the developer said, leaning forward, "the McKennas really have struck oil on that land."

"Report don't say nuthin' 'bout any oil, Boss."

"Idiot, what else could it be? Sprague doesn't test for much of anything else!"

"But didn't you sell that land to the McKennas?"

"You forget, Trig, I have a partnership agreement with the McKennas. Anything they find on the land must be split fifty–fifty with me."

"What about that masked feller Riff mentioned?"

Moreland's mind was too busy spinning with ideas about the McKennas to pay much attention. The developer looked at his henchman, archly. "Trig, I think it's time you and I pay a neighborly visit to the Circle K."

Later that afternoon, as Sheriff Grant sat working at his desk, he heard a slight knock at the back door. A moment later, the Lone Ranger entered followed by Tonto and Karen McKenna.

"How are you, Sheriff?" the masked man said extending his hand.

"Glad to see you, mister." Grant stretched out his hand to Tonto as well.

"Sheriff, this is a friend of ours," the Lone Ranger said.

"Why I've known Mrs. McKenna ever since she and her husband, Jim, bought the Circle K a few months back. Howdy, ma'am. I just sent a message to Sheriff Winslow in Cook County about you, mister."

"What kind of a message?"

"I asked him to explain about this." Grant handed the masked man one of the reward handbills and letter.

The Lone Ranger quickly read them both. "Have you posted this notice, Sheriff?"

"Tarnation, NO! I didn't want anyone to go gunnin' for ya."

"But why would anyone do that, Sheriff?" Karen wondered.

"To collect the 5,000 dollars re–ward, ma'am."

The Ranger continued to study the handbill more closely as the others speculated aloud.

"That just doesn't sound like the kind of thing Hank Winslow would do."

"You know Sheriff Winslow, Mrs. McKenna?" Grant asked.

"Know him, why he and my father rode with Teddy Roosevelt in the early days of the West. He's been like an uncle to me ever since Dad died."

"Mebbe you'd recognize his handwritin' if you saw it? Here," Grant said as he handed the note to the young woman. "Take a look at this."

"Why, this doesn't even look like uncle Hank's signature."

"Sheriff," the Ranger interrupted, "take a look at this handbill." He handed the notice back to the sheriff, then pulled another handbill from his pocket. "Now, compare it to the printing on this notice I brought with me."

"Hmm," Grant said squinting through his glasses.

The Ranger pointed to a small detail. "Notice how the letter 'D' is worn in the same place on both handbills?"

"By gosh, you're right!" Grant said. "That'd mean that both these handbills were printed on the same press."

"Mebbe printer work with con man," Tonto concluded.

"Who's a con man?" Grant asked.

The Lone Ranger's voice was crisp and sharp as he spoke. "These handbills have been circulated by a man named Blaine Moreland. He's been using them to cheat people by selling them land they think has oil on it."

"Why Moreland's got an office right here, in town. If you got proof he's a swindler, I'll jail 'em, pronto!"

"I don't have proof, Sheriff. But I do have a plan to make him repay what he's stolen."

"Does the plan include catchin' the jasper who sent this phony re—ward notice?"

Beneath the mask a slight smile showed on the Ranger's face. "Yes."

"Good!" Grant said.

The sun was touching the edge of the mountains when Trig Collins and Blaine Moreland rode through the gate of the

Circle K. Jim and Karen were finishing supper as they discussed the wire they received from Ed Sprague.

"If Sprague's report is as promising as he says, maybe we'll be able to turn this into a workin' ranch after all, honey." Jim grabbed some dishes from the supper table. "Here, let me help you with those."

Just then, they were interrupted by a knock at the door.

"Hello, Mrs. McKenna," the man grinned as the door swung open. "Mind if I come in?"

"Moreland!" Jim's lips compressed in anger. "Whadda you want?"

"If Trig and I can step in a minute, I'd be happy to tell you."

"You're not welcome here," Jim hobbled back near his rifle.

"Just a minute," Moreland pleaded.

"Talk fast, then, get goin'!"

"Well," Moreland began, "it's about that deal we had."

"What about it?"

Moreland sighed heavily, then put on his most sincere face. "Jim, I didn't know that well would turn out to be a duster. And I didn't know I was takin' the last cent you and Karen had."

"Well, you know it now."

The canny developer began wringing his hands in mock anguish. "I'm down right sorry and I wanna do something about it." He stopped pacing when he noticed a pair of Jim's overalls in the sink. "Say," he said, taking a closer look, "that looks like oil!"

"Make your point and get outta here," Jim shot back.

"All right," Moreland continued. "I know about the telegram you got from Ed Sprague today."

"Why, that's a private wire," Karen said.

Jim pushed into Moreland's face. "You have no right readin' anybody else's mail, Moreland!"

"It was quite accidental, I assure you, Jim. Trig here, was over at the telegraph office expecting a message from one of my associates in Cook county when he was handed the wrong wire by mistake. That's all."

Moreland's sincerity was beginning to wear a little thin on Karen. "What's your point, Mr. Moreland."

With all cards on the table, the well–dressed swindler dropped the last of any pretense. "The point, Mrs. McKenna, is that I know about the oil."

"The what?" Jim laughed.

"It's no use tryin' to cover it up, McKenna. Sprague has done engineering reports for me. I know you've found oil here."

"Get out!" Jim shouted. "Get out of my house, now!"

"If that's the way you want it." The developer casually pulled a paper from his pocket. "I'll just remind you of our agreement."

"What about it?" Jim said.

"The agreement specifically states that any profits from the sale of any minerals found are to be equally divided for a period of five years from the date of purchase. That's why," Moreland said, with dramatic pause for effect, "I sold you the land for less than what it was worth."

Jim exploded. "Why, it was never worth what you sold it for in the first place, you weasel, and you know it!"

"It really makes no difference, now. We're partners."

"We're no such a kind!" Jim shot back. "I didn't find any oil!"

"Really," Moreland continued in a softer voice. "Then

what about that report from Sprague?"

"And what about these pants," Moreland said, walking back to the sink. "I suppose you're going to tell me that this big oil stain is from machinery or something."

"Well, as a matter of fact..." Karen began.

"I won't be cheated, McKenna! We've got an agreement and I'm holding you to it."

"But we're not drilling for oil, I'm tellin' ya." Jim continued. "We already wasted enough money trying that once, remember?"

"Let's find out. I can have a drilling crew here in the morning."

"You do and I'll have men here to meet you with six–guns."

Karen quickly stepped between them. "STOP IT, BOTH OF YOU! Judge Peabody's in town. We'll take the agreement to him."

"Suits me," Moreland said.

"Fine!" Jim started to move then almost fell again.

Karen grabbed her husband's arm. "Jim, you're in no condition to go anywhere."

"I don't want this varmint getting one blasted cent more from us. I don't trust him, Karen!"

"Why don't you have your wife go in your place, Jim?" Moreland suggested.

The next morning, Karen and Moreland were busy going over the details of the agreement in the office of Judge Horace Peabody.

"As you can see, Judge," Moreland continued, "it clearly says that any mineral deposits found on the property are to be shared, fifty–fifty."

"I can read a contract, Blaine," the grizzled old judge barked.

Moreland backed off. "Course you can, Judge, sorry."

"But Mr. Moreland, we found no oil on the property," Karen added.

"Then how do you explain Sprague's report?"

"Mr. Sprague is testing for a water well. Nothing more."

"Water indeed. Your forgetting about those oil stains on Jim's pants."

"Now, hold on," Peabody interrupted. "You two came to me for an interpretation of an agreement and that's what I intend to do." The venerable judge adjusted his glasses, then carefully re–read the agreement. "Well, now," Peabody began, "according to this agreement, Blaine Moreland is entitled to a fifty percent share of any mineral found on the property known as the Circle K ranch for a period of five years."

Moreland smiled. "There, you see, Mrs. McKenna?"

"Hold on there, Blaine. I'm not finished, yet!"

The grin on Moreland's face started to fade as Peabody continued. "You're entitled to a fifty percent share of any oil found on the property, but you can't trespass on the ranch if they don't want you to!"

"And we don't want him to!" Karen replied.

"But that's not fair, Judge!"

"You can't TRESPASS on the land, Moreland, unless..." Peabody hedged.

"Unless, what?" Moreland asked.

"Unless, you want to *buy* the land back from them."

"That's ridiculous!" Karen said. "Besides, he'd never pay what it's worth, anyway."

"How much do you want for it?

"What?"

Moreland grabbed for the last opportunity he could see. "Name a price!"

"Well," Karen thought out loud. "I'd have to talk to Jim and..."

Moreland shifted tactics. "Wasn't the money used to buy the ranch yours, Mrs. McKenna?

"What's it to you, if it was?"

"Nothing. If you need permission, well, I can understand." The remark produced the exact response the shifty swindler was looking for.

"I don't need permission for anything, Mr. Moreland."

"Fine, I'll give you $10,000 cash for the whole spread."

The amount was enough to raise the eyebrows of even Judge Peabody and it left Karen stunned.

"Come, come, I'm offering you $10,000 dollars, Mrs. McKenna. That's three times what you paid for it. I can have the cash to you in one hour, as soon as the bank opens. Unless, of course," Moreland twisted, "you have to get permission."

"I'll take your offer, Mr. Moreland. Ten–thousand in cash in one hour."

Moreland grabbed his hat and moved toward the door. "Judge, draw up the papers. I'll be back in an hour."

Upon completion of the sale, it didn't take long for Jim and Karen to pack their belongings onto the big, single wagon they had and ride into town. The next morning they went directly to Sheriff Grant's office where they found the Lone Ranger waiting.

(Actually, there was another scene here, a "kegger" party Moreland held for his boys celebrating his acquisition.

Nothing of real importance. I mean, who cares about a bunch of bad guys having a good time? I was curious, though, as to how he knew, much less cared, about what Moreland was doing at this point. "Simple," he said. "Tonto always keeps an eye on things, just to be safe." So, you're really not missing anything here. Now, back to our story.)

"Well," Karen announced, as she pulled out a thick envelope with the money, "here it is, ten–thousand dollars in cash. Moreland signed the papers and Judge Peabody witnessed the sale."

"Good," the Ranger added.

"Here's the cash from the sale, less the three–thousand Jim and I paid out," Karen said, as she handed the balance to the sheriff.

"The rest of this money will go to Moreland's victims," the Ranger added.

Suddenly, the group was distracted by a clatter of sound outside.

"That'll be the stage from Cook county," Grant said. "Sheriff Winslow should be on board."

"And so will Moreland's man." the masked man said. "Tonto's waiting at the station to meet him."

Across the street, Riff Dening stepped out of the Concorde coach. He dusted himself off and stretched as he watched Sheriff Winslow exit the stage and walk over to Sheriff Grant's office. He was wondering what had brought the Cook County lawman to Mesa City as Tonto approached.

"You Riff Dening?" Tonto asked, politely.

"That's right. Whadda yuh want?"

"Me have message for you, 'bout man named Moreland."

The cowboy perked up. "Moreland!"

"That right."

"Well, spit it out, Injun. I don't have all day."

"Him think—um find oil. Buy McKenna ranch."

Dening smiled in anticipation of a generous slice of the newly acquired holdings. "I knew the boss'd find some way to get that land back." Dening said under his breath.

"What that?" Tonto asked.

"Nuthin'." Then, Dening's tone turned decidedly kinder. "Say, friend, can you take me out to this ranch?"

"Sure."

It didn't take long for them both to head down the street to where Tonto had two horses waiting. The two quickly headed east, out of town.

A short time later, another group of riders headed east. The Lone Ranger, and Karen McKenna were followed by the two lawmen and Judge Peabody.

Meanwhile, out at the Circle K, Moreland already had a rigging crew on the site making preparations to drill. Ted Hanson, the young foreman, walked over to where Blaine Moreland stood watching the work.

"Are you sure there's oil out here, Mr. Moreland? I thought Jim McKenna drilled here last spring and brought in a duster."

"Am I paying you to think, or to drill, Hanson?"

The young driller deferred to his client. "You're payin' the bills."

At that moment, Moreland caught sight of two riders coming through the gate of the ranch. They didn't waste time riding over to where he stood.

"...whoa, WHOA." Tonto and Dening reined up in front of the oil derrick.

Clearly, Moreland was surprised. "Riff, what are you doing here?"

"I came when I got the wire you sent me a couple of days ago."

"What wire? I didn't send any wire."

"Man who send message come this way, now." No sooner did Tonto finish his sentence than the group of riders led by the Lone Ranger reined up in front of the others at the drill site.

A confused Moreland mopped the sweat from his face as the group dismounted. "What's goin' on here?"

Dening was startled when he recognized the man walking toward them. "Boss, that masked man, he's the guy askin' all those questions in Sprague's office."

"Howdy, Riff."

"What are you doin' here, mister?" Riff asked.

The masked man smiled. "I came to talk to you, Dening."

"And so did I," Sheriff Winslow said, stepping forward.

"Oh, excuse me," the Ranger added, politely. "You know Sheriff Winslow, don't you Riff?"

The skinny henchman looked nervous. "We came over on the stage together. But I don't see what that has to do with..."

"Sheriff Grant sent for me, Dening, when he received this note and handbill sent to him with my signature on it. Only problem is," the lawman continued, "I didn't send any note to Sheriff Grant and this ain't my signature."

"Don't say anything, Riff." Moreland interrupted. "They can't prove a thing."

"Oh, we can prove it, Moreland." The Ranger removed the notices from his pocket. "These two handbills have the same crooked letter 'D' in the printing."

Moreland barely glanced at the papers. "I don't know what you're talkin' about, mister."

"It's no use, Dening," Winslow said. "Eustace Adams already confessed about your little scheme."

"And a handwriting expert will prove that the signature on the note you sent to Sheriff Grant will match yours, Dening," the Ranger added.

"I can't go back to jail," Dening balked. "I can't, I tell yuh!"

"Well, now," said the Judge, "just maybe you won't have to, son, if you got cash enough to pay the fine."

"Moreland," Dening pleaded. "You've got the cash."

"You idiot, my money's tied up in this drilling operation."

Suddenly, the drilling equipment ground to a halt as foreman Hanson walked back over.

"What's the matter? Why did you stop drilling?"

"I stopped drilling because there ain't nuthin' to drill *for*!" Hansen said. "It's a duster, like I told you before."

Moreland looked pale. "I don't understand."

"I told you before," Karen said. "There's no oil out here."

"But that report from Sprague..."

"Ed Sprague was testing for a water well Jim and I were digging. I tried to tell you but you wouldn't listen."

"The McKenna's cheated me, Judge!"

"Now, hold on there, Blaine," Peabody said. "I listened to you and Mrs. McKenna in my office. She never said anything about there being oil on the property. "

"You just assumed there was oil on the land," Karen said.

Moorland squirmed, "But those oil stains on Jim's clothes? I saw them myself!"

"Those came from cans of heating oil he knocked over when he had that fall a few days ago."

"Can you pay the fine, Dening?" the Judge asked.

Dening just shook his head

Grant stepped forward. "Then, you're goin' to jail."

"Mrs. McKenna," Moreland pleaded, "I'm appealing to your sense of fairness. I sold you this ranch for three–thousand dollars not ten!"

"Cheer up, Moreland," Grant continued, "the rest of the money is going back to the other citizens you swindled."

"Oh, no," the developer squeaked.

"Looks like you have everything in hand, Sheriff," the Lone Ranger said as he nodded to Tonto. The two men climbed back onto their horses. "Tonto and I will be heading out."

"Thanks, mister," Winslow said. "It was a pleasure working with the likes of... the Lone Ranger."

"ON, SILVER!" the masked man shouted.

"Gettum up, Scout!"

"I don't believe it!" Dening just shook his head as Hank Winslow secured him to the horse he rode in on.

"Don't believe what, son?"

"If I'd only known that that masked man was the Lone Ranger!"

(By the way, this last part is known in Rangerese as the "Benediction," punctuated by the startling pronouncement as to just who this masked do–gooder is. It's more or less equivalent to, "Ladies and Gentlemen, Elvis has left the building!" However, you gotta wonder, if the Ranger was so well known as a masked avenger and Dening sees a masked

*man early on who clearly does not show outlaw tendencies,
how come he never puts two and two together? I mean, when
Mike Wallace shows up asking questions, you know he's not
there to hand out the Publisher's Clearing House check.)*

~

Finishing my notes, I looked up to find the Ranger
interested in my stuff, especially my CD player. He
looked at me and I nodded an "okay" as he put the
headphones on, found the "start" button and immediately
blasted his ears with music. After a moment of recovery, we
got back to the value of the story.

By this time I already decided I was going to pay more
attention to the ethical value in the story and not just the
colorful expressions.

The previous story spoke of honesty. But what was I to
look for in this adventure? I flipped through my notebook.
Let's see, Moreland was a swindler who deceived people by
selling them land they thought had the possibility of oil on
it. Oh brother, these people had to be pretty dumb to begin
with.

"You're missing the point," he said.

*(The Ranger's minding-reading gimmick was beginning to
wear thin.)*

"Think about it," he said.

*(...? ? ?... This is me thinking, again. If he really could read
my thoughts, he'd give me a sign!) "...oh, very funny."*

The Ranger held up a sheet of paper on which was
written the following: What did Moreland ask Karen when
he learned the truth?

Suddenly, I flashed on the scene he was referring to.
"He said, 'I'm appealing to your sense of fairness.'"

"Exactly!"

"Fairness? Isn't that the same as honesty?" I asked.

"Not really, Jim. Being fair means treating all people fairly. When a conflict arises, a fair–minded person is willing to be open and listen to the other side of the story. He wants to understand what the other person is saying and feeling."

"Does this have anything to do with your sense of justice?" I asked him.

"Aristotle said, 'all virtue is summed up in dealing justly.' Justice, Jim, the quality of upholding rightfulness guided by truth."

"So, justice is upholding the quality of fair play for all."

"Exactly. The Lone Ranger disapproves of men who take unfair advantage of others," he continued, "men, who, even though within their legal rights, take unfair advantage of the mistakes or ignorance of others."

"So," I said, "even though Moreland had a contract with the McKennas, he had gone beyond the bounds of fair play in the way he sold them the property."

"Yes."

(Uh, oh, I feel another speech coming on.)

"The Lone Ranger advocates the American tradition, which gives each man the right to choose his work and profit in proportion to his effort."

"But you tricked Moreland into buying the property back," I said. "How fair was that?"

"My mother used to say that we are judged, condemned, or saved by our own acts. Remember the McKennas never told Moreland that there was oil on the property. He assumed there was from the report by Sprague and the stains on Jim's pants."

"Yes, but you set that thing up with the pants."

"Jim McKenna really did have oil stains on his pants, as Karen said. All the rest was Moreland's assumption. As a result, he suffered his own consequences."

That seemed to fit. The Ranger may have sent the message that called Riff Dening to Mesa City but it was Dening who assumed that Moreland had sent it. No wonder lawmen were glad to have the Lone Ranger's help. Not only was he there for the tough stuff but he could be relied on to reason out the proper plan to catch the crooks and all within his context of honesty and fair play.

"Notice anything else in this story, Jim?"

"Well, now that you mention it, there didn't seem to be the same amount of action as in the last one."

"Not a single shot was fired," he said. This seemed to be important to him.

"Yeah, I was a little disappointed," I said. "Kind of like going to an Arnold Schwartzenegger movie with a low body count."

"The Lone Ranger disapproves of bullets," he said.

"You're kidding!"

He shook his head. "I use them only when absolutely necessary and then, only to wound."

Saves on the silver. Well," I thought, "that's a good thing.

He looked past me smiling broadly. "That dessert of yours looks good."

"Yeah, in a minute," I said, finishing my notes. Just then, something occurred to me. "You know, both of these stories have one thing in common."

"What's that, Jim?"

"Everything is pretty black and white. I mean, it's easy

to know who the bad guys are and you sure can't confuse them with the good guys. A lot of things today just aren't that clear cut."

I leaned closer as I cut him a slice of Cheesecake. "A lot of good people have done bad things," I said. "And others are convicted of breaking the law but did it to help a friend, sometimes in a life or death situation. What about those kinds of things? How easy is it to determine who's right and who's wrong?"

"I never said these decisions were easy, Jim." He walked over to the fire and poured himself another cup of coffee. "There is such a wide difference of opinion in the world that it is virtually impossible to settle on one single standard of behavior. But we can tell what that standard has been in the past and what it is today. We can, for instance, generally agree that murder, lying, cheating and stealing are wrong and that consideration, truthfulness and honesty are right!" He paused for another bite of the cake.

"It takes great strength of character to face many of the challenges you speak of," he continued. "Strength of character is seldom developed in seclusion. The Great Teacher prayed, not that His disciples might be taken out of the world, but that they might go about their duties mingling with men, and at the same time be unscathed by the temptations with which they were surrounded."

"Knowing that," I said, "still doesn't make some of the choices any easier."

"It is by the choices and acts of everyday life that character is formed, more than by great crises," he said.

After serving up a second slice of the cheesecake, I felt that something was missing from my notes. "You mentioned your mother awhile ago. Is that who taught you all this stuff about honesty and fair play?"

I had to wait for him to finish chewing thoroughly, then

swallow.

(Yes, folks, the Lone Ranger even has amazing manners!)

"My mother, my father and my brother. But that's another story," he said.

MY NOTES:

- The Lone Ranger believes in being **Fair**.
- A fair–minded person is open and willing to listen to others.
- The Lone Ranger is committed to the equitable treatment of all.

EPISODE FOUR

The Masked Man's Teacher

I'd only been asleep an hour or so, when I heard footsteps barely crunching sand, voices whispering, then the clatter of pots.

"...careful, Kemo Sabay..." the masked man whispered.

This? This is the Indian, Tonto? Even though I was fully awake, I kept my back to them both. I just wanted to listen. What are they laughing at? Tonto said something but I couldn't make it out. They laughed, quietly.

"Yes, Tonto, he does pack a lot."

Maybe I should just turn around and... the whispers stopped. Everything was quiet again. I think they're going to sleep. Tomorrow's soon enough. I'll wait 'till tomorrow to meet Tonto.

What's that?

I rolled over and squinted a look. The Ranger's showin' him my stuff. Now Tonto's got the headphones on and... He's *skip/searching* my CD... how does he know how to use this stuff? ... thought they spent all their time out on the trail... Forget it. Just roll over and go back to sleep...... I thought Indians were only interested in mystical stuff, like eagle feathers or buffalo horns?... Drop it. Get some sleep.

I awoke the next morning to find the camp empty. No Lone Ranger or Tonto. I sat in the middle of the shelter with all my stuff right where I left it. Had I been dreaming? Was the whole thing just a figment from the cheesecake?

(Was I going to keep talking to myself like this for the rest of the episode?)

I climbed to the top of the canyon rocks and looked around. The sun had yet to break the horizon as I scanned the terrain. Looking west I saw nothing but mountains. Turning south... cactus, more mountains. East... cactus, two guys jogging, mountains. North... wait a second. I turned back and there, in the distance, I saw the Lone Ranger and Tonto, stripped to the waist and... what are they doing? They reached a cactus, turned left and continued in a circle. They're Power–Walking. Interesting. This must be one of the ways they keep in shape. I kept watching for several minutes. They're racing. For awhile Tonto was out in front, then... oh, nice move by the Ranger. Wonder if they ever thought of doing a fitness video. *Sweatin' Bullets to Get Buff with The Lone Ranger and Tonto.* What am I saying? They'd never make it on *Ricki Lake*.

I watched them for a couple more laps before I climbed down.

About the time I had my freeze–dried Eggs Benedict ready, I could hear them approach. They stopped at the stream to wash up. The Ranger waved to me as Tonto went under the water. A moment later, they were walking up to the cave. I tried to act casual but I must admit, I was nervous. I mean, this is Tonto, a legend in his own right. So what's the protocol, here. Do I shake hands with him, say "how?" No, no. That's not right. Just follow the masked man's lead.

The Lone Ranger pulled on a fresh shirt. Tonto was still toweling his head as they approached.

"Jim," the Ranger said, "this is Tonto."

I decided to put last night behind us and immediately extended a hand. "Boy, have I heard a lot about YOU!"

He walked right past me and helped himself to some of my breakfast. What's the deal, here? Oh, my God... he snubbed me. Tonto, the Indian, just snubbed me!

"Tonto didn't slight you, Jim. He just needs some time to get to know you, that's all."

"Really?" I wanted to believe this.

"Trust me on this," the Ranger said. "You see, Jim, Tonto is a little..."

"...moody?"

"No. He's shy, that's all. Give him a chance to get to know you. He'll come around."

I watched him as he took a plateful of food and sat off near a rocky overhang by himself. "Really?"

"Smells good, Jim," the masked man said.

"Yeah, help yourself." I stood there a moment longer watching him. He sure isn't shy about scarfing down my eggs. He paused long enough to nod approval of the food. I nodded back but he was already busy adding some sort of spice from a small pouch he carried. What's he thinking about? Forget it. The Lone Ranger said it takes time for him to get to know people and that's all there is to it.

After we finished, Tonto took the masked man's plate and mine and headed down to the stream to do the dishes. The Ranger pulled a blanket over toward me and sat down. "That was a fine breakfast, Jim", he smiled. "Tonto and I appreciate it."

"Sure," I said, as I watched the Indian wash the dishes.

"Would you like to continue our talk?"

"What? Oh, yeah." I turned back to the masked man and

grabbed my notes. "Let's see, you were about to tell me who taught you these values?"

I flipped to a clean page as the Ranger thought for a moment. For the last day or so, the Ranger had been quite open about sharing his adventures to help me better understand the principles that he and Tonto lived by. But now, he seemed more subdued, more studied. It was as if he were about to share something he did not let many people see.

"It was a long time ago," he began, "when my brother and I were young. My dad held a small ranch for a time. One of our neighbors was a man by the name of Bannerman."

~

Flint Bannerman sat at the head of the supper table with his wife Emily, and his foreman Shorty Stevens. My mom and dad, Frank and Amy Reid, along with my brother, Dan and I were guests. Something was on the mind of the crusty rancher and Flint, a bear of a man, was never one to mince words.

"By thunder, Shorty, I'm getting tired of those ornery nesters staked out on the north forty. Every time I turn 'round, they're buildin' more houses and farms. If you wanna stay on as foreman, you better clear 'em out and fast."

Shorty forked another piece of meat as he spoke. "Flint, I've tried every which way I know to get 'em out, but even threats won't budge 'em!"

Emily Bannerman, Flint's wife, rarely intruded in her husband's business, but this time her sympathies were clear. "Honey, I don't blame those folks. Those small farms are their homes. They're all they have."

"Figures you'd say something like that, Emily," Flint grumbled. "Wonder if you'd be so soft if'n they wuz takin' the food outta our mouths?"

"Flint Bannerman, you know that's just not so! Why, we have more than most folk and should be grateful to the good Lord."

"I should'a know'd better'n to argue with a woman." Flint glanced at the end of the table, to his neighbor and fellow rancher, Frank Reid, who remained strangely silent through most of the conversation. "What do you think, Reid?"

"You want me to be honest, Flint?"

"Course I do!"

"All right," Frank said, as he finished a bite of food and took a swallow of water. "The fact is, I'm not sure you really have legal title to that land anymore."

"What do you mean?"

Frank continued in an even voice. "When you let those first settlers farm out that section you never seemed to care."

"That's 'cause that rocky land was 'durn near impossible to do anything with. Thought the best thing was to leave 'em be. But now, it's gotten out of hand. Never figured they'd invite their friends."

"You should of thought of that before, Flint," Shorty added.

"Well, I'm thinkin' on it now, carnsarn it all!"

Frank Reid pushed his chair away from the supper table. "You know, Flint," he said trying a new tact, "you've got to give those farmers credit. They've not only cleared that land but have succeeded in making it fertile enough to produce a fine crop of corn. I've heard they've got quite a surplus this year."

"What're you drivin' at, Frank?"

"Winter's coming and with the price of feed from the east going up every season, the corn from those farmers might be a pretty good bargain for us."

Flint threw his napkin on the table. "I'll hear no such talk 'bout dealin' with the nesters. I want 'em out and that's final!"

"Just how do you aim to do that?" Shorty asked.

"I gave YOU the job of doin' it!" Flint thundered. "Dagnab it, Shorty, I don't know why I keep you on. To be a good foreman, you need a lot more gumption and..."

"Now, Flint that's enough," Emily scolded. "The Reid's are our guests and I won't have you spoilin' our supper with such talk. It's not Christian." Emily turned to the Reid boys and scooped another generous slice of pie onto their plates.

"Golly, thanks Mrs. Bannerman," the older boy said.

"Thank you, ma'am," the younger one added.

(Pssst! The "younger one" is the Lone Ranger, in case you weren't paying attention at the beginning.)

As the two youngsters finished their pie, Flint, Shorty and Frank rose from the table and moved to the fire as the women and two boys went to work clearing the table.

(During this last part Tonto returned with the clean dishes and now sits silently watching me. What can he be thinking about? I think he thinks he's getting on my nerves.)

Later that night, on the way back to their ranch, Dan, the older of the two Reid boys, spoke to his father about the gruff rancher. "Dad, why is mister Bannerman so mad at those farmers?"

"He's afraid, son."

"Afraid? Afraid of what?"

"He's afraid those farmers will take over more of his

property. He's afraid that if they stay, more farmers will settle in the area and push out the cattle ranchers."

"Gosh, are we going to lose our ranch?" the younger boy asked.

Frank Reid always spoke directly to his sons' questions. He never wanted them to know anything less than the truth, no matter how hard it might be. "I don't think anyone is going to lose their ranch, son."

"But mister Bannerman thinks so."

"I believe old Flint is mistaken. Those farmers aren't interested in anything more than farming the land they now occupy."

"How do you know that, Frank?"

"I met with some of them a couple of weeks ago, Amy, and they told me so. I'll take them at their word."

"Why did the farmers settle here in the first place?" Dan asked.

"I guess they chose the west because it's new and fresh and wide open. The same as we did. You see, son, if the west is to develop properly, we'll need farmers as well as cattle ranchers. And probably a lot of other businesses as well."

Frank Reid drew his wagon to a halt at the top of a ridge overlooking the small valley the farmers occupied. "Those farmers are working a piece of land that Flint has never used."

"But Dad," Dan asked, "doesn't mister Bannerman have a right to decide what he wants to do with his own land?"

"That's true, son. The land was once part of his holdings, but he paid no attention when the farmers settled there sometime ago. Now, they claim squatter's rights."

"He's not very understanding of the farmers side of things, is he?" Dan said.

"Perhaps, but we must also remember that to be understanding also means allowing a man like Flint to find his own balance in this situation."

"Flint doesn't need that land."

"I agree, Amy, but once Flint makes up his mind, he can be a hard man to change." Frank sighed as he looked down on the valley below. "I'm afraid he'll only stir up trouble if he decides to use force to move those farmers now."

Amy Reid looked down at the isolated little farms below. "Let's pray that mister Bannerman realizes that force isn't the answer."

That night, Flint Bannerman paid a visit to the bunkhouse to talk to his hands. "Men, I've been doin' some thinkin'."

"What's up, boss?"

"Those nesters are gonna clear outta that valley and pronto!" Flint said, pointing his finger for emphasis.

Rusty Gibson was the new man on the spread. "I reckon they got a right to make a livin' same as anybody else, mister Bannerman."

The old rancher's voice rose dramatically. "By thunder, they're settin' on Bar B land and they've got to go! I'm not puttin' it off any longer."

"Not puttin' off what, Flint?" Shorty asked.

"Why, makin' things so tough on 'em they'll be glad to pull stakes and leave."

"Just how you figure on doin' that?" Shorty persisted.

"I'LL TELL YOU HOW WE'RE GONNA DO IT!" Flint thundered.

Any doubts that remained in the bunkhouse left the room in a big hurry as the burly Bannerman moved to a table near the stove. "Now then, those nesters have their houses made up with a sorta main street with fences boarding the outskirts. Those fences are mighty weak. I checked 'em myself the other night. So, this is what we're gonna do. At dawn, I want you men to round up 'bout a thousand head of cattle. Then, we'll drive the herd down that narrow trail."

"But boss," Rusty said, "they'll break through those fences and spread out every which way."

"Exactly!" Flint said.

A low grumble stirred through the bunkhouse. Clearly, the men were not comfortable in riding the herd through the small settlement.

But Flint's strong voice quickly quelled the commotion. "Any cowpoke here who's skittish 'bout followin' orders, can get his gear and clear out. Savvy?"

The bunkhouse fell silent, again. Times were hard and no cowhand was eager to lose a good job.

Flint headed for the door. "Shorty, roust 'em at dawn. When you've got the cattle ready to move, let me know. I'll go along to help drive 'em." Flint stood at the door and peered into the crowd of cowpokes before leaving. "Now, that's all I gotta say on the matter."

The next morning, in the small town of Copper City, Frank Reid and his sons were busy packing supplies onto the back of their wagon with young Greg Baxter who worked for Billings Supply. "That's the last of it, mister Reid," Greg said hoisting a sack of flour onto the wagon.

Frank turned and shook the young man's hand. "Thanks for the help, Greg."

As Frank stirred his team forward, Ernie Baker, the telegraph master, came running down the street with important news. "Reid... Hey, mister Reid, hold up there!"

"Whoa!" Frank reined up.

"It's awful, mister Reid. Just awful."

"Slow down. What's awful?"

Ernie gulped air as he talked. "It's the train. The train from Chicago."

"The supply train?"

"Landslide hit the pass in the Rockies. Train's boxed in on all sides."

"Are the passengers and crew all right?"

"They're all fine, but the feed... boxcars of feed are all lost."

"Hmm, that's not good."

"Gotta go," Ernie said as he headed back down the street. "Gotta tell the rest of the ranchers."

"Looks like all of us will have to make a deal with those farmers sooner than we think." Frank grabbed the reins from Dan just as they caught sight of Shorty Stevens riding hard in their direction.

"Whoa, WHOAAA!" Shorty reined up in front of Frank bursting with news of his own. "Glad I caught you mister Reid. Amy said you were in town. You're the only one can help."

"Help with what, Shorty?"

"It's mister Bannerman. He's got me and the boys to round up a thousand head. He plans to run 'em straight through those nesters out in the valley."

"But that's crazy."

"Last night, me and a couple of the boys went out and warned some of the farmers, so's they can at least protect themselves."

"That's not enough. Flint's got to be stopped before anyone is hurt."

"I know, but you know Flint," Shorty said. "I've done all I can. Thought you might be able to get out there and talk sense. He might listen to you, mister Reid." The stocky foreman then ran inside the general store.

Frank climbed down from the wagon. "Help me unhitch these horses, boys. We've no time to waste."

A moment later, Frank Reid and his sons disappeared around a corner as Greg Baxter walked back out to the street. He scratched his head as he looked at the abandoned wagon.

Meanwhile, about a thousand head of Bannerman cattle were moving toward the valley where the farmers were located. Two cowhands, Jake and Speedy, noticed something up ahead. When they approached the entrance to the valley, they signaled the herd to stop, then turned and rode back toward Flint and the others.

"Jake, Speedy, what–in–thunder..." Flint barked.

Speedy raced through the news. "...mister–Bannerman–we–can't–go–on!"

"Slow down, Speedy. What are you talkin' about?"

Jake pulled his horse closer to Flint. "It's those nesters. They put a string of farm wagons across the entrance to the valley trail. Their blockin' the way."

"And the farmers are waitin' behind 'em with guns!" Speedy added.

"Guns!" Rusty said. "Looks like someone tipped 'em off as to what you wuz plannin', mister Bannerman."

"By thunder, we'll see about this. Let's get up there!"

At that same moment, Shorty Stevens had returned to the ranch. He had just finished telling Emily about her husband's plan.

"Doggone that old man!"

"Don't worry, Mrs. Bannerman," Shorty continued. "I've been to town and talked with Frank Reid. He's on his way out there now to see if Flint'll listen to reason."

Emily shook her head. "Maybe he'll listen and maybe not. I don't know."

"I better head back out there and see if there's anything more I can do, ma'am." The foreman tipped his hat then, turned his horse and galloped out in the direction of the valley.

Back in the valley, Flint Bannerman and his men had reached the front of the herd. They were met by a group of the farmers with rifles and six–guns behind a series of wagon barricades. Flint and the others drew rein at a respectable distance.

"HEY, YOU NESTERS! This is Flint Bannerman talkin'! Move those wagons out of there pronto or we'll do it for you!"

"Try it, Bannerman, and there'll be a lot of dead cowpokes," a farmer said.

"You got no reason to drive those cattle through this valley, Bannerman. You're doin' it just to ruin our crops."

Flint was not the type of man who liked being challenged. "I don't have to give you reasons for takin' cattle through my own property. Now, either move those wagons or pay the price!"

"Flint," Jake said, "cattle are gettin' mighty jumpy."

"Lefty, take some of the men and pull those wagons out of the way. We'll back you up from here."

Just then, one farmer, Judd Baxter, stepped out from behind the protection of the wagons with his rifle at his side. "First cowpoke that sets a hand on these wagons stops a bullet!"

Another joined him. "WE MEAN BUSINESS, BANNERMAN!"

The wranglers had every right to be nervous, now. "We better turn the herd back, mister Bannerman," Speedy said. "If shootin' starts, those cattle could stampede every which way."

Lefty nodded toward his boss. "Speedy's right, mister Bannerman."

"By thunder, I don't hold with no nester tellin' me what to do! Now, Lefty if you don't have gumption 'nuff to pull those wagons clear, I'll do it myself. Come on, men!"

Flint and his men slowly approached the farmers and their wagons.

"THIS IS YOUR LAST WARNING, BANNERMAN!"

"DRAW YOUR RIFLES, MEN!" Flint barked.

("Wait-a-minute, I know I'm interrupting in the middle of the big 'Face–off' scene but I've got a problem here. Flint's men have maneuvered about a thousand head of cattle down a narrow trail at the entrance to the valley where the farmers have it blocked, right? Right. Lefty, Rusty and Seedy all feel..."

"I think you mean, Speedy," the Ranger corrected.

"Right, Speedy, all feel the cattle are getting jumpy, right? So, what happened to the fencepost idea? Wasn't Flint just going to run the cattle through the weak fences, then straight through their town?

"Perhaps in my haste to move the story along," he said. "I forgot to mention that the geography of the valley was such that they were still a good distance from the fencepost area."

"Still... too... far... from... fenceposts," I wrote in my notebook. "Got it. Go ahead."

Tonto just rolled his eyes.)

For the moment, it was a total standoff. Each side had rifles pointed at the other. Unafraid, Flint walked his horse a little closer to the farmers, then waited.

From behind a barricade, Farmer Jones wasn't waiting any longer. "I'm gonna take care of that mangy, old man once and for all." The farmer drew a bead on Flint and started to squeeze the trigger when...

...C R A C K !

"Did you see that?" Lefty said.

"What a shot!" another cowpoke added.

Jake turned to look. There, halfway from the entrance to the valley Frank Reid holstered his rifle and began riding down to meet the others.

"Frank Reid saved 'ol Flint's life," Rusty said.

Followed closely by his two boys, Frank Reid drew rein alongside Bannerman and his men.

"Frank," Flint said, "you saved my life. I'm grateful."

"I'm here to do more than that, Flint."

"That's the spirit. Now, help us with these wagons."

"Just a minute. That's not what I meant. I'm not going to help you bring ruin to all these farmers."

Flint started to shove past him. "In that case, get outta here and mind your own business!"

Frank turned his horse in closer to Flint and looked at the crusty cattleman squarely. *(Uh, oh.)* "I'm making it my business to see that the rights of everyone here are respected. This small valley means little to you, and yet you're willing to drive these farmers from their homes just to prove your power."

Just then, Dan Reid turned to his father. "Gosh, Dad, the cattle seem restless."

Frank was too focused on what Flint was going to do next to listen.

Flint turned to two of his men. "Lefty, Pete, get some of the others and ride behind the herd. Keep 'em millin' 'till we're ready to drive 'em through."

"Okay, fellers," Lefty said. "You heard the boss. Let's git goin'!"

Some of the cowhands rode out to steady the herd while Bannerman and the remaining men once again began to advance on the wagons. "The rest of you hold your guns on those nesters while Rusty, Jake, Speedy, and me help move these wagons out of the way. And men, be prepared to throw lead, if necessary!"

"Flint...!" Frank started to say, but by this time, things were moving too fast to stop.

"We farmers have our rights, Bannerman!" Baxter said. "SHOW 'EM WE MEAN BUSINESS, BOYS!"

"WAIT, ALL OF YOU," Reid shouted.

Immediately, the two sides began to open fire on one another.

The uproar of the shooting startled and confused the herd, causing them to quickly turn and stampede in the opposite direction. In all the pandemonium, the cowboys could barely control their own horses.

Suddenly, panic swept over Lefty Rodgers as he glimpsed the horizon. "MISTER BANNERMAN, LOOK WHO'S RIDIN' RIGHT IN THE WAY OF THE HERD!"

Flint strained to look through the flying dust and dirt. "Great Scott... EMILY! Git–up, there." He took off with a couple of his men as fast as they could toward the head of the herd.

"You boys stay here." Frank Reid quickly turned his horse and headed out to help.

Try as they might to outdistance the racing cattle, Flint and his men were simply no match alongside the frenzied herd.

However, Frank's excellent horsemanship and the speed of his trusty horse soon passed Flint and the others. "C'mon, big fella, we've got to reach Emily."

Quickly, Frank found himself galloping closer to the leaders of the herd. In the distance, he saw Emily stop her horse in alarm when she realized the cattle were moving in her direction. "We've got to make it. Faster, boy, FASTER!"

Emily Bannerman tried to move safely out of the way of the uncontrolled herd. Suddenly, her horse stumbled and though she didn't fall, Frank watched as Emily lost the reins. Terrified of the fast moving cattle, her horse stepped on the trailing reins, then stomped in a circle as Emily tried frantically to reach for them.

Frank sensed he was not going to reach her in time. He pushed his horse harder when he glimpsed a figure riding over the ridge toward Emily.

Young Greg Baxter, having learned of the trouble in town, was riding back to the valley when he spotted Emily Bannerman. Without a thought to his own safety, he rode like lightning to help the woman.

"Why, look at that," Frank thought. "They still won't make it, unless... FLINT," Frank shouted, "USE YOUR GUNS... FIRE OVER THE HERD!"

Frank began firing over the herd and Flint and his men quickly followed his lead. Slowly, the cattle started to swerve, not much, but enough to buy some time for Greg.

Young Baxter pulled closer to a desperate Emily Bannerman. "GRAB HOLD," he shouted. "IT'S OUR ONLY CHANCE!" He slowed his horse, lowered his right arm and scooped her up onto his side. By this time, Greg felt some of the herd pressing hard against his leg. Valiantly, he urged his horse on. But inspite of his effort, things didn't look good.

Flint heard screams. "My God, EMILY!!"

By now there was so much dust and dirt kicked up from the cattle that it was impossible for Flint to see clearly.

"YAAA!" The cowboys spurred their horses, charging forward as fast as they could.

As the heard moved away, the dust settled. Flint and his men reined up at the place they last spotted the rancher's wife. "Where is she?"

"Boss," Lefty said, pointing off to one side down the ridge. "Looky there!"

Greg reined up near a tree before he gently set Emily down.

She was out of breath and still shaking. "Sakes alive, that was close."

Greg climbed down from his horse. "If the cattle hadn't swerved, we'd have been goners for sure, ma'am."

Frank Reid was the first to reach them, quickly followed by Flint and his men, and the two Reid boys.

"Greg, Greg Baxter," Frank said. "That was a brave thing you did back there. I'm proud of you."

"What's goin' on here. Let me through." Flint said, pushing his horse through to his wife. "Emily, EMILY, are you all right?"

"This young man saved my life." Emily gave the boy a grateful hug.

"I don't know who you are, son, but..."

"Baxter, sir. Greg Baxter. My father has a farm down in the valley."

"Who did you say?"

Many of the farmers rode up to join the others. Judd

Baxter was the first to break through the crowd. "Let me through. Greg, are you all right, son?"

"I'm fine, Dad," Greg said accepting a hug from his father. "We're all fine."

Frank Reid turned to Flint. "Bannerman, your actions toward these farmers almost brought about your wife's death."

The crusty cattleman sighed as he turned to his wife. "You're right, Frank." You could almost see the big man's eyes water as he looked into Emily's eyes.

Flint extended his hand to Greg Baxter. "Son, I'm pleased to shake your hand. It was a brave thing you done and I'm beholdin' to you." Then, he turned to acknowledge Judd Baxter, who but a few short moments ago stood at the other end of a rifle. "Judd, I don't know what to say, 'cept that I'm sorry about all this."

Silence hushed the cowhands who were stunned to hear an apology fall from the lips of their boss.

"Judd," Flint said, looking the farmer square in the eye. "I'm man enough to admit when I've made a mistake and I made a whopper." He turned to Emily. "Guess I let my pride get in the way."

Flint now looked at Frank and the others. "Mebbe I'm gettin' soft with the years. Mebbe the happenin's today have made me see things more clearly. Mebbe what Frank said 'bout them havin' rights and such, changed me. At any rate, I feel different 'bout these nesters... uh, farmers. Judd, you and your friends are welcome to stay in this valley as long as you like."

"You mean it?"

"I'll have deeds drawn just as soon as I get to town," Flint added.

"Well, thanks, Mister Bannerman," Judd said shaking

the rancher's hand.

As the rest of the farmers began to cheer, Shorty Stevens moved through the crowd until he reached Flint. "Now that we've got that settled, what are we gonna do about the train from Chicago?"

"What train?"

"Why, the train carryin' all our winter feed," the foreman continued. "Big slide closed the pass. Railroad don't know when they'll get another through."

"Dagnab it all, Shorty!" Flint said. "Rusty, Pete, better get the wagons together. It's a long ride to Durango to get these critters fed."

"Flint, that's more'n a hundred miles!" Rusty said.

"Hold on there." Judd turned to the other farmers who held a brief conference among themselves. It didn't take long for them to reach agreement.

"You know, Flint," Judd said. "We've got quite a storehouse of corn from last season. The boys and I would be pleased to supply you with all the feed you can use."

"You'd do that for me?" Flint said. "After all that's happened?"

Judd smiled. "Sure, why not? After all, we're neighbors, now!"

The grizzled old rancher just shook his head. "Guess I've been a fool 'bout this whole thing."

"You can sure say that again'," a cowpoke volunteered from somewhere in the crowd.

A few of the others joined in a good–natured laugh until Flint's eyes pierced the crowd sharply. "So, that's what everyone thinks of me, that I'm mean and stubborn?"

Just then, Emily put her arm around her husband. "Oh, you're not so bad. But do you really want everybody to go around calling you Flint? A name like that would make anyone sour. Why don't you use your given name?"

The news caused a stir among the men.

"Now, hold on, there, Emily."

"Oh, go on, honey. It's a wonderful name."

"What's your real name, mister Bannerman?" Lefty asked.

"C'mon, boss."

Flint was on the spot. "Well, all right. But if'n any of you buzzards start to laugh, I'll..."

"We won't laugh, mister Bannerman," the youngest Reid said, "honest."

"Well," Flint said taking a deep breath. "My given name is... *Francis*."

The boys couldn't believe their ears. A few almost let fly with something that sounded like a hoot, until...

"Fran for short," Bannerman snapped.

Judd Baxter gave the rancher's hand a firm shake. "Pleased to meet you, Fran."

Then each of the farmers stepped forward to shake hands followed by Flint's own men. Finally, Shorty Stevens extended his hand. "Pleased to be workin' for you... Fran," he smiled broadly.

Flint shot a hard look to his foreman. "It's MISTER Bannerman to you, Shorty!"

Suddenly, the smile drained from Shorty's face. "...uhhh, sorry, boss."

Then Fran laughed harder than he'd done in years and everyone joined in.

~

"So, your dad was a rancher?" I asked him, as I finished my notes.

"For a while."

"Where did your folks come from, anyway?"

Suddenly, we were interrupted by a wailing sound. "Hey–uh–hey–ahh... ya–hey–uh–hey–uh... heeeey–aahhh–heeeeey–ah..."

"What's that?"

"Tonto," the Ranger said.

I turned and looked outside the cave and there, facing the rising sun stood Tonto high on a rocky outcrop.

"We'll have to stop a moment," he said. "I have a great deal of respect for the ways of Tonto. Whenever he does his morning prayers, I stop anything I'm involved in and quiet myself." With that he closed his eyes and sat silently as the Indian continued his chanting.

I sat quietly, too. After all, I didn't want to be disrespectful. But I also wondered how much of this was prayer and how much was something else.

The Indian's voice moved from a low moan to a series of high pitched screams. It all sounded like some weird song but the lyrics needed some work. He went on like this for several minutes. Actually, it sounds pretty soothing once you get into it. His voice grew lower as he seemed to return to the sound he started with. Then it was over.

The Ranger drew a deep breath and exhaled before opening his eyes again.

"I like it," I said. "But what's it all about? What does it mean?"

"It helps you concentrate on *Wakan Tanka*."

"Walkin–talkin? What's that?"

"Waaakan Taaanka," he said, slowly. "You'll have to ask Tonto about it. He explains it better than I. Shall we get back to the story?"

A feeling I can only describe as a kind of clarity came over me. I read through my notes. "I think I know what the value is here. I think it has something to do with understanding."

"Understanding, yes and caring," he added.

"Caring. Of course. Next word out of my mouth. Bannerman didn't have much sympathy for the plight of the farmers, huh?"

"Well," he smiled. "While sympathy is certainly one aspect of caring, Jim, I see it as something more."

"Oh?"

"True caring is consideration of the feelings, needs and desires of another. A caring person treats others with kindness, generosity and compassion. A person who cares offers understanding especially in the light of another's shortcomings."

"How so?"

"Remember when my dad said, that to be understanding also means allowing a man like Flint Bannerman to find his own balance."

"Yeah, what did he mean by that?"

"He meant that he had to let Flint come to terms with the situation himself, without hearing all the opinions from others on what he should or should not do.

That's an aspect of caring."

"You mean instead of giving him some big lecture about what to do, Frank tried to get him to look at something positive about the farmers?"

"Yes. But notice that Dad never tried to force Flint to see his point of view," the masked man added.

"At least, not until that farmer was about ready to shoot Flint," I said.

"You only use force as a last resort, Dad told us. Even then," he continued, "he couldn't prevent what ultimately happened."

"Yeah, the part where Emily Bannerman was riding right smack into the frenzied herd! For awhile there, I didn't think the kid was going to make it."

"It took the imminent loss of Emily for Flint to see just what was important to him."

"Old Flint was a hard-head, all right."

"But look what happened to Flint after that experience.

"He decided he was going to give deeds to all the farmers for the property that was his."

"See how one act of caring grows from another?" the masked man said.

"Then, hearing about the train accident," I said, "the farmers decided to help Flint and the other ranchers by offering them their corn."

"Sharing and helping is the best course of all," he said. "Because if we don't care about each other, Jim, who's going to care about us?"

MY NOTES:

- The Lone Ranger is **Caring** toward others.
- Caring is showing kindness, generosity and compassion toward others.
- It's treating others the way you want to be treated.

"One more thing?" I asked. "How did Greg manage to get his horse out of the way of the herd? You said yourself that they were pressing in on him and it didn't look good. The next thing, poof, they're sittin' all safe and sound by some tree?"

The Ranger just shook his head. "You sure get sidetracked by details, Jim."

"All right! You wanna know what's bothering me? I'll tell you. Tonto hasn't said word one to me! You tell me he's shy, needs some time. Fine. But he just sits there watching me without saying anything and it's getting to me. Why doesn't he say something? Would it be so much to maybe shake my hand, SOMETHING! That's what's bothering me."

"Maybe you need to tell Tonto that, yourself."

"Don't think I won't!" I turned and there stood the Indian facing me.

"I think I'll give Silver a good run, now."

I think I'm having a *Maalox* moment.

EPISODE FIVE

The Medicine Tree

"Welcome to another edition of *Matter of Fact.* I'm your host Debbie Knowsit. Here are the categories, players: Anatomy, U.S. History, 60's TV, Chemical Additives, and finally... Grab Bag."

"I'll take U.S. History for three–hundred."

"In 1974, this organization of countries lifted the oil embargo."

"OPEC," I answered. "Piece of cake."

"60's TV, one–hundred, Debbie."

"This TV islander was the Skipper's 'little buddy.'"

"Gilligan! Boy, givin' 'em away, today, Debbie."

I noticed Tonto's reflection in the screen of my Watchman as he sat behind me.

(Here's what's going on. He still hasn't said a word to me. Nice people skills, huh? So, I'm still ignoring him.)

"Let's try Anatomy for three–hundred."

"This bone forms the pectoral arch in humans."

"Clavicle. C'mon, Debbie, you can do better than this."

"Chemical Additives, five–hundred."

"And you've hit our first Double Down, Bob. You have the lead with twelve–hundred. How much of that would you like to bet?"

"Bet it all," Tonto said.

Oh, so now, he's a Trivia expert. "Don't chance it, Bob. Betty's only..."

"I'll bet it all, Debbie," Bob said.

"Let's see if it pays off for you. 'A common constituent of animal and plant tissues, this emulsifier is also an antioxidant?'"

Tonto casually sucked down another noodle. "...lecithin."

"Lecithin? Give me a break."

"I think it's... Lecithin?" Bob said.

"Correct!"

How does he know these things?

"Let'd try Grab Bag for two–hundred, please, Debbie."

"This popular board game is played by two players, each with fifteen markers, or stones."

Tonto slurped another fat noodle without missing a beat. "Backgammon."

"Correct!"

"Grab Bag, three–hundred."

"A simple looped bridle, used chiefly in breaking colts."

"Hackamore."

"Well, of course you're gonna get that one," I said. "It's a horse question!"

"60's TV, four–hundred."

"This show by, 'Master of Disaster' Irwin Allen, was really out of this world."

Like–a–shot, "LOST–IN–SPACE!"

Tonto gave a respectful nod.

"On a roll, boy. On. A. Roll!"

"U.S. History, one–thousand."

"A member of a North American Indian confederacy comprising the Mohawks, Oneidas, Onondagas, Cayugas and Senecas."

I snapped off the TV.

"Hmm. To be honest, I'm not sure if it's the Iroquois or not." He shrugged a look as he got up and walked down to the stream to wash out his cup.

What is *with* this guy? How does he know all this stuff? Uh–oh, he's coming back. I got busy pretending I was busy. Eyes in my notebook. Not going to give him the satisfaction of...

"The Ranger and I have a pretty decent library of books," he said.

"What? Sorry, I was..." pointed to my notebook.

He tapped his head a couple of times when it clicked. He's got that same mind thing the Ranger has.

"I pick up things to read, here and there," he said. "Most weeks I prefer *Time* or *Newsweek*, *Rolling Stone,* a local paper. And if I can squeeze it in, I like to catch *Larry King*. I find it comes in handy to keep up with current events both locally and nationally." He just smiled.

I tried not to react but I must admit, I was more than a little astounded at his coverage. I smiled back. Finally, it seemed, the ice had been broken and from then on we talked about all kinds of stuff. For instance, I found out that all things pertaining to trailing, woodcraft and first aid were left to Tonto. He also acted as the Ranger's Intelligence Unit, handling surveillance, gathering information. He cooked most of the meals the two ate because the masked man is, "what you'd call, cooking–impaired, Jim."

I found out the secret behind his warm buckskins–
Capilene underwear.

I pulled out a current copy of the *Patagonia* catalog and
we had a lively discussion about the virtues of *Synchilla*
versus buffalo robes which, he said, sometimes he still
prefers. He pulled one out and let me try it on.

"Nice but a little heavy, don't you think?"

"It's not meant for warmth alone, Jim."

"Oh?"

He pulled the buffalo skin from my back and adjusted it
so that the fur part was on the outside and the buffalo head
covered my head. "This buffalo robe was given to me by an
elder in my tribe, Walks About Early. All animals carry
medicine from *Wakan Tanka,* Jim."

"Yeah, what's with this *Wakan* thing?" I asked.

"*Wakan Tanka* is the Great Mystery. The Spirit behind
all that is."

"Okay. So, what's the big deal about a dead buffalo
skin?"

"The buffalo is Chief of all animals. His spirit carries
great medicine."

"I see." *(but I really didn't. I just said that I did.)*

"You ask a lot of questions."

I felt uncomfortable but I didn't want to look stupid.
"Well... it's how my people learn," I said.

"It's not how the Lone Ranger learns."

"Well, he's different."

"I think I will try this question way, too," he said. "Why
are you here?"

"What, you mean on the planet?"

"No. HERE," he said, indicating the campsite.

"Oh. Well, I wrote this seminar on values and I had some questions about those things."

He sat silent for a moment. "Why?"

"WHY?" I said, looking at him, *squarely*.

"Yes," he continued. "If you wrote the seminar, why do you ask the questions?"

"Well... because I still have more questions and I thought, being a fighter for truth, freedom and all that stuff, he might be able to give me a few answers."

"What is your intention?" he asked.

"I want to learn about honesty, fairness, caring..."

"Yes, but what is your *purpose* in learning these things? What's the pay-off for being honest, fair or caring?"

"The pay-off?" The nerve of this guy, that he should... whoa, hold it. Don't forget he can hear what you're thinking. I just smiled at him.

He smiled back.

Then, I smi... "I'm not sure I know what you mean."

He sat there quietly studying me for a moment. "I think I'd like to read your stones."

"Excuse me?"

"Have you ever had your stones read?"

I glanced down at my crotch.

"No, no," he laughed. "Not *cajones*." He looked around and picked up a rock nearby. "These! Look," he said, "lets try something. Go out and search for a stone, such as this." He held one up.

"You want me to go and look for a rock?"

"Pick it up. Feel it. Move it between your hands. Make sure you find one that feels good to you."

"You want me to find a rock that feels good?" I repeated.

"When you find one you like, I want you to look for another."

"You want me to find *two* rocks that feel good?"

"Right," he said. "Move them between your hands. Compare the one with the other. As you do this, don't be afraid to let go of the first if it doesn't feel right with the second."

As he continued I tried to visualize all this, using my hands as scales, making sure I was holding my "air" rocks right.

"When you've found two stones that you are completely happy with, come back."

I got up and started walking around, repeating his instructions. "I go around the camp."

"Anywhere you want. As far as you want." He pushed me to walk farther.

I moved outside the campsite, searching the ground as I went.

"Go, farther!" he shouted. "Find some good stones."

I walked around a boulder and into an open area of the canyon. How will I recognize the right ones, I thought... too small... too round... hey, what's this? I picked up a black rock. "It's a piece of asphalt, for crissakes!"

I walked deeper into the canyon. Can't find anything here. These are rocks. I need two stones. "Wait a second." There, on the far side of the canyon wall, I spotted an interesting gray stone a little larger than my hand. It was speckled with black and white and brown spots. But the shape. It looked like a lopsided pyramid. I moved it back and forth in my hands. "Feels... good." What am I saying? It's a rock! No, it's a *Stone* and a damn good one!

I continued on, around another corner, all the time moving my stone back and forth, keeping my eyes on the lookout until... I spotted another one, similar to the first. Straight angles. It was white, mainly with black speckles like the first but the sides had some shiny bits. Looks sort of like the Matterhorn after a binge. Let's try the "moving" test. I shifted the stone back and forth between both hands. "Feels good." Now, for the crunch test. I hefted both of the Stones, together. "Nice."

"Found 'em." I said, as I returned to the campsite. "Found my stones."

Tonto was chewing on a piece of my expensive *Hickory Farms* jerky. "Good."

I wasn't sure if he was referring to the rocks or the jerky.

"Let's see what you've got?" he said, as I handed him my Stones. "Hmm, All right. Sit down here and we'll get started."

He began by drawing a circle in the sand. "Now," he said. "I want you to place each of your stones in the circle."

I started to follow his instructions, when...

"BUT," he added. "Place the stones in the circle with the side that looks best facing you."

This whole thing was beginning to sound a little too *Carlos Casteneda* for me.

He snatched the stones from me. "Of course, if you don't want to learn about your purpose, we don't..."

"No, no," I said, grabbing them back. "I want to know my purpose." I studied the circle before setting them down. "Place them the way I want, facing me, right?"

"There is no wrong way."

This really didn't take long since they looked pretty good the way I had them. But I wanted to make sure they were right. So, I kept my hands on top of them both as I carefully analyzed all possible moves—as if they were chess pieces in the final match against grandmaster, Nick Maffeo. Then, slowly, I eased my fingers off. "Your move," I said.

He dusted his hands clean and began his assessment. He examined their place in the circle. He observed their position to the sun. Then he picked them up, one at a time. He analyzed the texture, the color, the faceting. He looked at the footprints they made in the sand. Suddenly, I felt nervous, like I was watching a teacher grade my final and I silently wished I had studied more. When he seemed to have extracted all available information, he returned them to the circle exactly as I had placed them.

"Let me tell you what I see," he began. "You are a deep thinker. And you have many qualities that do you credit."

Jeez, now he sounded like *Madame Rozinka* reading my tea leaves down at the pier.

"Shh," he said. He picked up one of the stones, and looked closely. "You like to read and learn. You carry with you many questions. You are in good health but... uh–oh..."

"What?" I leaned forward to hear his diagnosis.

He kept turning it in his hand and shook his head. "...too many cheeseburgers."

Do I really need to hear this?

He picked up the second stone. "You have worked very hard to achieve something, " he said. "Very hard. And you have achieved it, but you still have many questions. But they are sincere questions." Then he stopped. "That's all."

"That's all? That's everything?"

"For today."

"So what does it all mean?" I asked.

"Stone reading is a way of learning about yourself by knowing how you are aligned with the natural forces. Even though you may think that they have no life," he said. "the stones carry Spirit. All things are part of *Wakan Tanka,* Jim.

"We believe that if we can see how our stones align with the natural forces, we can become aware of our present strengths and weaknesses. We can be better trackers and hunters, better farmers, better story tellers. We can benefit by invoking our strong attributes and strengthening our weaker ones."

"So, what about me?"

"The questions you ask are valid and important. You are on a quest."

"For what?"

"That's for you to answer. You're in training."

"Training? Training for what?" But before he could say another word... "I know, I know, that's for me to answer. So, what do you and the Lone Ranger have to do with it all?"

"According to *Wakan Tanka,* we are here to help you, guide you."

"So, what's next?" I asked.

"You must ask *Wakan Tanka,* Jim."

This is where I came in—when he was on that rocky outcrop this morning. I began by taking several deep breaths... relaxed... rolled my head around slowly a couple of times, closed my eyes then............ they popped back open. "Okay, he told me."

Tonto stopped in mid–chew. "You asked *Wakan Tanka?*"

"Yes."

"And he answered you?"

"Of course. Isn't that what you said to do?"

"Yes, but..." he paused. "I just never saw it happen that fast before."

"What can I say, when you're aligned with the Great

Mystery *things* happen! Nice guy, I might add."

"So, what did he say?"

"He said to ask anything I like. He said, you'd be more than happy to answer any question I had." I pulled out my notebook and pencil. "So, let's begin."

"What would you like to know?"

"Let's see," I said looking at his buffalo skin. "Why don't you start by telling me what you first learned from that elder, you know, what's–his–name–that–walks–somewhere."

"Hmm," he smiled. "Interesting choice."

~

A long time ago, there lived a group of people who had no laws. They had no rules of behavior or other things of value. They hardly knew enough to survive. They did shameful things out of ignorance, because they did not understand how to live.

(Couple of points of interest here. For one, Tonto doesn't tell stories like the Lone Ranger. His style is different, more direct and pithy. And his voice. Well, it's hard to describe but when he speaks his voice is very relaxed, and... well, it just made me want to listen without thinking about anything else.)

There was one among this tribe who was worse than the others. He would take whatever he wanted from his people without asking.

"Hey, where are you going with my buffalo robes?" a man asked.

"I like these robes," the young boy said. "And mine are looking a little worn. So, I think I'll take yours."

On another occasion, a woman had just finished

grinding a great deal of corn. The young boy walked up and took the pot of freshly made meal for himself without so much as a word to the woman. This is why his people gave him the name of Young Boy Who takes Without Asking.

This young boy's ways carried over to his hunting, as well. Sometimes, he would kill animals just to show how clever he was.

"Dear hunter," said the fox, "why do you kill me? It cannot be for food. You look well fed. It cannot be for clothing, for you already possess fine buckskins."

"It was your own stupidity that caused you to be caught," said Young Boy, "and now you must be killed."

Worst of all, he never gave thanks or made sacrifice to the animals he killed.

"How can we get rid of this awful boy?" one man asked.

"Yes," said another. "He takes anything he chooses."

"What you say is true," an elder said, "but he is the best hunter we have. He is the *only* hunter we have. He brings back many deer and buffalo for our people. Who are we to say *no* to him?"

They were a weak people. Not only did they let this young boy do their hunting for them but they let him act with little regard for others.

"Here, Owl Nose, you must be thirsty. Take my pot of water to drink," Young Boy said offering the pot to his companion.

Owl Nose started to drink from the pot when he heard several others around him laughing. He looked down to see that water had spilled from the pot all over his clean buckskins.

Young Boy howled with laughter. "It's a dribble pot. Great, huh?"

One day a member of the tribe came to the elder to

speak. "Hey, he's gone too far, this time."

The elder sighed. "What has he done?"

"He has taken my daughter. What are you going to do about it?"

"Do?" said the elder. "What do you want me to do? This boy who takes without asking provides most of our food. We cannot survive on only what we grow. If we kick him out, we lose our supply of buffalo and deer. Do you want our people to starve?"

"Well, no," the man said. "But why can't we send some young braves out to follow the boy. They could see where the best deer and buffalo live. They could learn how he kills the animals. Then, we would have no use for this boy."

And so, the elder called forth three young braves. They really weren't all that brave because they had never distinguished themselves either in battle or on the hunting field, but they were called braves, nonetheless.

"You three must go forth," the elder said. "and follow Young Boy Who Takes Without Asking."

"Why?" asked the first brave.

"I want you to see where he goes."

"Then, what?" asked the second brave.

"Then," said the elder, "I want you to watch him carefully and learn how he hunts the animals."

"Then, what?" asked the third brave.

"Then," said the elder. "I want you to *kill* Young Boy."

"WHAT?" the three said. "Why should we do this?"

The elder wheezed. "It seems like the best thing to do. He is causing too much trouble."

"So, he takes a few things without asking," the first brave said.

"I would gladly give him anything he wants," said the

second. "He provides us with many deer and buffalo and we don't have to do anything to help."

"I agree, too," said the third. "So, he takes without asking..."

"ENOUGH!" said the elder. "I have given you your task and if you want to BECOME braves of this tribe instead of wannabes, you'll follow my orders."

The three looked at each other, then at the elder. They didn't say anything for several moments but secretly, they thought: who is this elder to tell us what to do? He is old and weak and probably going to die soon, anyway. Why follow his orders? We could get lost, or starve or worse yet, get caught by Young Boy. Finally, the first brave stepped closer to the elder. "Why should we do this?"

The elder closed his eyes. Then he wheezed and coughed. He coughed harder and louder. The braves stepped closer. They thought, this must be it. His last breath will surely follow.

Suddenly, the elder pulled back his robe, jumped to his feet and held a big knife, ready to attack. "If you don't do this, I will kill you all and eat you and there is nobody here who will care that I do it!"

The young braves quickly agreed to the elder's wishes.

"We were just leaving."

"We'll just get a few supplies."

"No problema!"

The three braves were two days out on the trail of Young Boy Who Takes Without Asking when they stopped to rest.

"This is too much," said the first. "He goes too far."

"Besides, we're running out of corn to eat," said the second.

"I'm tired of this whole thing," the other added. "Besides, how are we going to kill him once we've learned his secrets?"

"I don't know," said the first. "My task was to follow him."

"Don't ask me," said the second. "My job was to watch and learn how he hunted."

The third looked at the other two and said, "I didn't even see him after he passed those trees. I'm for turning around and forgetting the whole thing."

Suddenly, Young Boy jumped from behind and killed them all. Then he gathered their heads together and when he returned to the village, he dropped them at the feet of the elder. "Next time," he warned. "I will add your head to this pile."

Once again, he left on another hunting trip. He hunted for days and weeks. He ate only what he needed and left the rest to rot. Along his journey one could find the remains of fox, elk, deer, and an occasional buffalo.

Late one afternoon, after a fine meal, he drank from a stream. Looking into the water, he noticed a fish swimming. In the blink of an eye, he pulled the fish from the water and was about ready to eat it when the fish spoke to him.

"Dear hunter," said the fish, "why do you eat me when you have just finished such a fine meal of deer?"

"It was your own stupidity that caused you to be caught," said Young Boy as he prepared to eat the fish.

"Truly, you are a great hunter," Fish said. "such a hunter would be worthy of a great gift."

Young Boy stopped a moment. "What gift?"

"If you put me back into the stream unharmed," said Fish, "I will tell you where you can find a great medicine tree."

"What good is a medicine tree to me?" Young Boy said. "I have everything I need and what I don't have, I take."

"I am sure you are correct," said Fish. "But this tree can provide you with the finest clothing ever made."

"I already have a fine set of clothing."

"Oh," said Fish. "And yet this tree can provide you with all the game you wish to hunt."

"Maybe you should re—read the last few pages of the story. I already HAVE all the game I can hunt," Young Boy said.

"Indeed, that would seem so," the fish said, nervously. "And yet this tree can provide you with..." Fish thought hard, "...eternal strength and power. Yeah, that's it! Imagine, hunting, fishing, going everywhere you want with all your great skills intact forever?"

"Hmm," thought Young Boy.

"After all," reasoned Fish, "you are a mighty hunter today, but tomorrow, you might not be so quick."

"That's a possibility," said Young Boy.

"From this tree you will gain strength and power over all forever."

"How do I know this to be true?"

"If I'm lyin', I'm dyin'," Fish said.

And so, following Fish's directions, Young Boy set out to find the source of his gift. They traveled along the stream for sometime until they came to a magnificent tree by the side of the water.

"Here, HERE," Fish said. "This is it. Stop!"

The young boy looked and, indeed, saw a great tree before him.

"Well," said Fish, "I told you I would lead you to the medicine tree. What do you think?"

"I think," said Young Boy looking at the tree, "you better come up with a better gimmick."

"What are you talking about? Did I not tell you I would lead you here?"

"You took me to a tree, that is true. But how do I know it is a medicine tree and how do I know it will give me the gift you spoke of?"

"I don't believe it!" said Fish. "I'm not hearing this! Do you hear what this young boy said to me, Tree?"

The tree said nothing.

"Fine," said Fish. "Go ahead, eat me. Let's get it over with. Open up!"

"...young boy... ?"

"Who said that?"

"No, you don't believe me. So, just go ahead, eat away."

"Hello, there!" the voice said more distinctly.

Young Boy turned and walked closer to the tree until he stood directly under it's many branches and leaves.

"Up here," the voice said.

"Where? I can't see you."

"First, you must return Fish to the stream."

Young Boy looked at the fish. "How did you do that?"

"What? Do I look like a ventriloquist or something?" Fish said. "Stupid. Stuuu–pid! Your name should be Young *Stupid* Boy."

"Before I can give you the gifts you seek," said the tree, "you must return Fish to the stream."

"Get the picture, Stupid Boy? NOW!"

Young Boy did as the tree asked and put the fish gently back into the water. "Okay. I did it."

No answer came from the tree.

"All Right!" he said, louder. "FISH IS BACK IN THE STREAM!"

"You don't have to shout," Tree said. "I'm right here."

The young boy looked and though he could see no outward signs, he clearly heard someone talking, but who or what he did not know.

"Climb," said Tree.

Young Boy followed the tree's command and climbed into the tree. He got to a place a few limbs up and stopped.

"Climb higher," Tree said.

Young Boy again followed the bidding of the tree and climbed higher. He climbed to the highest point of the great tree and stopped. "I can climb no higher."

"Climb out," Tree said.

"What?"

"Did I stutter? C L I M B   O U T!"

Young Boy looked and saw only one narrow limb in front of him and began to carefully climb out on it.

"I don't think it's going to hold me."

The tree did not answer.

Young Boy climbed out until the limb became a slender branch that began to move and bend and then he stopped.

"Good," said Tree. "Now, reach."

The only thing that remained in front of Young Boy was the end of the branch he was sitting on, but he did as he was instructed and reached out as far as he could. Suddenly, a small red bird perched on the end of a branch jumped onto his finger. The weight of the tiny bird was enough to cause the branch to begin to break and it was all Young Boy could do to hold on with his other hand. Carefully, he moved back to the center of the tree with the small bird in his hand.

Back on the ground, Young Boy examined the tiny red bird, then turned to the tree again. "All right, I did as you asked. I WOULD LIKE MY GIFTS NOW."

"No need to shout," the bird said. "I'm right here."

Young Boy looked down at the little, red bird. "You?"

"What? You actually thought a tree could talk?" Bird rolled his eyes. "Why do I always get the bimbos?"

"Excuse me?" Young Boy asked.

"Skip it, Einstein. Now, then, what gifts were you promised?"

"I'm supposed to get the gifts of eternal energy and power?"

"Wouldn't you rather have a nice new pair of buckskins?" But Bird didn't get to finish this part because Young Boy began gripping him tightly.

"All right, all RIGHT," said Bird. "I just wanted to see if you were paying attention. You'll get it. You'll get it! Just let go!"

Young Boy let go and the bird fluffed his feathers. "First, we have to take a little trip."

"Another trip?" Young Boy moaned as he gripped the bird, again.

"Not far. Just over this hill," Bird coughed. "Please... the circulation... you're cutting it off!"

Young Boy loosened his grip and held the small red bird in the open palm of his hand. Then, Bird led the young boy over the hill to a darkly forested area where there were many hills. Standing a way from the others was a large mountain in the shape of an enormous tipi.

"This is it!" cried Bird. "We're here. All you have to do is go inside and head for the gift counter."

"You're going with me, right?" Young Boy said, gripping

the little bird tightly, again.

"Yeah," Bird coughed. "Sure. Absolutely! Only let go."

The two approached the foot of the great mountain tipi and after looking around, could find no entrance. Bird faced the mountain and whistled a few notes. Suddenly, the great mountain opened and the two entered. "You gotta know the code," Bird said.

It was hollow inside and very dark. It was the home of many animal spirits but Young Boy could see nothing.

"Come in," said a spirit voice. "We have been expecting you."

As the door closed behind him, Young Boy slowly walked to the center, drawn to the mysterious glow of a fire. Suddenly, he found himself surrounded by many animals.

"Around you are the spirits of the many animals you have killed," the spirit said.

Young Boy looked and saw coyote, elk, and buffalo. Fox was there and so were many deer. Everything that Young Boy had killed surrounded him in the great tipi.

"Young Boy," said Fox. "You have taken everything and given nothing. Worst of all, you have never thanked us."

Young Boy looked around the group. Their numbers were many. How was he to escape, he thought.

"We animals have led a good life, a happy life, until you came and made it miserable," said Deer.

"You have taken our lives without respect. WHO GAVE YOU THE RIGHT TO DO THAT!?" Buffalo thundered.

For the first time in his life the young boy was truly scared.

"Many times," continued Buffalo, "we offered you the chance to change your ways but you refused."

The others growled in agreement.

"Wait!" Young Boy said. "I can change. Really I can!"

"How can we believe you," said Buffalo, "with a life such as yours?"

"He's got you there, pal," Bird added.

Buffalo turned to the other animals. "I'm all for stomping the living beejeepers out of him."

The animals cheered, wildly, sounding like the half–time crowd at a 49'rs game.

"Wait, WAIT!" Young Boy said as the group closed in around him. "I have already begun to change."

But the animals were on all sides of him, now. Deer grabbed his feet. Elk held his hands.

"Nice knowin' you, kiddo," Bird said jumping out of his hand.

The animals started to tear and pull him in different ways. It was awful. They were all acting like, well... like a bunch of wild animals!

"...p r o o f... i've... got... proof..." Young Boy said.

"STOP, ALL OF YOU!" Buffalo roared.

Young Boy dropped to the ground and sat terrified.

"All right," Buffalo said, leaning closer. "Where is this proof?"

Out of breath and still shaking, Young Boy stood up and pointed to Bird.

"This tiny red bird will tell you."

"Whoa, hold on there, killer. Don't get me mixed up in this," Bird said.

"Tell them," said Young Boy. "Tell them about Fish."

"Huh? Oh, the fish," said Bird in a low voice. "He let the fish go."

Murmurs of shock rippled through the great tipi.

"Hey," continued Bird, "no big deal. It was just one fish."

Groans now came from the animals.

"SILENCE!" Buffalo commanded. He walked slowly to the small bird and stared down at him. "Is this true? Did he let Fish go?"

Even Bird was nervous around such a mighty animal. "...yes... your buffaloness."

Buffalo rubbed his chin in thought. "All right, call off the stomping."

A collective cry, much worse than before came from the animals: "OOOOOOHHHHHHHHhhhhhhhhhh!"

"Young Boy," Buffalo continued, "maybe you have changed."

"But what if he goes back to killing without respect?" asked Elk.

"Yes," said Deer. "What if he's just bluffing?"

"I'm not bluffing. Really!"

Once again, the great tipi was beset with the sound of animals arguing amongst themselves. Buffalo stepped to the center and once more, silence fell over the animal spirits. "We'll give him... one... last... chance." Buffalo stared straight into Young Boy's eyes. "DON'T BLOW IT!"

"...I won't," squeaked Young Boy. They all stood there, frozen for several moments.

Carefully, Young Boy placed one foot in front of the other as he slowly made his way back to the entrance. Not a single animal made a move against him. He was almost there, now. He couldn't believe it. Another thirty feet... twenty...... ten.

"Don't you want your gift?" Buffalo asked.

Young Boy turned and bowed respectfully to the buffalo. "I thought I was getting the gift of life, here, sir?" he volunteered meekly.

They all laughed.

"No, no, not that gift," said Buffalo.

Young Boy looked around. He wasn't at all sure what the right answer was. After all, he didn't want to say the wrong thing. But then, again, I'm only ten feet from the entrance, he thought. They're too far away to catch me, now. I can make it. Yes!

"WELL?" thundered Buffalo.

"I'd love to have the gift, sir." Young Boy ran back like a shot.

Buffalo extended his hoof. "This is the gift we are giving to you."

Young Boy looked down and was surprised to see Buffalo holding four small arrows.

"With these sacred arrows," Buffalo continued, "your village will prosper. They have great powers. Two are for war and two for hunting. But there is much more to these sacred arrows." Buffalo put his hoof around Young Boy's shoulder as he continued. "They contain the rules by which men ought to live. We will teach you how to use them. We will teach you the wise ways of animals and man alike."

And so the animals took Young Boy under their collective wing and trained him in the ways of the sacred arrows. For the next year, Young–Boy learned many things. He learned how to set up rules in his village. He learned how to honor the animals on the land and in the sky. He learned how to honor the fish in the water. He learned how to honor women. He learned how to prosper and survive in service to others and how, when necessary, to make war with those who would be his enemies.

The great buffalo animal built a sacred fire and taught Young Boy how to build such a fire and how to pray. The animals taught him how to give thanks. They taught him respect for all things through many lessons. One day, Young Boy placed his sacred arrow bundle on his back and began the long journey home to his people.

While he was gone, famine had claimed the land. The animals had gone into hiding. They were angry at all the people who did not know how to live and were behaving without respect. When Young Boy arrived at the village, he found several children eating scraps of buffalo hide and mud. Using his spirit bundle, he changed the hide and mud into meat and corn. Soon, there was enough to feed the entire village.

The next day, Young Boy sat in front of a fire with the sacred arrows. He sat there in quiet gratitude until all of his people came out of their tipis. He sat there until one by one, they joined him in the great circle. Then, he began to share with them what had happened to him. He told them about Fish and the Medicine Tree. He told them about Red Bird and the great mountain tipi. He told them what the animals had taught him. Then, he began to teach his people the ways of behavior, the rules of honor and respect for all.

Over the weeks and months that followed, the people listened and followed the lessons that Young Boy taught them. Then, they took that understanding to other villages. When asked by others where they came by so much knowledge and wise ways, the village elder said, simply, "we learn from he who is called Young Boy Who Gives And Respects All.

~

I sat there quietly for several moments. I stared at the stones in front of me. "I think I'm beginning to understand what my purpose is. I guess I want to find out what I stand for."

Tonto smiled. "As a small boy, it was instilled in me to be silent and restrained. It was an essential quality in the character of my people. I was shown that this restraint was necessary for patience and self–control. It was okay to have fun and play jokes but the first rule was always respect. I was made to *respect* all things: man, woman, animal, earth. I was taught generosity to the poor and reverence for *Wakan Tanka*."

He paused for a moment. He seemed to be looking inside himself for something more. "Silence is meaningful to my people," he continued. "Silence before speaking was done in true regard of the rule that earnest thought comes before all worthwhile speech."

I considered what he said. "I would like to learn more."

He bit off another piece of jerky. He seemed to be deliberating and I couldn't help wondering, what with all that happened so far—I mean, with my attitude and all—could he put it all behind him? Would he take my request seriously? Would he be willing to share what he knows?

He glanced at a small stack of CD's by my pack. "Got any *Hootie and the Blowfish?*" he smiled.

MY NOTES:

- Tonto believes in **Respect** for all things: man, woman, animal, earth.

- Respect means not only being courteous and polite but not taking advantage of others.

- It means that you care about how your actions affect others.

EPISODE SIX

Tonto 101

The time seemed to go quickly. Occasionally, I would take notes. But most of the time I just listened. Somehow, writing it down seemed to get in the way of the whole experience. So, what you are about to read is part notes, part reconstruction.

First off, everything Tonto spoke of seemed to be part of a way, a path, or a journey. According to Tonto, the whole experience of life was like some great classroom in which we were all here to solve problems. And our experience along the way was a process through which we gained knowledge or wisdom. He liked that word, wisdom. He used it a lot to describe what one gains from an experience and takes with him along his journey.

"From *Wakan Tanka,*" he said, "there came a great unifying life force that flowed in and through all things: wind, sand, mountains, flowers, trees, birds, animals. This same force had been breathed into the first man. Thus, all things were related, and carried equal importance because all things were filled with the essence of the Great Spirit. This view of life," he said, "was humanizing, and gave to my people a reverence for all life. The Great Spirit sees and hears everything, Jim and never forgets."

"Never?"

"Never."

"Well, what happens if, you know, make a mistake or something? Is there a way you can say, 'Sorry, Wakan,' 'excuse me' or something?"

"Those words are not in our language, Jim. If someone injures another, the word *wanunhecun* is spoken. This is enough to show that no disrespect was intended and that whatever happened was accidental. The Great Spirit listens and watches this, too; for in the next life, you will get according to what you give in your heart."

The Ways of Living –

"Walks About taught me many laws. He taught me that these laws were for the good of all. He taught me to treat all people as they treated me; that I should never be the first to break an agreement; that truth should be the only words spoken and that good words do not last long unless they amount to something."

Tonto's manner throughout all of this was very straight–forward, and calm. He wasn't trying to convince me of anything as much as he was describing those things that mattered most to him. But it was more than that. It's hard to describe, but the *way* he explained things as well as the things themselves had a soundness and natural quality to them.

"When I was very young," he said, "I was taught that true politeness was defined by actions rather than words. We were never allowed to pass between the fire and an older person, to never speak while others were speaking and to respect the words of an elder."

The Path to Knowledge –

He picked up one of my stones. "Knowledge is basic in all things. It only differs in form. The world is a library and its books are the rocks and rivers, plants and animals that we share this life with. My people never get angry at natural conditions such as storms or the cold snows of winter. To do so would only intensify human futility. No matter what happens, we respect the condition and adapt ourselves without complaint."

Respect seemed to be the cornerstone of everything he spoke of, but I became increasingly interested in his teacher, the one he called, Walks About Early.

"Walks About was very instrumental in my spiritual growth," he said. "He was part medicine man, and part...... doofas."

"Excuse me?"

"Well, what would you call someone who got up in the middle of the night, tripped over pots and baskets and talked to invisible animals? "Boy, what a doof!"

"If it wasn't for his amazing insights into dreams, the chief would have dumped him long ago."

"Dreams?"

"Much wisdom comes to us in dreams, Jim. It is the job of the medicine man to interpret these visions in order to keep the people of his tribe on their true path. Much of what I have learned comes from Walks About Early."

When I asked him to tell me what one thing was most important, he didn't hesitate.

"Loyalty is held to be the most important test of character."

"Test?"

"It is easy to be loyal to family and tribe, those whose blood is in our own veins. But to have a friend and to be loyal under all trials, that is the mark of true character."

"Did you ever undergo such a test?" I asked.

He sighed deeply. "It is a time and place that remains alive in my heart, forever. It was a season that brought forth many changes. It started with the death of a friend."

~

It was very cold that day. The burial procession wound its way slowly up a hill from our camp. At the head walked my father, White Hawk. He was burying his closest friend, Looking Elk.

In the years that saw an ever increasing amount of settlers from the east, the peace between the white man and our people was constantly at odds. Having moved from their lands again, a tribe to the east had settled in an area where the game was plentiful. But, as more settlers entered the area, the game animals fled. In order to feed their starving families, these tribal hunters found it necessary to travel north and west into Sioux hunting grounds. Intertribal fighting broke out.

While out hunting one morning, Looking Elk was ambushed and killed by a band of rival hunters. In spite of the great loss he felt, my father spoke only of peace.

"What has happened," my father said, "cannot be changed. We must find a way to live in peace with ourselves as well as the white man." Then he told me of a time when he was young and lost his father to war. While dying, his father had a vision for his young son. His vision was that he would follow the path of peace, that he would lead his tribe to a time and a place where the peace remains unbroken forever. This was his purpose, he said.

At the top of the hill, my father stood before Looking Elk's burial mound. He looked at Song of Delight quietly weeping for her dead husband. "Do not grieve," he said. "Misfortune happens to the wisest and best of men. Death will come always out of season. It is the command of the

Great Spirit and all people must obey. What is past and what cannot be prevented should not be grieved for. Misfortunes do not flourish particularly in our lives. They grow everywhere. Look not at the misfortune but seek the quiet wisdom on the other side. Each soul must meet the morning sun and the Great Silence alone."

That night, I had a vision. I was in a strange land but things seemed familiar. I was alone but there was another presence. I was preparing the burial mound of a friend but the mound was empty. Then a voice called to me. I turned and stared into a strange and powerful darkness. The voice called my name four times. I walked slowly toward the darkness then stopped.

"So," Walks About asked, "did you enter the cave?"

"I never saw a cave."

"It's a cave, alright. Did you go inside?"

Tonto thought for a moment. "I don't know. I woke up."

"Hmm, I'd sure like to know what's in that cave."

"What does it mean?"

"I don't know," the medicine man said. "I will think on it."

Tension between the tribes continued to build during the long winter. A group of elders led by White Hawk held a Medicine Council. Its purpose was to find some agreement and put an end to the fighting. All had grown tired of war amongst themselves as well as the white settlers. They listened to the words of peace offered by White Hawk.

After he sat down, Little Bear, an old and respected Cheyenne chief, rose to speak. "My brothers, I look around this council with much sadness. Where are the Narragansett, the Mahican, and many other once powerful tribes of our people? They have vanished before the greed and oppression of the white man, as snow before a summer sun."

He turned slowly toward White Hawk. "I too, grow weary of war with my brothers as well as the white settlers." He motioned his medicine man to step forward. "Red Cloud has received a vision from the *Gitche Manitou* that I wish all to hear."

Red Cloud stood and faced the elders. "The other night I spoke with the Great Spirit." He closed his eyes. "He said, 'the land on which you live I have made for you, and for no others. Why do you suffer the white men to dwell among you? They come only to rob you of your hunting grounds, and drive away the game. You must lift your hatchet against the white eyes. Wipe them from the face of the earth. Then you will win back my favor and once more be happy and prosperous.'"

All sat in quiet reflection at Red Cloud's vision, for many had believed, as he, that the white man was a scourge to be destroyed.

"...yeah, right..." a voice said.

"Uh—oh," White Hawk groaned.

Red Cloud looked around the council. "Who said that?"

"I think some bad bird has given you ill news of the white man," Walks About said.

"Are you questioning the words I received from the *Gitche Manitou,* the Master of Life?"

The others began to stir. White Hawk leaned closer to his medicine man. "This is not a good time, Walks About."

"Trust me," he whispered back. He rose to address the council. "Red Cloud says that the only way to have peace is to destroy the white man."

"That's what Spirit told me!"

"And we all know that Red Cloud is an honorable medicine man from an honorable tribe. But let's face it, this wouldn't be the first time he got his metaphors mixed, now would it?"

"What disrespect is this?" Red Cloud said.

"Anybody remember the time when the *Gitche Manitou* told him that we would endure the cruelest snows ever?"

"It could have happened."

"In the summer?" said Walks About.

"An honest mistake." an elder added.

"Maybe, but it sure caused a lot more work to grow and store all that extra corn."

"Red Cloud was a young medicine man, then," said another. "He has grown in power over the years."

"I had hoped he would grow in wisdom, as well!" Walks About's words were met with only hard looks, now. The Medicine Council was a tough room.

"Better try something else," White Hawk whispered, "You're losing them."

Walks About looked into the eyes of each of the council members. "You all know me. You know I believe in the Great Spirit. I look for his signs in every leaf and rock. I listen for his wisdom in the wind. Has not the Great Spirit always provided for us?"

A few nods of agreement slowly moved through the group.

"Has He not taught us how to grow and hunt for our food?"

More nods.

"Has He not shown us the way of peace among ourselves?"

They're all nodding, now.

"And has not the Great Spirit put the white man on the earth, as well?"

Everyone stopped nodding.

"WELL!?" he snapped.

Reluctantly, they agreed.

"We have all seen these white settlers. And," he shrugged, "I'll be honest with you, I am not crazy about them. But the white man is many. When one is killed, fifty take his place. There is no end to this white man. But who among us can say what the purpose of the white man is? Who can say what the whole of the wisdom of the Great Spirit is?"

Walks About looked at White Hawk. He was making points and he knew it. "I am Walks About Early, medicine man to White Hawk, chief of his tribe and peacemaker to his people. And I say that if you wish to make a strong and lasting peace with the white man we must follow the wisdom of White Hawk. It is the only true way. It is the only way for that of our sons and daughters."

Slowly, one by one, each member of the group began to nod in agreement. All except Red Cloud. Walks About stood for a moment, basking in the respect of the council. It was a good moment for him. If they had "highlight" tapes back then this would definitely rate a featured spot.

Back at camp, White Hawk congratulated his medicine man for pulling another game winner out in the last two minutes. Since the death of Looking Elk, the medicine man had grown to be a trusted friend. But the look on Walks About's face told another story.

"What is it?" asked White Hawk. "You do not seem pleased. We turned the tide. The council voted for peace."

"I fear it will be short–lived," the medicine man said. Then, he walked to his tipi to be alone.

Later that night, White Hawk was disturbed by the commotion of pots and baskets being knocked over. He looked outside his tipi to see Walks About communing again with his spirit animals. White Hawk watched for awhile. He tried to listen, so that he might understand, but he could not. This night more than any before, the medicine man seemed greatly troubled.

Over the next several days, White Hawk gave instructions that Walks About be left alone, that no one approach him for any reason. The medicine man's activities were repeated over many nights. Each time White Hawk tried to listen more closely to the conversations. Walks About seemed to be arguing with the spirit animals.

Early one morning, White Hawk awoke to find his medicine man sitting outside the chief's tipi. His solemn look told the chief that he wanted to talk privately. Actually, it was Walks About that did most of the talking. After much time had passed, the medicine man left quietly.

Something was happening but I did not know what. A short time later, White Hawk emerged from the tipi and I was asked to call everyone together this night. We were to have a Ghost Dance.

I had been part of many ceremonial dances of my people but the Ghost Dance was one that I had never seen before.

"It is a special prayer for peace, my son; for courage and strength in the face of great challenges," my father said as he removed a ring from his finger and placed it in my hand.

After seeing to the preparations, I went to Walks About's tipi. He seemed to be expecting me. In the hour before the Ghost Dance he told me many things: of his pride for me, of the many lessons I had learned, of the respect he held for my purpose that was about to unfold. "We are about to go on a journey, Tonto."

"I understand." I said. Maybe, now I was to learn the key to my future, my place in the circle.

"No, you do not. Your journey lies along a different path.

I have seen it. In time, you will lead many in a peace with the white man, but at a great price." He put his hands gently on my shoulders. "You will not understand everything now, but soon it will become clear to you. It is the wisdom of the Great Spirit that this be your true purpose."

I stood there as he removed his Ghost Shirt and carefully placed it over me. The Ghost Shirt meant divine protection in the face of great danger. "*Wakan Takan* will show you the way. It is up to you to enter the cave of darkness and claim your destiny."

That night, my people danced and chanted in the circle of the Ghost Dance. They danced into the next morning, and through the next day. Men, women and children all took part. All danced and chanted but me. I remained in Walks About's tipi undisturbed. At the end of the fourth day, the dancing stopped. It was silent for a long time. I stepped outside the tent and found everyone asleep in a circle. Apart from the others stood Walks About. As I approached him, the man who had been my friend and teacher remained strangely silent. I looked up into the clear night sky and could find no stars.

"Do you think we will ever meet again?" I asked him.

He studied my eyes for a time before answering. "I do not know." Then he smiled, putting his hands on my shoulders. "I believe good friends will meet somewhere."

Next morning they were all dead. Poisoned by the false visions of Red Cloud, Little Bear's warriors attacked and killed everyone. I remember running around during the confusion, fighting as best I could, but we were badly outnumbered. Fighting off two braves attacking my mother and sister, Walks About stopped an arrow directed at me. I turned and watched my father take down three warriors only to collapse under the blows from several clubs. I held him in my arms until I felt a hard fist slam into me, then I collapsed.

Somewhere, I remember a night bird's call. Was this what dying was like? I remembered what Walks About said about one's past going by as the spirit departs. I remember hunting with my father, laughing with my sister and riding with my friends. Everything seemed so vivid. I could hear the horses approach.

"This one's still alive, Dan!"

I hurried to finish the empty burial mound but the darkness stretched out its arms and beckoned, again.

The night bird continued calling. She held me and caressed my wounds as she sang. "The Lord is my shepherd. Yea, though I walk through the valley of the shadow of death, I will fear no evil."

The next thing I remember is waking up in a room made from wood and the gentle hands of a woman tending my wounds. White settlers had found me and watched over me as if I were one of their own. I do not remember how long I had been there. That night, I awoke to discover the boy who found me. He was asleep beside my bed. He was there the next night and the night after that.

Soon, I was strong again, strong enough to help hunt for game. The youngest boy seemed genuinely interested in who I was and what I knew. Although he lacked knowledge in the ways of hunting and woodcraft, I was impressed with his eagerness to learn. I taught him to hunt and fish and he showed me how to plant and grow different kinds of food.

In the days that followed, we grew closer, spending many hours climbing hilltops, sometimes just sitting and talking. He would point things out and I would tell him what it was in the language of my people. It wasn't long before we began to speak using each other's words.

At night, after the *supper*, his mother would read to us.

It is from her that I learned about the wisdom of the book that helped me through my great sadness. "In their death they were not divided," she would read. "Many are called, but few are chosen."

The book seemed to have an understanding of the Great Spirit and although her wisdom came through different words, it reminded me of Walks About Early.

Alone on the hilltop, I would share with my brother all that I had learned from my teacher. "Silence is the sign of balance," I told him. "He who preserves his selfhood ever calm and unshaken by the storms of existence, his is the ideal attitude and conduct of life."

For many hours over many days he would sit and listen.

"One who is true sets no price upon either his property or his labor. His generosity is limited only by his strength and ability. He regards it as an honor to be selected for a difficult or dangerous service and would think it shameful to ask for any reward. This I believe and all my people believe the same."

The time I spent with the people called Reid was one of the happiest of my life. I had not known any white settlers before. I did not know their ways. They seemed not like the others we had heard about. They respected the land. They valued the animals. And although their words were different, they offered their prayers to the Great Spirit every night.

"He that searcheth the hearts knoweth what is the mind of the Spirit," the father would say. "A person of strong character nurtures that character through fruitful action."

Late one afternoon, on the crest of a ridge, I sat looking in the direction of the camp of my people. Once more, my heart filled with sadness. When my brother came upon me, he sensed my uneasiness. For a long time, we sat silently looking into the distance.

At the home of the Reid people, I put things in order. "I give thanks for all that you have given Tonto. To you, my mother, I give the mimbres shell necklace of my mother. You have fed my spirit with love. Without love, my courage fails. To you, my father, I give the eagle feather of my father. If all would talk and do as you have done, the sun of peace would shine forever. To you, my older brother, I give my knife made from buffalo bone, as strong and true as your heart. In my pain you came to help me. My face shines with joy, as I look upon you."

I turned to my young brother. Although his eyes were pained, he remained silent. I had nothing left to give, except... I removed the silver ring my father had given to me and placed it in his hand. "Long as I live, you will always be... *Kemo Sabay*."

"Kemo Sabay?"

"It means, *faithful friend.*"

He stared at it for a moment before looking into my eyes. "Will we ever meet again?" he asked.

I, too, felt the sadness. "Good friends will meet somewhere."

I returned to the camp of my people and was overcome with emptiness. Along a line of sycamores, I saw many burial mounds. In the center, where my father fell, stood a mound of stones. Turning around, I discovered the Reid people standing at a respectful distance. During the time of my recovery they had spent many hours in the burial of my people.

I got to work cutting the saplings I would need for the final ceremony. Without a word, they began to help me. I showed them how the burial of a chief was to be prepared. It took most of the night. They helped me construct the raised platform and place bundles of twigs around the bottom.

When the morning came, the Reid people stood solemnly as I set fire to the twig bundles. A leader of his people in this life, the spirit of my father must be released through the smoke of the fire in order that he may lead his people to the next life.

Watching the flames begin to move up the scaffold I became aware of my brother standing beside me. After a moment, he slowly walked to the pile and tossed his own stick into the flames. As I had accepted his father, so he had accepted mine.

Then, he turned and whispered to me in the language he had begun to learn. "Do not grieve," he said. "Death will come always out of season. It is the command of the Great Spirit and all people must obey. Each soul must meet the morning sun and the Great Silence alone."

I stood there for some time, watching the smoke slowly wind its way up to the sky. "The Lord is my shepherd; I shall not want. He leadeth me in the paths of righteousness for His name's sake. Yea, though I walk through the valley of the shadow of death, I will fear no evil, for thou art with me. Surely, Goodness and Mercy shall follow him all the days of his life and he will dwell in the house of the Lord forever."

~

"Tonto," the Lone Ranger said in a voice that showed complete surprise. "It was *your* voice I heard in the cave."

I turned and saw the Ranger standing against the wall of the campsite. I looked back at Tonto who never said a word. He just smiled as the two of them stood quietly. It was a real Kodak moment.

MY NOTES:

- Tonto believes **Loyalty** to be the most important test of character.

- Loyalty means to stand by, support and protect your family, friends, community and country.

- It means a faithfulness to commitments or obligations but most importantly, to principle.

EPISODE SEVEN

Blade of Honor

The Lone Ranger, Tonto and I talked late into the night on a variety of subjects. Contrary to my earlier impressions, the masked man appeared well informed on a variety of current events. He expressed equal interest with conditions in Bosnia as well as the Middle East. But the illegal alien issue in his own desert southwest was of special concern.

"The color of skin makes no difference," Tonto said. "All men are made by the same Great Spirit Chief. They are all brothers and sisters. What is good and just for one is good and just for the other."

"That's one of those, sounds–good–in–theory things," I said, "but in practice..."

"In practice, Jim," the Ranger added, "all actions come back to us."

"Easy for you to say," I said paging through my notebook at the last few adventures. "I hate to tell you this, masked man, but everyone in your stories is either good or bad, Black Bart or Swell Sam. People aren't always like that in real life."

"You're right, Jim. There are many people who are a

mixture of traits. Tonto and I have known such people; people who don't break any laws but choose to close their eyes to other principles, just the same. I recall a man who was upstanding, honest and helpful in many ways. He was one of the richest men on the west coast. Remember, Tonto?"

The Indian nodded.

"Gavin Grayson had many fine qualities, Jim, but he had a blind spot when it came to certain fundamental truths."

~

Tonto and I had ridden hard for two days to get to the mission of our good friend, the Padre. However, before we arrived, another man stood in the cool shade of the patio watering his horse and filling his canteens.

"It is very hot today, my son."

The bearded man looked up at the sky. "So it is, Padre."

"You would do better if you rested awhile and continued your journey in the afternoon, when it is cooler."

"Hmm, not a bad idea."

"Fine. I will have a meal prepared."

"Much obliged."

"Are you... traveling far?"

"Headed back to Frisco," the bearded man said, hesitating a moment. "Why do you ask, Padre?"

"I do not wish to pry into matters that are personal. It is just that... if you were heading the other way, east, toward Texas..."

"East?"

"To all who travel east from here I give a message, a plea."

"What kind of message?"

"There is a friend whose wealth and position is great. Many times he has put forth both his money and effort in helping those less fortunate. But he would gladly give all of his wealth to the man who could deliver his young son safely to his home and purge the demons that threaten him and others."

"What demons?"

"They are led by a man whose name is as evil as his heart, Claw Craddick."

"Craddick!" the bearded man said in astonishment. "Tough hombre, Padre, but what's this got to do with Texas?"

"In Texas there is a man whose strength and courage is like an army of angels, a man who helps people in a time of desperate need. He rides like the wind on a magnificent... white..." The Padre stopped, staring at something in the distance. "...out there," the priest pointed. "Do you see?"

The stranger followed the Padre's gaze. "I don't... wait. Looks like someone riding hard, this way. And he's on a... *white* horse. Who is that?"

The priest crossed himself in thanksgiving. "The answer to a thousand prayers, my son."

The image that both men saw looked almost surreal. A great white spirit appeared as a shimmering apparition against the vast desert landscape. Nonetheless, it was real; the white horse, the masked rider and his Indian companion were very real.

A few miles to the west in San Francisco harbor, Craddick's ship, *El Diablo*, rested at anchor. Young Billy Grayson sat tied to a chair in the Captain's quarters. His only companions were a small Chinese deck slave and two hard–

looking sailors. The taller of the sailors, a Frenchman with a rapier at his side, spoke with cruel authority. "Now, Chinaman, you keep zee lad comfortable while 'ee eat 'eez dinner and zee that 'ee does not escape or, your skin, I will strip away an 'eench at a time."

The Asian spoke a few indistinguishable words.

"He can't understand a single word yer sayin', Frenchy!" the other sailor said.

The Frenchman quickly pulled his epee from it's scabbard and held it tightly to the Asian's face. "You understand what I zay, China." With that, the Frenchman pricked the Asian's cheek with the tip of his blade. "Now, zee that you do as you're told or my blade, she will bite you again."

The Asian bowed respectfully.

"I gotta hand it to you Frenchy, you sure have a way with words."

"I've always believed in zee diplomacy."

The two men laughed as they left the cabin and bolted the door behind them.

The Asian listened quietly at the door, then moved back to young Grayson.

"You stay away from me!"

Ignoring the plea, the Asian examined the bindings around Billy's wrists.

"Keep away from me, I say!"

"I'm just as much a prisoner on this ship as you are, Mr. Grayson," the Asian whispered, "but I do not intend to remain so."

"You speak... English."

The Asian turned to the stern window and carefully signaled with a lantern. "I've got a plan," he continued, "but we can do nothing now. I have loosened the ropes so your hands will be more comfortable."

"Who are you?" Billy asked.

The Asian placed a finger to his lips to finish the conversation.

Meanwhile, after learning about the cruel slave trader Claw Craddick and the disappearance of Billy Grayson from the good Padre, the Lone Ranger wasted no time in making plans. The following day, dressed in the clothes of a successful businessman and with his unmasked face hidden beneath another of his many disguises, he entered the office of Gavin Grayson.

"I understand from the Padre," Grayson began, "that you can deliver a message to the Lone Ranger."

A small smile of assurance crossed the Ranger's disguised face. "You can be sure that he will hear whatever you have to tell me."

Grayson leaned forward to examine the man more closely. "Well, if the Padre trusts you, I guess that's good enough for me."

Grayson relaxed a bit. Without understanding why, he trusted the stranger sitting across from him. "Several weeks ago, my young son, William, sailed out of Boston on a ship called the *Morning Star*. I purchased his ticket myself weeks ago without realizing that the ship was owned by Claw Craddick, the most ruthless, savage..."

"Go on."

"Not content to steal goods or money, this scum deals exclusively in human cargo. He buys and sells human lives, mostly chinamen and darkies but somehow, he found out who my son was. Several days ago, a ship put into the harbor, the *El Diablo*. A sailor from that ship delivered this letter to me."

The Ranger read the letter carefully. "Hmm, it's obviously a ransom note. Are you going to pay it?"

"I'd pay it gladly if I thought it would bring Billy home, but a man like Craddick, I don't trust him."

"This letter doesn't say where he is right now."

"No. He could be anywhere up and down the coast. I'm at my wits end. I want my son returned safely but I need assurance, the kind of assurance that I can get from a man like the Lone Ranger. Do you understand?"

"I think I do."

"Do you have any idea how he can find my son?"

"I'm not sure," the Ranger said, thinking out loud. "I have to visit a friend who may be of some help, Meng–Tze Chou."

"Who's he?"

"One of the finest men I have ever known."

"I'm afraid I don't know much about the Chinese in this city. To be honest, I've never cared much for foreigners."

"Meng Chou is not a foreigner. He's an honest, Chinese–American citizen."

"Just as you say. But I tend to concur with the poet, Rudyard Kipling. You know, 'east is east and west is west.'"

"You should meet Meng. His philosophy is more powerful than any poetry."

Grayson's face was deeply lined from worry. "Do you really think he can help?"

"I don't know. He and his family run a successful import business here in San Francisco. His many contacts may know about the comings and goings of your Captain Craddick."

As the Ranger and Grayson continued their conversation, two men were meeting in a darkened alley not far from the harbor. The two were careful to speak in low voices so they could not be heard.

"...his plans were to visit a chinaman named Chou after speaking to Grayson," the bearded man said.

"You sure 'bout all this?"

"Sure as I can be, Claw." Just then, the big man slapped the bearded man so hard it caused him to fall to the ground. "What did you do that for?"

"Ya gotta loose mouth. Mention my name like that again and I'll..."

"Sorry, boss. "

"All right," Craddick continued. "If that masked hombre's in on this, we gotta take steps to get rid of him, see? I don't want him spoilin' my plans for the Grayson kid. Now, this is what I want you to do."

Later that night, in more familiar clothes, the Lone Ranger and Tonto paid a visit to an old friend. After respectfully taking them into his home and serving tea, Meng Chou's expression turned more serious. "My friends, you have come at a time of great need."

"It would be an honor for Tonto and I to help such a great friend in any way we can."

"I know that your courage is great, otherwise I would not ask." The venerable Asian folded his hands in his lap and began. "Three days ago, I sent my daughter, Li, to deliver some shipping bills to a local captain. She made the unfortunate mistake of entering the *Yellow Dog* Saloon. It is a place from which many are shanghaied. I have only just learned that she is being held captive aboard that ship of the devil run by Claw Craddick and his fiends."

The Lone Ranger put down his tea and leaned forward. "Do you mean the *El Diablo*?"

"You know the ship?"

"Tonto, that's the ship owned by the same man that delivered the ransom note to Gavin Grayson."

"Please," Chou interrupted, "I do not understand."

"This afternoon, I spoke with a wealthy banker whose son has been kidnapped and is being held for ransom by Craddick. The ship that docked a few days ago, the ship from where the ransom note came was *El Diablo*."

"What can we do, my friends? Craddick is a most resourceful man. His ship is filled with many cut throats and slaves who gladly do his bidding."

"Yes," the masked man continued, "and any attempt by us to storm that ship could prove fatal to both your daughter and Billy Grayson."

"You think the boy and Li are aboard that ship, Kemo Sabay?" Tonto asked.

"Craddick wouldn't trust such precious cargo anywhere else, Tonto. Hmm..." the masked man thought. "I've got to get aboard that ship and there's only one place I can go to do that."

Suddenly, the keen eyes of the Indian caught the shadow of a gun barrel at the window. "Kemo Sabay, LOOK OUT!"

Instantly, there was an explosion of action. Shots barked from both sides. The room went dark. More shots. Then silence.

The vast underbelly of the wharf district paled in comparison to the scum and villainy in the *Yellow Dog* Saloon. Known for being a safe haven for the most notorious, it was also the headquarters for Claw Craddick.

Craddick sat at a small table in the back room. With him was Squint Jackson. "I'm fixin' to shove off just as soon as Grayson settles up for the kid. Have you got all the men I need, Squint?"

"After word got out about that Lone Ranger character, the town has closed up some."

"Well, you better UN–CLOSE it!"

Just then the two men were distracted by loud voices outside. Craddick opened the door to see what was going on.

"THEY GOT THE LONE RANGER!" one sailor yelled.

"What!"

"Are ya sure?"

A wave of commotion quickly rolled through the bar.

"Pipe down, ALL OF YOU!" Craddick bellowed. "Now, what's going on?"

"Just heard the news, Cap'n," a sailor said. "The Lone Ranger's dead!"

Then, another, louder voice came from outside the bar. "...me see Cap'n Craddick. MOVE ASIDE!"

Craddick turned to Squint. "Who's that?"

"A rough looking Indian of some kind, Claw, and he's headin' this way."

"Feller outside say I find man name of Craddick, here."

The steely–eyed captain slowly approached the Indian. His hand rested on a gun sticking out of his belt. "I'm Craddick. What can I do for ya?"

"Someone kill masked man at house of chinaman, tonight. Me learn, you send him there!"

"Talkin' kinda careless for an Injun, ain't ya? So, what if I did."

"Him good man. Now, Tonto kill you!" Moving fast

enough to surprise even Craddick, the Indian pulled a knife from his belt and ...

Instantly, a slug from a six–gun whizzed by Craddick and shattered the blade of the knife.

"Did you see that?" a sailor said.

"Not tonight, Indian!" A tall, hard looking bearded stranger, dressed in a dark hat and dingy shirt, moved quickly to the side of Tonto and shoved his gun against the Indian's side.

Craddick remained suspicious. "Who are you, mister?"

"A man who's been looking for you, Craddick," sneered the stranger.

"Any man who can draw and fire like that's got my attention and my thanks, mister."

Squint moved forward to grab Tonto. "We'll take care of this Injun, for ya."

"I don't think so," the stranger said, shoving Squint aside. "He may be wanted by the law. If so, I'm plannin' on collecting the reward."

"Sure, you take 'em," Craddick laughed. "You the one responsible for killin' the Lone Ranger, tonight?"

"You see me wearing his boots and mask, don't you?" the stranger said.

Craddick eyed the man carefully. "Just how'd you come to be in on this, stranger?"

"Your man, Griffin, talked to me. And it was a good thing, too." The stranger grabbed Tonto by the back of the neck. "This Injun warned that Ranger fella and he wound up gettin' Griffin first. But they didn't figure on me finishin' the play for 'em."

"Good enough, mister," Craddick said. "Gettin' rid of that masked hombre's worth a lot to me, 'bout three–

hundred?"

"You were going to pay Griffin five," the stranger said cooly.

Craddick grinned. "You're not only fast but smart, too. I like that. Five–hundred it is. You know, a man like you could be valuable to me."

"Do I get my money?" the stranger pressed.

"Sure, sure. I gotta go to the safe in my office. It'll just take a minute. Jake. Hey, JAKE," Craddick called to the bartender. "Set up a bottle for my friend, here."

"Thanks."

Craddick and Squint went to the office as the masked stranger and Tonto approached the bar. The Lone Ranger poured two glasses as he continued the ruse. "Drink up, Indian. It may be the last you have for some time."

"He's a tough one, Claw," Squint said, watching the tall man and Indian through a peep–hole.

"Yeah, I think he'll make a great First Mate."

"First Mate! What if he don't wanna go?"

"You think I'm stupid or somethin'? Jake's given 'em the knock–out drops even as he's swiggin' that rum."

"Gotta hand it to you, Claw, you don't waste no time."

"I gotta load of slaves due up the coast and I ain't gettin' any richer sittin' round here jabberin' with the likes of you!" Craddick barked.

Squint took another look through the peep–hole. "I was just wonderin'..."

"Wonderin' what?"

"...wonderin' if he might be the real..." Squint's words were cut short by more loud voices out front. The two men walked back out to the bar.

"...my head," the masked man said as he began to fall

away from the bar. "...that... drink... drugged!" The Lone Ranger lunged at Craddick but fell before he could reach him.

Then, Tonto, slumped to the floor.

Craddick laughed. For him it was just another day's work and he was anxious to get on with it. "All right, Squint. See that he and the Injun get on board my ship. And see that Cookie keeps these two out for some time. I don't want 'em wakin' up 'till we're well out to sea."

An hour later, a longboat approached the side of a ship anchored a few hundred yards off shore.

"AHOY THERE, El Diablo!"

"Who goes there?" Scar shouted back.

"It's me, Dusty, with a couple more for the cap'n. Gimme a hand, lads."

The Lone Ranger and Tonto were placed on deck with about two–dozen other men in similar condition. But now, something else caught the attention of Scar who stood watch on the top deck.

"Frenchy, what was that?"

"What 'eez what?"

"You see a light over there?"

"I do not zee anyzing. You, too much rum."

At that same moment, in the Captain's quarters, the Asian turned from the window to Billy Grayson. "That's the signal. Many friends will come this night."

"But how will we get out of the cabin and on deck?"

"We will need a diversion."

Meanwhile, back at the *Yellow Dog*, Craddick was finalizing his plans with Squint. "So, with that Lone Ranger fella out of the way, Grayson will pay up or..."

Just then, the two were interrupted by a frantic knock at the door. "Craddick, CRADDICK! Open up, it's me... GRIFFIN!"

"Griffin!" Craddick opened the door. "Say, what's goin' on, here? Your partner was just here an hour ago. Said you were dead!"

"Partner? I don't have any partner. That was the Lone Ranger!"

"WHAT?"

"The masked man only winged me. I was tied up and held at the chinaman's house 'til just a little while ago when he left and I escaped."

"But the man who came here saved Claw from being stabbed by an Indian," Squint said. "We all saw him shoot the knife from the Indian's hand."

"It's a trick, I'm tellin' ya! They planned it."

Craddick eased back in his chair. "Don't make no difference, anyhow. Jake gave 'em the rum with the knock-out drops. He and the Injun are aboard the *Diablo* with the others."

"But the Lone Ranger don't drink," Griffin pressed. "He never drinks!"

You could see the anger quickly build in Craddick's eyes, now. "Hmm... did it just so's he and the Injun could get on board and rescue the kid. He's a smart one, all right. Squint, get all the men together, everyone you can trust."

"Right, boss."

"So, the Lone Ranger wants to join the crew of the *Diablo*, eh? Well, I'll make sure we show him a good time."

Back on board the *El Diablo*, among the many men

sprawled on deck, the Lone Ranger and Tonto cautiously moved below a railing, out of sight of any sailors on watch. They were careful to speak in whispers.

"Tonto, Scar and Frenchy are moving to the portside. There's a dim light coming from that passageway. I believe it leads to the Captain's quarters. My guess is that's where we'll find Billy Grayson."

Suddenly, Tonto froze. "What's that?"

"AHOY THERE, El Diablo!" a voice bellowed.

The Ranger pulled the Indian to the side as he carefully looked, portside. "Several small boats are coming this way."

"You think they're bringing more slaves aboard, Kemo Sabay?"

"AHOY, ON DECK. IT'S CAP'N CRADDICK!"

"Something's wrong, Tonto." The masked man had to think fast. "We'll have to move quickly. Here, help me."

Craddick's boat was the first to reach the side of the ship. "Is that masked man still on board with the Injun?"

"*Oui,*" Frency said, throwing a line over the side. "They arrived an hour ago."

Craddick quickly climbed to the main deck. "Shoot any man who tries to make a move off this ship."

"*Oui, mon capitan!*"

"That masked man and Injun ain't any more asleep than I am."

It did not take long for the rest of Craddick's men to reach the ship and climb the ropes to the main deck. Quickly, the men assembled to listen to their captain's orders.

"You, you and you... go 'round that way. Squint, you, Rusty and Griffin head over that way. The rest of you men, fan out. I want the masked man and Injun alive!"

Instantly, the men split up and did as they were instructed as Craddick leaned closer to his first mate. "Frenchy, what about the kid?"

"I got one china watching 'em inzide and anozther outside zee cabin."

"Good. Now, I want..."

"CAPTAIN!" Squint shouted. "We found him. We found the Lone Ranger!"

Craddick and the others all rushed to the starboard side.

"All right, Rusty," Squint commanded, "pull 'em to his feet."

"Still playin' possum, huh! Shall we kill 'em now, boss?"

"Hold that lantern close. I wanna take that mask off and... there!"

"Boss," Dusty interrupted. "This ain't the same man we brought aboard!"

"What do ya mean, not the same?"

"This man's... too short."

"Yeah," Griffin added, "that masked feller was much taller. And his clothes were different."

It didn't take Craddick long to figure things out. "WHAT ARE YOU ALL STANDIN' AROUND HERE FOR? FAN OUT! And search every square inch of this ship 'till you find 'em both! Frenchy, come with me."

"Oui, capitan!"

Below deck, in the Captain's cabin, the Asian was busy untying Billy Grayson. "This could be the diversion I'm looking for. Stay ready."

Suddenly, there was a knock at the door followed by a strange voice. As soon as the door opened, the Asian skillfully swept Tonto to one side, then moved on the Lone

Ranger, when...

"No, you don't," the Ranger said as he flung the charging Asian to the deck of the cabin.

"Ohhh..."

"Kemo Sabay, look! Small feller... girl!"

Her dark hair was knocked loose from beneath a hat. But she still had enough energy left to make another charge at the masked man.

"WAIT!" the Lone Ranger cried. "You must be Li Chou."

The Asian girl stopped her attack but stood prepared for any sudden move by the two men. "Who are you?"

"We were sent here by your father Meng. We're here to rescue you and Billy Grayson."

"Nobody's rescuin' nobody!" Craddick snarled as he came up behind the Ranger and Tonto. "Drop those guns or the kid gets it first!"

The masked man and Indian had no choice but to do as they were ordered.

"Now, kick 'em outside, here," Craddick barked. "Frenchy, get the kid."

But as soon as the Frenchman moved between Tonto and Craddick, the Lone Ranger turned and struck a hard blow to the captain's chin, knocking him out. In the calamity, Tonto quickly picked up his gun but the Frenchman drew his sword and stung the Indian's wrist causing the six–gun to fall in the dark passageway outside.

With their backs against a cabin wall, the Frenchman approached the unarmed men with his blade. "Now, I will have zee privilege of running you both through." Frenchy lunged at the masked man when his sword unexpectedly crossed with another.

"Not yet!" Li Chou said as she pulled a sword from the

wall of the cabin and successfully parried the Frenchman's attack.

"*Sacrebleu!* YOU?" The Frenchman laughed, wildly. "Why, you are just a girl."

In a flash, Li Chou swung her blade back and forth in front of the Frenchman until a brass button flew from his coat.

"All right, my little china, you asked for 'eet... *EN GARDE!*"

As they watched helplessly, the Lone Ranger realized that Li Chou was risking her life against a well–trained opponent.

"Quickly, Tonto, we must get our guns in the passageway."

The rapid footwork between the Frenchman and the Asian girl kept the masked man and Indian blocked from any forward movement. But as the swordplay continued, the Lone Ranger began to see that Li, too, had been well trained in the use of the blade and continued to press forward.

The Frenchman parried, thrust after thrust. "Ah, you do well, little china, but not... well... ENOUGH!" Suddenly, the Frenchman leaped to the side and pressed a more deadly attack.

For several moments, the fencers seemed well matched. Then, gradually, through a combination of swift moves and the relentless use of a dazzling *parry* and *riposte*, Li forced the Frenchman back across the room.

"NOW, Tonto!" said the masked man as he and the Indian quickly moved to the corridor to locate their guns.

Then, in one rapid flurry of action, a rapier flew across the room.

"Mercy, please. I beg of you!" The Frenchman shrieked

sinking to his knees before Li's blade. "Do not kill me!"

"Tonto, did you see that?"

"Girl pretty good, Kemo Sabay!"

All at once, Meng's men could be heard scrambling onto the slave ship from all sides. Shots were fired and moments later, the fight was over. With guns at their backs, the Frenchman and Craddick were escorted on deck by the Lone Ranger and Tonto in a final round up of the gang.

"Good work, Meng," the Ranger said. "You will find more men in that forward hold, below decks."

Craddick just shook his head. "I don't get it. What are you doin' it for? You got the kid. The rest are just a bunch of chinamen and darkies. What are they to you?"

"Men like you, Craddick, are more than brutal. You see people as cargo rather than human beings deserving of respect no matter who they are or what their background."

Later that evening, at the Grayson estate, the distinguished banker could not hold back the tears in his eyes when he was reunited with his young son. He then turned to the Lone Ranger. "I have you to thank for this."

"You really should thank Li Chou."

"Oh?"

"Tonto and I were unarmed when Craddick's first mate was about to move on us with his sword. If it wasn't for her skill and courage, I hate to think what could have happened." The masked man gave a gentle nudge to the slender girl who reluctantly stepped forward.

"Well, I'll be," Grayson said in amazement. "Why, you're just a girl."

Meng Chou smiled at the banker. "There is an old expression in my country, Mr. Grayson: 'Yellow cat, black cat, as long as it catches mice, it is a good cat.'"

"Hmm," Grayson smiled at Li. "I see your point, sir. I see it very clearly."

~

"Cool! I liked the part about the guy who turned out to be a girl who turned out to be Errol Flynn. Nice touch. Four stars!"

The Ranger smiled.

"How'd that last part go, again? 'Black cat, orange cat, somethin', somethin'...?'"

"'Yellow cat, black cat, as long as it catches mice, it is a good cat,'" Tonto said.

I finished scribbling this down. "That reminds me, I got a quiz for you: how many Chinese does it take to do a load of laundry?"

"I have a better one," Tonto shot back. "A big white guy and a skinny white guy jump from the top of a tall rock at the same time. Who hits the ground first?"

"I give up. Who?"

"Who cares?" he grinned.

I looked at the Ranger for a clue. "I don't get it. What's so funny about that?" This time they both looked at me. It was the kind of look my fifth grade teacher, Mrs. Riggs, would give us whenever we did something wrong. "What did I do?" They remained silent. "What... the Chinese joke?" Bingo! "You guys can't be serious? It's just a *joke*."

"Would you be willing to tell it to a Chinese, Jim?" the masked man asked.

"Well... no." I said, sheepishly. "It wasn't meant to hurt anyone."

"Perhaps, but there are enough individuals who find it convenient to reduce people to a cliche. Too many people show a lack of tolerance by believing that one race is lazier than another, or that one is more tightfisted or that another is less intelligent. And when you do that, even under the pretext of a joke, you take something away from your own credibility."

"I never really thought about it like that before." I took a moment to think this over. "But how do you remain unprejudiced? Is that even realistic?"

"Unfortunately, most of us hold onto some prejudices, in one form or another, Jim, but that doesn't mean we have to give in to them. We are a country of many nationalities, many races, beliefs and ideas bound together by a single unity, the unity of freedom and equality. Whoever seeks to set one nationality against another, seeks to degrade all nationalities."

I felt embarrassed but the point he was making was a good one. I never fully realized how casual comments, even jokes can really chip away at our own character.

"You look like you have another question, Jim."

"I guess I have trouble with that word, *tolerance*. It sounds like 'putting up' with something or somebody."

"Our nation was founded on the principle of freedom from oppression. Much of that oppression, Jim, came in the form of religious persecution. The idea of tolerance was put forth in order that people with one set of religious beliefs would not reject their neighbors because they happen to hold beliefs different from their own. What's important to remember is that people be willing to be open toward another who may be different." He turned toward Tonto.

"Many years ago, Jim, Tonto and I pledged a friendship and a partnership that has remained unchanged to this day. It is a partnership based on equality, trust and respect."

Tonto nodded. "Kemo Sabay, as long as you live, as long as I live, I ride with you."

"Yes, Tonto, I couldn't carry on without you. As long as we ride, we'll travel together."

MY NOTES:

- The Lone Ranger is **Tolerant** of others.
- Tolerance is the ability to accept differences and not judge people harshly or negatively because of those differences.
- It's having a fair and open–minded attitude toward others.

EPISODE EIGHT

Bullets of Silver

"Whoa, wait... do you think this is a good idea?"

"Relax, Jim. Silver will do all the work."

"Well, it's just that..."

"Yes?"

"I've never been on a real horse before."

"What do you mean?"

Out of the corner of my eye, I could see Tonto trying hard to keep from breaking up. I leaned closer to the masked man. "I mean, the burro ride at *Knott's Berry Farm* is the depth of my riding experience."

When I sat up, he made sure my feet were well placed in the stirrups.

"But I did that maybe six times."

"Grab the reins, like this."

"Wait!"

"Ready?"

If I didn't know the Ranger was so upstanding, I'd swear he was enjoying this. "Why don't I just practice walking around first."

"Don't worry, Jim. Silver will take care of you."

Just then, Silver whinnied funny.

"That's what worries me!"

"Hold on, now. ON SILVER!" he cried.

With that, the great stallion took off like a shot. Instantly, I felt my whole body stiffen. Then, "uuuhhhhhhhhh!" I almost fell off the back end but somehow Silver sensed this and adjusted accordingly. Before I knew it, I was... we were off and awaaaay! I looked back over my shoulder. Incredible. In a blink we left the Ranger and Tonto in the dust.

"All right, let's road–test this puppy." I drew the reins to the right. Silver veered to the right. I pulled lightly to the left and he moved easily back. "Niiiiice." I crouched lower. "All right, Silver," I whispered. "Let's see what you've got. Okay, get ready, boy. KICK IT!!!!.. ohhh, shhhhhhhhhhh..." He pulled away so fast, it just about knocked out every ounce of oxygen left in my lungs.

Slowly, I tried to sit up a little more, then, "...good..." I started leaning forward then... I was in the zone. "SSSSSSSSSSMOKIN!"

Just then, I heard the Ranger whistle some special signal in the distance. The horse responded by instantly circling back. "GET READY, JIM!"

"...ready... for what?"

He whistled again. Silver slowed and...

"Hold on, TIGHT!" he shouted.

Tight? I'm holdin' on as tight as...

All of the sudden, the great horse began to rear–up on his hind legs and... "Oh, no, I can't do this... NOOOOOOOOOOOO WHOOOAAAAA!!!!" And then we were up. I mean, UPPP!

And it was some classic image, too: Silver with his front legs up in the air, me with my arms clinging desperately around the saddle horn. "All right... I get the idea... that's good... you can go down, now." This horse has longer hang time than Michael Jordan. "Good, Boy! THAT'S ENOUGH!!!"

Then, just as effortlessly, he set down, again. "Thank God."

"HERE, SILVER!" the Lone Ranger called, again.

We shot off toward the masked man and Tonto some fifty yards away. As the great stallion came to a halt, I remained fused to the reins when the Ranger approached. "Are you all right?"

I climbed down, slowly. "...yeah..."

He patted Silver. "Good boy."

I tried to pat him but missed.

"You weren't scared, were you, Jim?" Tonto asked.

"No!" I sat down on a rock with my head bent, still trying to catch my breath. "I just have a sensitive stomach, all right?"

The masked man chuckled. "Don't worry, Jim. I'm sure it'll be easier next time."

"NEXT time! Are you crazy?" I stopped when I saw his expression change. "I mean... well, riding Silver is a great privilege. It should only be allowed... once." I started feeling queasy, again. "Let's head back. I think I need something."

The Lone Ranger grabbed Silver's reins as the three of us headed back to the canyon.

"I think I've got some Pepto or something back at camp, Jim," Tonto said, walking alongside me. "Only six burro rides, huh? I'm impressed."

Back at the campsite the sun had been down about an hour when Tonto handed me a hot cup of coffee.

"Ahhh, thanks." I took a big swallow and "...Uuucch! What is this stuff?"

"Tastes awful, doesn't it?"

"Yes, it does."

"Bitterroot tea. Supposed to be good for you."

"Good for what?"

"I don't know," he shrugged. "I could never get past the bad taste."

"What happened to the rest of the coffee?"

I watched as the Ranger drained the last of a pot near the fire. He walked over and sat down on a blanket near me as Tonto continued to work on dinner. "How's the tea, Jim?"

I just stared down at it. "Strong."

He leaned closer. "Personally, I don't care for it. But don't tell Tonto."

I pulled my blanket up around me. "Oh, don't worry. It'll be our little secret."

After a moment, he stood up and looked out at the horizon. "You know, Jim, I never get tired of this." He seemed to be gazing at something. "'Here lies a most beautiful lady...'"

"Where?" I grabbed my glasses and quickly stood up, looking around, when I realized he was referring to the striking sunset.

"'Light of step and heart was she; I think she was the most beautiful lady that ever was—this West Country.'"

We stood there, together, watching the sun silently retreat behind the mountains. I have to admit, it was pretty spectacular. Bathed in the warm, orange light, nothing else seemed to matter much. A moment more... and it was gone.

He took another swallow of coffee. "Let's see, where did we leave off?"

I returned to my notebook. "We've covered honesty, fairness, caring, respect, loyalty and tolerance."

Tonto walked over with a couple of plates of food. But after that bitterroot tea thing, I was a little...

"Go ahead," he said. "I think you'll like this."

The masked man and I looked at each other.

"Did you try this?" I watched him, before I took a forkful. "Hey, this is good."

"Curried pasta with chicken and golden raisins," Tonto said. "Found it in this month's *Martha Stewart*." He sat down alongside us. "So, what value are we up to, now?"

"Duty," the Ranger said.

"I thought I'd tell Jim about the time we closed in on Butch Cavendish."

"Cool! Butch Cavendish. This should be good."

"Hmm..." Tonto thought. "How about the time you almost lost your fastball in Boulder City?"

"Whoa, wait a second. You made a mistake?"

"You think that illustrates the point more effectively, Tonto?"

"I don't know what would underscore duty better, Kemo Sabay."

The Ranger deliberated a moment. "Okay," he said.

"ALRIGHT! The Ranger's mistake." Unfortunately, he didn't share the same level of enthusiasm I did. "Sorry, it's just that I've never heard of the Lone Ranger making a mistake before." I smiled, again, at the thought. "Sort of makes you... I don't know, more like me, I guess." I settled back down on my blanket. "Okay, I got it out of my system now. Go ahead."

~

Tonto and I were traveling through the Copper Hills on our way to the town of Crestwood when without warning Silver's cinch broke and I fell to the ground.

Tonto quickly spun Scout around and drew rein alongside his masked friend. "Kemo Sabay, what happen?"

"The cinch broke."

"Ohhh, you told me three days ago about that worn cinch. I meant to fix it."

"It's my fault, Tonto. I should have checked it this morning." Just then, the masked man stumbled a bit. "My ankle. I must have twisted it when I hit the ground."

"Hmm," Tonto thought, looking around. "This looks like a good place to make camp."

"Good idea," the masked man said as he and Tonto led Silver and Scout behind several trees and started to unpack their saddle bags. "We'll continue on tomorrow morning. I want to see Marshal Mark Nelson."

"He's the marshal at Crestwood. I've heard he's a pretty good lawman."

"One of the best, Tonto."

"Kemo Sabay! There's a small town not far from here, Boulder City. How about if I ride there and pick up a new cinch for Silver?"

"Good idea, Tonto. I'll have supper ready when you return."

Dusk was falling as Tonto turned the corner on the main street of Boulder City. After securing Scout to the hitchrail, the Indian was distracted by a loud voice coming from the Boulder Cafe. He moved closer to investigate.

"Leave me alone, Smitty! I know when I've had too

much to drink!" A shaggy–haired man finished pouring what was left of a bottle of whiskey into his glass. "I'm sick and tired of people tellin' me what to do. Sick of that partner of mine tellin' me what to do! Well, Charlie Eaton's not takin' it no more. No more, YA HEAR ME!"

"Simmer down, Charlie. You don't mean any of this," Smitty said.

"Oh, I mean it, all right. I'm tired of always bein' broke. Tired of workin' that worthless hole in the ground. I'm pullin' stakes just as soon as I get back."

"But, Charlie," Smitty wondered, "if you're broke, how you gonna leave town?"

"Gil is gonna buy me out, that's how!"

"With what?"

"Insurance money! He's going to cash in that policy of his, OR ELSE!"

"Easy, settle down. Let me get you some coffee. Whadda ya say?"

Holding onto the empty bottle, Charlie just stared straight ahead.

"Sure, a little coffee'll fix you right up. I'll be right back."

Smitty disappeared for only a moment when Charlie suddenly jumped from his chair and burst out the door of the cafe. He nearly knocked Tonto over as he headed for his horse.

Without a word, Charlie was on his horse and rode out of town just as Smitty Doogan reached the door. "Doggone it all! Did you see which way he went, Indian?"

"Him, big hurry. Go that way," Tonto said, pointing north.

Smitty looked worried. "Dadrat it! Headed back to the mine, I 'spect. I've never seen him like this before."

"Him, plenty mad."

"It's more'n that, I'm afraid. No tellin' what he's likely to do, this time."

"What you think him do?"

"He's drunk enough and crazy enough to hurt 'ol Gil, that's what! I better notify Sheriff Beachum."

A short time later, Tonto hurriedly rode into camp where the Lone Ranger waited. "Whoa, Scout! Easy, fella. Kemo Sabay, maybe trouble!"

"What's happened, Tonto?"

"I overheard some angry words from a fella by the name of Charlie Eaton. Says he's planning on leaving town with the insurance money of his partner Gil Loomis or else! He was plenty angry."

"Did you notify the sheriff?"

"Sheriff Beachum and his posse are out looking for some outlaw gang."

"Do you know where this mine is?"

"The Loomis mine is not far from here. North."

Quickly, the masked man called Silver. "We've no time to lose, then."

"But I haven't had a chance to fix that cinch, yet, Kemo Sabay."

"I'll just have to ride bareback." The masked man carefully stepped alongside Silver and gently grabbed a fistful of mane. "Easy, steady, big fella," he said as he mounted the stallion in one swift move. "Lead the way, Tonto. I only hope we get there before there's trouble. On, SILLLVER!"

Later, that evening, the Lone Ranger and Tonto quietly

approached the cabin and found Charlie Eaton engaged in an angry debate with his partner, Gil Loomis. The masked man and Indian carefully watched the two figures against a curtained window. "Tonto, you were right," the Ranger said.

"I want out, Gil, and I want out, NOW!" Charlie shouted.

"But I told ya, Charlie, everything I own is in this mine. I don't have no cash to buy you out."

"You 'ol weasel, you got that life insurance and that's just as good as cash."

"But, Charlie," Gil said, desperately. "I borrowed on it already."

"You WHAT?"

"To the hilt! That's what we been livin' on for the last two months."

Charlie's eyes narrowed on Gil.

The Lone Ranger and Tonto watched the shadows of the two men as they began grappling back and forth. But things happened more quickly than even the masked man and Indian were prepared for.

"You stay out of this!" Charlie shouted.

"NO!"

Suddenly, two shots rang out from the cabin. Instantly, the masked man pulled his gun and approached the window. "Don't move. I've got you covered."

Just then, the remaining shadow turned toward the window with his gun pointed.

"DROP IT, OR..." But before the Ranger could utter another word, the gun behind the curtain fired. The masked man returned fire. A random shot barked from the man's gun before he fell to the floor. At that same moment, the Lone Ranger and Tonto could hear the horses approaching.

"Those shots came from over there. Come on, men!" Sheriff Wes Beachum rode into view, quickly followed by several more riders. "Whoa, WHOA! ... a masked man and Injun! Hold it, you two, you're covered."

The Lone Ranger holstered his gun and walked slowly toward the lawman with his hands raised. "Sheriff, I can explain."

"That mask and gun explain quite a lot, mister."

"Hold on, Wes," a member of the posse said, riding forward. "I recognize that man."

"You know this owl–hoot, Jack?"

"He's no outlaw, Sheriff," Jack Sanders said. "There's only one masked man in the west that rides a horse like that white stallion over there and travels with an Indian. That's the Lone Ranger."

"The Lone Ranger!" Beachum quickly dismounted followed by three of his posse. "Tarnation, I've heard of you, mister. Sorry, for the mistake."

"That's all right, Sheriff."

"But what are you doin' out here?"

"Tonto overheard Charlie Eaton at the Boulder Cafe make some threatening statements. When we rode up, Charlie and his partner Gil Loomis were arguing about an insurance policy. Shots were fired. When I tried to stop Charlie, he turned and fired at me. I returned the fire just as you and your men rode up."

"Well, what are we standin' around here for, boys? Let's git inside."

The men walked through the door of the cabin. Tonto immediately went to the side of Gil Loomis. "Him dead, Kemo Sabay."

"Looky there," Jack said, pointing to the far wall. "It's Charlie Eaton. Appears you killed him, mister."

"I aimed for his shoulder. I'm sure of it."

"Wait a second." The sheriff held up the head of the man on the floor who was starting to come to. "You're right. You only winged 'em, but he's got some lump on his head. Must've fallen backwards and hit this table, here."

The man on the floor groaned as a six–gun dropped from his hand.

"Charlie, CHARLIE EATON," Beachum said. "Ya crazy fool, you killed Gil Loomis!"

The man on the floor remained silent as he grabbed his shoulder in pain.

Suddenly, another rider approached, dismounted and quickly entered the cabin. "Sheriff, SHERIFF! Gol' durn it, I'm too late!" Smitty Doogan pushed through the crowd of men gathered inside and stopped when he recognized Tonto.

"What are you doin' here, Injun?"

"This here is Tonto, Smitty," a posseman said, "and his masked friend is the Lone Ranger."

"The Lone Ranger!"

"Never mind that now, Smitty," Beachum said, as he took a look out a back window, then closed it. "Tonto says he overheard Charlie at the cafe tonight makin' threats against Gil, here."

"That's right, Sheriff," Smitty said. "He wuz awful mad. Drunk mad!"

"Sheriff, look at this!" A member of the posse pulled a paper from the wounded man's shirt pocket.

"What is it?" Beachum asked.

"It's an insurance policy stuck in Charlie's pocket, here."

"Guess that settles it," Beachum said as he turned to the Ranger. "I'm obliged to you, mister. If you hadn't gotten out here, quick as you did, Charlie just might have gotten away with murder." Beachum pulled a pair of handcuffs from a vest pocket. "Charlie Eaton, I'm placin' you under arrest for the murder of Gil Loomis. Whadda gotta say fer yorself?"

Charlie started to fidget with his hands but Beachum had the cuffs on him before he could do anything else.

"Keepin' silent, eh? Reckon mebbe yu'll have more tuh say in court. Well, you won't have long to wait. Judge Hackett's in town and with as many friends as 'ol Gil had, we won't have no trouble roundin' up a jury."

Early, next morning, the Lone Ranger and Tonto were riding into Boulder City.

"The town looks empty, Kemo Sabay."

"I expect most people are at the trial of Charlie Eaton, Tonto."

The masked man and Tonto reined in their horses a short distance from the Boulder Cafe. As they approached, they could hear prosecutor Gage Cooper call Charlie Eaton to the stand.

"Now, Charlie, isn't it true that last evening you were at this very Cafe drinking with one, Smitson Doogan?"

Charlie remained nervously silent. He tried to fidget with his hands again, but the handcuffs made this difficult.

"Isn't it true, Mr. Eaton," Cooper continued, "that you had quite a bit to drink?" More silence. "And you said, in a loud voice, that you were going to ask Gil Loomis to buy out your share of the mine, or else?"

Charlie closely watched Cooper's face but everything was happening too fast for him.

"Well, mister Eaton?" Finally, Cooper turned to Judge Hackett. "Your honor, would you kindly instruct the witness to answer the questions?"

"Kemo Sabay," Tonto said, watching from a rear window with the Lone Ranger. "He's refusing to speak."

The Ranger studied the accused man closely. "It would appear so, Tonto."

Judge Hackett glared at Eaton. "Charlie, you are instructed to answer Mr. Cooper's questions."

Charlie didn't look at the judge.

"Mr. Eaton," Hackett continued. "Do you understand what I just said?"

Charlie looked forlornly at Cooper and the others in the courtroom.

"I don't know why we're even botherin' with a trial, Judge. We all know Charlie Eaton's as guilty as sin," one man said.

"Yeah, let's hurry up and find him guilty so's we can string 'em up!"

Others in the court quickly agreed until Judge Hackett rapped his gavel hard on the table. "NOBODY'S STRINGIN' UP NOBODY! And if you all don't quiet down, I'll find the lot of you in contempt and send you ALL to jail!"

The crowd quickly settled down again as Charlie's defense attorney, John Henderson, motioned to his client on the witness stand. "Go ahead, Charlie," he urged. "Tell your side of things."

A sudden, overpowering fear gripped Charlie as he stared at the faces of prosecutor Cooper and the others in front of him.

"Been like this since last night, Judge," Beachum said. "Hasn't spoken a word since the murder."

"Well, he'll speak today or be held in contempt. Is that what you want, young man?" Hackett's patience was at an end. He rapped his gavel on the wooden table, again. "Done! Sheriff, remove the prisoner from the courtroom. I'm holding him in contempt."

Suddenly, Tonto noticed something. "Kemo Sabay, look closely at Charlie."

It didn't take the masked man long to come to a similar conclusion. "Tonto, I think I've made a terrible mistake!"

Charlie was suddenly horrified that everyone, including the judge was angrily looking at him. He started to fidget again when Beachum grabbed his cuffed hands and pulled him along.

Not long after he was returned to his cell, the Lone Ranger and Tonto entered the back door of the sheriff's office.

"Oh, it's you," Beachum said a little surprised. "Good to see you again, mister. Headin' out of town today, are ya?"

"Not just yet, Sheriff. Tonto and I stopped by to see if we could talk with Charlie Eaton."

"Talk?" The sheriff laughed. "You can talk all you want. Don't know as Charlie'll talk back. But go ahead if you think it'll do any good."

Beachum opened the door to the lock–up and started to walk back with the two men when the Lone Ranger stopped. "Sheriff, if it's all right with you, Tonto and I would like to be alone with the prisoner."

Beachum shrugged. "Suit yourself." He then closed the outer door and locked it behind the two men.

Charlie looked surprised as the masked man and Indian stood facing him.

"Are you ready, Tonto?" the Ranger whispered.

Tonto nodded.

"Charlie," the Ranger said in a clear voice. "Tonto and I

would like to talk with you."

The Indian closely observed the young prisoner's hands. Freed from the handcuffs, he started to fidget again. "He said, he doesn't understand what's happening."

"So, you *can* talk. Tonto and I have a few questions to ask of you, Charlie," the masked man said softly.

The prisoner nodded.

Later, that morning, the Lone Ranger and Tonto drew rein in front of the cabin alongside the Loomis Mine.

"You think the killer is still in the area, Kemo Sabay?"

"I'm hoping he is, Tonto."

After entering the empty shack, the two men began to look around.

"What are we looking for?"

"Anything that might give us a clue to support..." Just then, the Ranger noticed something that had fallen behind a chair. "Take a look at this, Tonto," the masked man said as he handed a framed and faded tin–type photograph to the Indian.

"Hmm, it's a picture of a mother, father and two, small boys. Wait!" Tonto examined the photo more closely. "The boys are... twins!"

"Yes, Tonto," the Ranger continued. "Charlie and his brother *Rick* Eaton."

"Then the man in jail is not lying!"

"It's a little difficult to fake deafness after Judge Hackett rapped that gavel on the table as hard as he did, Tonto." The masked man walked to the other side of the cabin. He was examining a window that opened outside to the rear of the cabin. "Look at this."

Tonto looked closely as the edge of the window. "It looks

like a black heel mark. Do you think it belongs to the brother of the man in jail?"

"Yes, Tonto. And I'll bet he's still in the area."

"How can you be sure?"

"I'm not." The masked man walked around the cabin as he thought. "I think we were supposed to see Charlie shoot Gil Loomis last night. But there is something else. The killer already knows he can't collect on Gil's insurance. So, there must be something else he wants. We need to find out what that is and flush him out."

"How, Kemo Sabay?"

"By posing as Gil Loomis, Tonto." The masked man quickly collected a few objects in the cabin. "I'm heading back to town. I'm going to send a wire to Crestwood. Then, I'll tell Sheriff Beachum of our plan. I want you to follow Charlie's backtrail. When you find him, I want you to tell him that Gil Loomis is still alive."

"He'll be pretty surprised when he finds out that Gil is not dead."

"I'm counting on that, Tonto."

Later that day, after completing some business at the Boulder telegraph office, the masked man explained his objective to Sheriff Beachum.

"That's a pretty slick plan, masked man," Beachum said. "Don't think folks ever heard Charlie Eaton to have a brother, let alone a twin! What do you want me to do?"

"I'd like to have a couple of your deputies ready when Charlie shows up."

"I'll go myself," Beachum offered. "I'd like to catch this varmint. But what makes you think he'll show up?"

"I think there's something he wants, Sheriff."

"Oh, what's that?"

"I'm not sure. But whatever it is I think he wanted to stop Gil Loomis from talking about it."

Meanwhile, south of town, Tonto was following Charlie Eaton's backtrail. "Hmm, tracks disappear behind rock ridge." Suddenly, a shot snapped near his feet.

"THAT'S FAR ENOUGH, INJUN!" a voice shouted.

"If you lawman, you not take Tonto, 'live!"

"Just keep your hands out where I can see 'em!"

A moment later, the real Charlie Eaton headed down from the ridge and held his rifle straight at the Indian. "I'm no lawman but you'll wish I were, if you make a move."

"You!"

"What's the matter, Injun?" Charlie smiled. "You look like you've seen a ghost."

"I know you! You... Charlie Eaton. Me see you in jail, yesterday."

Charlie just laughed. "You must have me confused with someone else."

"Tonto not confused. Man in jail look like you!"

Somehow, Charlie felt safe enough to relax a little. "That's because we're twins, Injun. How's 'ol Rick doin' these days?"

"Him in jail. Try to kill partner Gil Loomis."

"What do you mean, tried'?"

"Gil fella, still live. Testify in trial as soon as him recover."

"Recover! No one told me..." Eaton quickly stopped before anything else slipped out.

"What you say?"

"Never mind." Charlie quickly changed tracks. "What's the law interested in an Injun like you for, anyway?"

"Lawman don't like Injun, this territory. Think, steal paint horse."

"Hmm," Charlie said. "That is a pretty fine horse, at that. Might be the kind of horse I'd like to have." Eaton leveled his rifle on Tonto, again.

Instantly, the Indian whirled his leg around and kicked the rifle out of Eaton's hands, then mounted Scout and took off.

Before he knew what had happened, Charlie was clearing the dust from his eyes. "Dang it!" He picked up his rifle and readied to squeeze the trigger, when..." Forget it. I've got more important things to take care of."

Later, that evening, at the Loomis cabin, Doc Murphy bent over the blood–stained bandaged head of the Lone Ranger posing as Gil Loomis. Suddenly, something caught his attention. "What was that?"

"Don't turn around, Doc," the masked man whispered. The Ranger started moaning in a low, painful voice just as the door swung open and Charlie Eaton walked in. "Don't move, Doc. There's a gun pointed straight at your back." Charlie walked around toward the front of the bed.

"Well," Charlie continued. "Looks like that Injun was right after all."

"Eaton if you had any sense of decency left in you, you'd..."

"But I don't, Doc!" Eaton shoved his gun deeper into Murphy's back. "The last of my decency is at the bottom of that mine over there."

"So, you're just gonna let your twin brother take the blame. Is that it?"

"And why not, he's been just as much a burden to me as that old man, there. As soon as I make sure he can't testify, I can start over and..."

"You not start anything." Suddenly, Tonto stood in the doorway to the cabin with his gun in Charlie's back.

"What the? That you, Injun?"

"Me, Tonto, friend of Lone Ranger."

"Good work, Tonto." At that moment, the masked man sprang out of bed and held his gun on Charlie.

Eaton couldn't believe his eyes. "The Lone Ranger! Thought you cleared out of town."

"You thought wrong, Charlie," the Ranger said. "You can come in now, Sheriff."

Beachum entered the cabin just behind Tonto.

"I trust you heard everything the *real* Charlie Eaton had to say?"

"Didn't miss a thing, mister."

"You see, Sheriff," the Ranger continued. "What really caused Charlie to be upset was a letter he had received from a lawyer in Denver. His mother had died and left the balance of her family estate to Charlie on condition that he take care of his brother, Rick. Charlie wasn't too happy with that."

"You seem to know a lot, mister," Charlie said.

"He'd already spent the better part of his life taking care of his brother. Then, when Charlie discovered that Gil Loomis overheard his plan to get rid of Rick, he decided to kill Gil and frame his twin brother for the crime."

"There's just one thing you left out, masked man."

"What's that?"

The sheriff poked his gun into Tonto's side. "Me! Now, hand over your guns or your Indian friend gets it!"

"I thought you were on our side, Sheriff?"

"Thought wrong, mister," Beachum smirked.

"So, you must be Charlie's partner," the Ranger added.

"You catch on fast, mister," Beachum said as he collected the guns and handed one to Charlie.

"I don't understand, Wes," Doc Murphy asked. "Why are you in on this?"

Beachum laughed. "You think I want to sit back and collect that lousy forty dollars a month forever, Doc? I'll never get rich that way."

"Get rich? I don't follow ya, Wes."

The Lone Ranger carefully edged toward Charlie and Beachum as they talked. "Why don't you tell the doctor how you were Charlie's outside man; the one person he could count on to see that things happen the way you had planned?"

Charlie's voice grew anxious. "How'd he know 'bout our plans, Wes?"

"Relax, Charlie. He's just tryin' to get your goat. He's the Lone Ranger and he think's he's figured it all out, see."

The masked man leaned closer to the two. "Figured out how you'd be out of town, supposedly hunting an outlaw gang, while Charlie was at the Cafe in town telling Smitty Doogan loud and clear how he was getting tired of Gil Loomis."

"What?" Murphy said, in disbelief.

"Sheriff Beachum and Charlie had it all planned out, Doc, until..."

"...until," Beachum interrupted, "you and your Indian friend happened to step in."

"Yes, when Tonto and I showed up, we did your job for you."

Beachum smiled. "What better evidence than to have me and the posse tell Judge Hackett that the Lone Ranger and Tonto captured Gil's murderer."

"You see, Doc," the Ranger continued. "It was Rick that I shot, thinking he was Charlie. Then, Sheriff Beachum arrived on the scene at the right moment to stop us. That gave Charlie a chance to get out by this back window and hide in the hills for a time. Later, Charlie would give Beachum a share of the inheritance money for his help."

Now, it was Beachum's turn to look nervous. "Say, you do know a lot, mister. How'd you find out about that will?"

"From me, Wes." Marshal Mark Nelson and two of his deputies quietly stepped in behind Beachum and Charlie with their guns drawn.

"Why, you're a lawman, same as me!"

The marshal's expression stiffened. "Not the same as you, Beachum!"

"Good work, Marshal," the Ranger said.

Next morning, they all gathered in the Boulder jail along with Judge Hackett. Beachum and Charlie stood quietly in separate cells.

"And that's what happened, Judge," the Ranger said. "Charlie's brother Rick is deaf. When he was on the stand the other day, he wasn't fidgeting with his hands, he was trying to use sign language. Unfortunately, no one knew that."

"Well, I'll be!" Hackett said, scratching his head. "Then the boy couldn't hear me!"

"Exactly. Tonto and I spoke with him using sign language. Using Rick's information of his family, I wired the lawyer in Denver who sent the information to Marshal Nelson."

"They as good as confessed, last night at the cabin, Judge," Nelson added.

"I'll throw the book at both of 'em! Nothin' worse than a lawman going bad."

They all started to leave the lock–up as Charlie turned to Beachum. "I can't believe I was loco enough to listen to that plan of yours, Wes."

Marshal Nelson paused a moment. A slow smile ran across his face. "You fellas just picked the wrong man when you tried to pull the wool over the eyes of the Lone Ranger."

From out back they all heard a familiar cry, "Hi–Yo Silver, Awaaaayyy!"

~

"It's time to think about updating that line," I said. The Ranger winced.

"Now, don't take it personal. It's a classic. But even *Coca–Cola* comes up with a new tag line every few years. It's a competition thing," I explained. "You gotta stay fresh, on the edge. I come up against this sort of thing all the time with my advertising clients."

He turned to Tonto who shrugged a "what–have–you–got–to–lose" look.

"What would you suggest, Jim?"

"Let me think on it, some." I wrote this down before turning back to my story notes. "Duty," I continued. "So, what *is* duty?" I asked.

"What does it mean to you?" he asked.

(Uh, oh. That's just the sort of thing my teacher, Mrs. Riggs, would pull. She'd always figure a way to turn a hard question around and ask it back.)

"Hmmmmm..." *(I was trying to buy some time here; to think*

of something..) "...mmmmmm..."

(They're not buyin' it.)

"Relax, Jim. This isn't a test," he said.

"Maybe," I hesitated, "it's seeing what needs to be done and doing it."

The masked man smiled.

Tonto nodded. "Sounds good to me."

"Yes, well, doing what needs to be done. What could be more dutiful?" I said, a little more confidently.

"But more than that, Jim," the Ranger added. He pushed another log onto the fire. "People who have a sense of duty are responsible and accountable for their actions."

"Like when you mistook Rick Eaton for Charlie."

"Yes, but duty also means doing one's best."

"But you did the best you could, at the time. You could have walked away when Charlie Eaton was arrested. Why didn't you?"

"Responsible people better themselves when they see a chance to correct any mistakes they've made. Tonto and I stopped in town to get a new cinch strap. But also to take another look at things at the trial."

"You suspected the sheriff, then?"

"Not yet."

"Then why?"

"People of character are answerable for their actions, Jim. They accept responsibility for the choices they make and the consequences that come from those choices. They persist to the end and find out if something is wrong. Sometimes that means going beyond the demands of the law."

I glanced down at my notes. "Boy, if Rick Eaton had really wanted to press the matter he could've had a heck of a wrongful arrest suit going for him. You'll have to admit, his rights were sure given a shellacking."

Tonto groaned.

"What did I say, this time?"

The Ranger looked at me squarely. "There seems to be a lot of focus on people's 'rights' these days, Jim."

"Yeah, well that's part of living in a democracy. You know, '...all men are... endowed by their Creator with certain unalienable rights.'"

Tonto just shook his head.

"What's wrong with that?" I asked.

"We have spent so much time emphasizing rights," the Ranger said, "that many have forgotten the responsibilities that go along with them."

He stood to reinforce his point. "A community driven by rights is oriented toward acquisition and confrontation, Jim. A community driven by *duty* is oriented toward service, acknowledging other points of view, compromise and progress."

He paused a moment. "If we were more committed to pulling together in a spirit of service and citizenship instead of focusing only on personal gain, a greater sense of community would exist. Youngsters would see this example and do nothing less." Suddenly, the Ranger became aware of something and glanced over at Tonto. "Do I sound like I'm giving another speech, Kemo Sabay?"

The Indian nodded and the masked man sat down.

I looked at Tonto for anything else.

"I can only add what my father, White Hawk, said to me. 'I am responsible,' he said, 'To be true to myself; To be loyal to my principles; To keep an open mind; To be of service to my brother; To recognize that others have a right to live their own lives; To listen not just with my ears but also with my heart; And to make all I do worthy of pride.'"

The Indian glanced over at the masked man. It looked like the Ranger was giving him the same, "sounds–like–a–speech" look. Tonto sat down.

I looked at my notes, then gave them both a look. "Jeeez, Louise! How the heck am I going to remember all of that!? There ain't a memory peg long enough to fit all that in!"

The Lone Ranger held up a small, shiny object. "Each of these bullets, Jim, is solid silver. They reaffirm my duty to strive for the highest standards for myself." He placed it in my hand.

"Do your duty in all things, Jim. You cannot do more. You should never wish to do less."

I smiled as I rolled the gleaming metal between my fingers. "Nice memory peg."

MY NOTES:

- The Lone Ranger believes in doing his **Duty**.

- Doing one's duty means doing what is expected or needs to be done for ourselves and others.

- Responsible people accept their duties and are obliged to do them.

- They think before they act.

- People who do their duty make all they do worthy of pride.

EPISODE NINE

The Black Arrow

With his head outside the window of the engine's cab, the Lone Ranger, disguised as a railroad engineer, peered through his goggles at the track ahead. Through the soft fog, he saw two men standing alongside their horses near the Northfield spur. One of them waved a signal flag.

"There they are," the Ranger said, as he closed the throttle and applied the brakes. Suddenly, he recognized the man who was signaling. "Chet," the masked man said to the fireman behind him, "it *is* Dolan!"

When the locomotive halted about ten yards from the men, Chet spoke sharply. "Don't touch your guns."

"What!"

"Hoist your hands and turn 'round slowly. You're covered, mister Jones."

"What's this all about, Chet?" the masked man asked.

Chet smiled slowly. "You're the railroad detective, you figure it out."

Another of Dolan's henchmen climbed down from the coal car joining his friend just as a voice called from outside the cab. "Chet? Ringo?"

"UP HERE, RED! We gotta little surprise for yuh."

A moment later, the notorious "Red" Dolan climbed into the engine cab.

("Hey, what happened to the intro?" you're probably asking. "How come we're already in the middle of something and what's it all about?"

I know we're in the middle of somethin', okay? I just don't have any notes for the first part. What happened? I had to go to the bathroom is what happened. By the time I turned around and got back to my notes, the Ranger was well into his next story and I sure wasn't going to ask him to stop and start over. What's it about? The Black Arrow. Great title, huh? Really grabbed my attention, too. So, let's not waste any more time.)

Quickly, other members of the Dolan gang swarmed over the coal car and engine cab.

"Good work, boys," Dolan said. "Who's that critter?"

"Railroad detective, posin' as engineer," Chet said.

"I'll take those guns, mister. You won't be needin' 'em." Dolan took a closer look at the twin six–guns the detective wore. "Say, these look mighty fancy for a..." Suddenly, the outlaw jumped back. "Hold your guns on 'em, boys!"

Some of the others acted surprised. "Kinda jumpy, ain't ya, Red?"

"You idiots. That's no railroad detective." Dolan snapped the chamber closed to one of the six–guns. "There's only one man in the west that carries twin, pearl–handled Colts and fires special bullets like these." Red held a silver bullet out to the others. "He's the Lone Ranger!"

"The LONE RANGER!!!" the men echoed.

"You'll never get away with this, Dolan," the Ranger said.

The outlaw's steely eyes narrowed on the masked man. "You're the one that put me away four years ago after that robbery in Topeka and the time before in Texas."

"And you'll go back to prison after this."

Dolan smiled slowly. "Mister, this time you poked your head into somethin' you have no idea about."

"I know enough," the masked man continued. "I know you plan to run this train right through the east gate of the Northfield prison when the prisoners are out in the yard; that you have guns and men to overpower the guards, so you can take the prisoners and head out the same way you came in."

"Hey, boss, he knows everything!" Ringo said.

Panic swept through the gang members.

"SHUT–UP!" Dolan moved closer to the Ranger. "If he knew all this before, this train would have been crawlin' with law dogs, boys."

"The boss is right," Ringo added.

Dolan stared straight into the eyes of his enemy. "I say, you're bluffin', mister Ranger, bluffin' to buy time."

"You're smart, Dolan," the Ranger said, defiantly. "You figure it out."

Dolan's hand came down hard across the Ranger's face. The masked man instantly responded with a right cross that sent the outlaw reeling. But before he could get in another blow, Dolan's men were all over him.

"Go ahead, Red," Chet said.

"We got his arms, boss," Ringo added. "Let 'im have it!"

The outlaw stood up and rubbed his jaw. "So, you wanna fight, do ya?" The outlaw rolled up his sleeves revealing powerful arms. "I've thought about this for a long time, mister; through those long, cold nights in prison; the prison you sent me to!"

"You sent yourself to prison, Dolan, when you chose a

life of crime."

The big man shrugged as he turned away from the masked man for a moment, then spun around sharply and struck the Ranger's jaw with a hard right.

The Lone Ranger buckled at the blow. "You'll pay for that, Dolan."

"Oh, I'll pay, huh? Pull 'im up, boys." With that Dolan began a barrage against the masked man with all the vengeance and fury that was bottled up inside him for the last four years. Blow after blow, the outlaw pounded the Ranger with his fists. The cruel blows to his chin and body were more than human endurance could tolerate. Finally, he lost consciousness.

"He's out cold, Red."

But that didn't stop Dolan. "I'm not through with him, yet!"

"BOSS!" Ringo cried, grabbing Dolan's arm. "We're gonna be late."

After one final kick, the outlaw backed off. "Alright. Let 'im go."

The Lone Ranger slumped to the floor of the cab and lay motionless.

Dolan jumped down from the engine cab. He felt strangely refreshed from the beating and the night air.

"What'll we do with him now, boss?" Ringo asked. "Plug 'im and throw 'im over the side?"

Catching his breath, Dolan was more than eager to end the life of the man who had stood in his way too many times. "Yeah, finish 'im. Finish 'im and let's get goin'."

"With pleasure." Ringo held his gun to the head of the Lone Ranger. He cocked the hammer and...

"No, wait!" Dolan interrupted. An evil gleam came to the

outlaw's eyes. "I've got a better idea."

Meanwhile, at the Northfield Prison, Warden Stockton stood talking to an Indian on top of the prison walls overlooking a large gate and the railroad tracks that led to it.

"Train seems a might late, Tonto."

"Hmm, I don't like it."

"What do you think we should do?"

"Have you done as the masked man has asked?"

"Yes," Stockton said. "I've had all the prisoners taken from the yard early and locked in their cells."

"Good."

"And all available guards have been stationed inside the gate and along the section of track within the prison walls."

"Warden!" a guard yelled from the tower. "Train's comin'!"

"YOU MEN AT THE GATE," Stockton shouted. "GET READY. WHEN I GIVE THE SIGNAL, YOU KNOW WHAT TO DO!"

As agreements were called back, Tonto spotted something as he looked through the Warden's field glasses. "Warden, LOOK THERE!"

"Lemme see." When Stockton's eyes focused in the distance, he was stunned at what he saw. "GREAT DAY! It's the masked man. And he's tied to the front of the locomotive!"

"Quick," Tonto said running down from the wall, "No time to lose!"

At that moment, the big train headed straight for the prison gate.

"Almost there, Red!" Chet said.

Dolan leaned over and gave the throttle another push, increasing the engine's speed.

"What are you doin', boss?"

"I want our friend to get the full effect when we smash through that gate."

"We're goin' plenty fast as it is, and I don't..."

"Who's runnin' this outfit, you or me? ALL RIGHT, MEN!" Red shouted. "Hang on to somethin' so's you won't be thrown when we hit the gate. Now, remember, as soon as we're inside the wall, Ringo, you and your men hold off the guards while Frisco and the rest toss out the guns to the prisoners."

"Right boss!"

"Sure, Red!"

Chet looked out the side of the cab. "I see the guards on top of the walls."

"Are they gonna shoot?"

"Don't act like it. One of the guards is waving to us."

Dolan let out a laugh. "Boys, I think we've surprised 'em. Brace yourselves."

"WAIT, boss! He's not waving at us. He's waving at somebody inside... HEY, THE GATES ARE SWINGIN' OPEN!"

"WHAT!" Dolan leaned out for a closer look.

"The yard's crawlin' with guards and they all got rifles and shotguns."

"It's a trap! HIT THE BRAKES!"

Chet quickly pulled back on the throttle and slammed on the brakes. "We're goin' too fast! WE'RE NOT STOPPIN'," he screamed. "We're gonna slide right through the gates."

"DO SOMETHING!" Dolan shouted. "PUT'R IN

REVERSE!"

It was too late. With sparks flying from frozen wheels skidding along the rails, the big train slid past the wide open gates and well within the prison walls.

"WE'RE TRAPPED!"

"SURROUNDED!"

"What'll we do?"

"MAKE A RUN FOR IT, BOYS," Dolan screamed.

With guns blazing, Dolan and his men jumped from the train and began running toward the prison gate, their only hope of escape.

"Fight for the gate, boys. Come on!"

One by one the outlaws fell under an unrelenting barrage of gunfire from the prison guards.

Meanwhile, Tonto quickly ran to the front of the locomotive with his knife and cut the ropes that held the Lone Ranger. "Kemo Sabay, are you all right?"

"Yes, Tonto. Come on, let's join the fight." With that, the Lone Ranger grabbed a pair of six–guns the Indian had for him and along with the prison guards, began to push back Dolan and his men.

As the giant gates closed, the outlaws were powerless to continue. Stockton called down to them from above. "PUT DOWN YOUR GUNS OR WE'LL SHOOT ALL OF YOU!"

"I got my hands up," Chet said.

"Don't shoot," Ringo said. "I give up!"

"HOLD YOUR FIRE, MEN," Stockton yelled. "YOU OUTLAWS KEEP YOUR HANDS HIGH WHERE WE CAN SEE 'EM!"

Amid the confusion in the yard, Red Dolan was making his way through a group of men, until...

"Where do you think you're going, Dolan?" the masked

man said as he cut off the outlaw's escape.

"Why, you!" Dolan swung wildly at the masked man who dodged the big man's fist.

"Search 'em, men!" Stockton said, as the guards began rounding up Dolan's gang.

The Lone Ranger and Tonto with Red Dolan in tow approached the others.

The warden smiled. "Well, Dolan, didn't expect you back so early. Must be the food, huh? Cuff 'im."

Three guards rushed over and put cuffs on his hands and binders on his feet. But the outlaw just smiled as he glared at the Ranger. "If you think this is the end of it, you're crazy. You have no idea what you're up against this time, mister."

"Take him inside, men," Stockton said.

The Ranger held up a hand. "Wait!" He walked over and faced the outlaw directly. "Exactly, what do you mean, Dolan?"

The outlaw leaned closer. "It's bigger than even you can imagine."

"Oh?"

"In the weeks to come you're gonna see a lot of jail–breaks and robberies AND murders. Whole towns will be taken over, then territories throughout the entire West! You think this is over?" he laughed. "It's not over!"

"All right, Dolan, I'm sick of listening to you! Take him inside," Stockton said.

But the outlaw only grew louder and more defiant as he was led away. "This is just the beginning and there's nuthin' you or your Injun pal can do about it... not if there were a HUNDRED Lone Rangers... NOT IF THERE WERE A THOUSAND!!" Dolan laughed harder than before. "I'LL GET OUT AND KILL YOU, LONE RANGER. I'LL KILL

YOU IF IT'S THE LAST THING I DO!"

The masked man returned Dolan's steely look. "If you ever do get out of prison, Dolan, I'll be waiting for you."

("Whoa! This Dolan guy's a pretty tough hombre. But you got 'im behind bars, right?"

"For now, Jim," the Ranger said. "But over the weeks and months that followed, things began changing in the West. Lawlessness was on a rampage: robberies, murders, and sabotage. As soon as Tonto and I moved into an area to fight one criminal element, the gangs would scatter and move on. Those that were caught, well, for every two or three we caught, more were on the loose. Thirty men broke out of a Kansas prison; fifty escaped from a train in Texas. That's when I began to wonder, wonder if 'Red' Dolan's prophesies were coming true. But it was deeper than that. Local governments were crumbling under the oppression of the lawlessness. Communities were breaking down. It seemed as if there was a plan underway."

"What kind of plan?"

"A plan to subvert the very principles this country was founded on." The Ranger took a slow swallow of coffee and stared into the fire. "When I learned from the Padre that a high official in our government wanted to meet with me, Tonto and I hit the trail at once.")

"Kansas is quite a ride from here, Kemo Sabay."

"Yes, Tonto. We have no time to lose."

The two riders broke into a steady gallop as they headed east.

Riding all day and late into the night, the Lone Ranger and Tonto rested but a few hours and were well on the road early the next morning.

Late in the afternoon on the third day, high on a ridge overlooking the growing metropolis of Kansas City,

Missouri, they paused.

"Kemo Sabay, this meeting's important. What does it mean?"

"There are vague rumors about some kind of uprising. I don't have to tell you what's happened in the last several months."

Tonto nodded.

"And it seems to be growing by the week. There's an evil force at work, Tonto, a force so strong and powerful that it crushes any resistance that stands in it's way."

The Indian's eyes narrowed.

The masked man looked toward the horizon. "It'll be getting dark soon."

"You need me to go with you?"

"From here on I must ride alone, Kemo Sabay. I need you to make camp and wait..."

"...help... Help, HELP!"

Suddenly, the two men turned and saw a girl frantically reaching for the reins on her horse.

"Tonto, look, that girl's on a runaway. And she's heading straight for that ravine. ON, SILVER!"

Instantly, the two men took off after her. The Lone Ranger raced ahead of Tonto and tried to pull up alongside the girl's horse. But for every approach Silver took, the girl's horse seemed to veer at the last minute. Closing in again, the horse raced off even faster toward the on–coming gorge.

"Only one chance." The masked man pulled out his lariat. After a couple of quick overhead circles, he maneuvered as close as he dared. Then, expertly, he threw his rope around the horse's neck and gently reined it to a stop. "Whoa... WHOAAA!!" The two horses came to a halt near the edge of the ravine. The Ranger quickly dismounted. "Are you all right, miss?"

She seemed dazed. "I don't know what happened. Ginger has never acted like... oh, my goodness, a masked man!"

"Don't be alarmed by my mask, miss. I'm here to help."

At that moment, Tonto reined up alongside the two. "Kemo Sabay, girl all right?"

"Yes, she's just out of breath."

"...and an Indian!"

"As I said before, miss, we're friends. Tonto and I..."

"Tonto!" the girl exclaimed. "Then, you must be... the *Lone Ranger.*"

"You've heard of us?"

"Who hasn't? I'm all right, now."

"It's lucky for you, we were riding by when we did." The Ranger held her arm as she climbed down off her horse and walked to the edge of the ravine. "Another few feet and..." With that, she collapsed into his arms. "She's fainted, Tonto. Get some water."

After a few moments, she came around. "Ohh, I wasn't dreaming, then."

The Ranger chuckled. "No, Miss Devlin, you weren't dreaming."

"You know my name!"

"I took the liberty of looking through your saddle bags and came across your credentials. You're a reporter for the Kansas City Sentinel. And by all accounts, Tonto, a good one."

"Why, thank you." Laura Devlin smiled at the recognition.

"It is through many of your reports, miss Devlin, that

I've followed the increase in crime in the West."

"Well, I sure hope you can do something about it."

"I hope so, too. Now, if you'll excuse me. There's something I need to do." The masked man turned to his Indian friend as he grabbed Silver's reins. "Tonto, take care of Miss Devlin for me."

"Oh, I'll be all right, masked man."

"I'd feel better if you'd let Tonto fix you some tea and rest for a while."

(Pssst! Skip the tea.)

"I appreciate that, but I'm expected home soon and I don't want to be late." The girl mounted her horse then smiled at the Ranger. "I hope we'll meet again, sometime."

"Perhaps we will," the Ranger said, smiling back. "Adios."

The girl quickly disappeared into the distance.

"She seems a bit nervous, Kemo Sabay."

"That horse gave her quite a scare." The Lone Ranger continued to watch her a moment longer with a little more interest than usual. Then, he remembered his meeting. "I've got to go, Tonto. Keep a low fire burning for my return. On Silver!"

Swiftly, the great stallion galloped through the approaching darkness to the waiting train. When they were but a few hundred yards away, the masked man reined up, then carefully led Silver to a place not easily seen by anyone approaching. Continuing on foot, he moved through the darkness like a gray ghost. He passed sentries on duty, soldiers at a campfire but no one heard him, no one saw him. He slipped between railroad cars until he reached the spot where he was to meet his contact.

After a moment, a thin man in a dark suit approached.

He watched the man nervously pace back and forth, looking in opposite directions. Convinced that the man before him fit the description of whom he was to meet, he called out. "Mister Secretary."

The man turned around, sharply. "Who's there?"

"I think you're expecting me," the masked man said stepping out from the shadows.

"The Lone Ranger! But how did you get through without being seen?"

"I was told that the fewer people that saw me, the better."

"You truly *are* amazing, sir. Here, put this cape around you. I'll lead you through the sentries to the car where your meeting is to be held."

In the darkness, covered with the cape, no soldier questioned the secretary's companion. In a moment, they stepped inside a guarded train. After securing the door behind him, the secretary moved to an inner compartment door and knocked softly. A voice inside beckoned and the secretary entered. "He's here, sir." The secretary paused before turning back to the Ranger. "You may go in, now."

The masked man stepped into a compartment that was fitted as a private office. His eyes were drawn to a man sitting behind a desk lighted by a single lamp. Although the man's face was in shadow, there was no mistaking his importance and dignity. The Lone Ranger's voice was deeply respectful. "Mister President."

"Good evening. Please sit down." The President turned to his secretary. "Very well, Thomas. You may leave us."

"I shall be outside if you need me, sir."

As the Ranger sat down in a chair opposite him, the Chief Executive's eyes tried in vain to penetrate the mask. "You are the one they call the Lone Ranger?"

"I am, sir."

The President paused a moment to reflect. "What I have to say is vital to the security of our country." Then, he tossed a single object on the table.

The Ranger's eyes widened when he saw it. "A *black* arrow!"

"It was found in the back of one of our best scouts and... my best friend; a man I've known for more than twenty years. He gave his life to provide us with what information we now have."

The masked man never took his eyes off the President as he spoke.

"This arrow is more than an instrument of death. It's a symbol; a symbol for an evil group who conspire against this great country of ours."

The Ranger's jaw tightened. "Mister President, you have my allegiance and that of Tonto to help in any way we can."

"Before you agree, sir, you must know what you're up against." The Chief Executive leaned closer. "What we face is no less than war; a secret war that threatens the very core of what this country stands for. It is an enemy that is unafraid to use any and all means to achieve their goal. They teach hatred and intolerance, breed mistrust and false ambition. They spread poverty, undermine local leaders and, when necessary, resort to murder itself.

"Behind this movement, we believe, is one man. This man threatens to destroy all the principles that many have fought to save and hold dear."

"What do you know about this man, sir?"

"Very little, I'm afraid. I'm sure you've noticed how crime out West has grown?"

"Tonto and I have done our best but, I'm afraid it hasn't been enough."

"I've followed your deeds with great interest."

"Do you have any clues as to who they are, sir?"

The President fingered the object on the table before him. "They are a group of outlaws, murderers and thieves who have banded together and call themselves... the *Legion of the Black Arrow*. Their aim is to take over those states west of the Mississippi."

"Incredible!"

(They want to take over the West? Obviously, these Black Arrow guys haven't been to L.A., yet.)

"Last week, we intercepted a coded letter and arrested the man who received it. Although we were unable to determine the leader of the plot, the man confessed to his part in the plan and convinced us that it's genuine.

"In six months time they intend to have all the outlaws united in one effort to help enforce their new government; a government of complete oppression." The President pounded the table at the mere thought of such a thing. "Every way imaginable to infiltrate the plotters has failed." He looked the masked man straight in the eyes. "Maybe, if one man, a man who's identity is unknown, who couldn't be bought off or, heaven forbid, killed..."

"I understand, sir."

The Chief Executive paused before continuing. "I know that I am asking a great deal of you."

"I'm ready to serve in any way possible, Mister President."

"I'm relieved to hear you say that. But beware. This man, whoever he is, has built a vast organization. They seem to work from the inside, undermining the confidence of town leaders. Then, slowly gain control of those towns until they are ready to join them under one new empire; an empire born of greed and oppression."

"What do you want me to do, sir?"

"Your mission is to try and penetrate this Black Arrow. Find out what you can of their conspiracy and help formulate a plan to defeat them."

"I understand, sir." The masked man stood to leave.

The President grabbed his arm. "Lone Ranger, I believe that if anyone can carry out this assignment, you are the one. But I warn you, it's dangerous."

"I can assure you, sir, that Tonto and I will do everything humanly possible to bring an end to this group."

The President then produced a piece of paper from his jacket pocket. "On this paper is a list of names of my most trusted aids. Please look it over carefully, then destroy it. If you wish to contact me at any time, you can reach me through any of these men." The President extended a warm hand to the masked man. "I wish you God's speed, my friend. The future of our country depends on it."

"Tonto and I won't let you down, sir."

("So, that was it, right? You got the President on your side and everything worked out, huh?"

"Not quite," the Ranger said. *"The President gave us his blessing but the secrecy behind our assignment meant that he could offer no direct aid or protection if we got into trouble."*

"So what did you guys do? How did you find out about this Black Arrow? And how did you stop them from taking over the West?"

"I wish it had been as easy as previous missions, Jim. Many weeks went by with very little information to go on. Those few trails Tonto and I did find disappeared whenever we got close."

"Someone knew of your plans?"

"Tonto kept a sharp look out for anyone trailing us but he

saw no one. Somehow, information kept getting out, spoiling our plans at the last minute. We started eliminating those names from the list the President had given me as his trusted aids.

"Then, something happened that changed everything, something quite unexpected. In town for supplies, Tonto overheard something.")

A non–descript cowboy sat at a table near the corner of the Cactus Saloon. "Everything's set. The train'll be settin' just outside of Memphis next Tuesday. There won't be many guards that night."

"Ya sure nuthin' can go wrong?"

The cowboy spoke confidently in a low voice. "You do your part and nothin' will go wrong."

Tonto hurried back to camp. He was so interested in the news that he didn't realize that he was being followed.

"Kemo Sabay, I just overheard something terrible."

"What is it, Tonto?"

"I watched two men talk softly at table in a saloon. I hid in hallway as they made plans."

"What plans?"

"Plans to kill... the President!"

"What! Are you sure?"

"One cowpoke said, 'everything's set for Tuesday in Memphis.'"

"Hmm, the President is going to be in Memphis next Tuesday for a speech. We've got to get there, Kemo Sabay. We've got to get there and..."

Suddenly, Tonto signaled that he heard something in the brush.

Instinctively, both men drew their guns in the direction of the sound. "Whoever you are, come out with your hands up. You're covered!"

Laura Devlin stepped into the light of the campfire. "I'm sorry to have crept up on you like that."

The Ranger lowered his gun. "Miss Devlin, what are you doing here?"

"I simply had to come when I heard the news." Moving closer, the reporter's eyes tried to see the face behind the mask but it was too dark.

"Oh, what news is that?" the Ranger said, glancing at Tonto.

"Why the news about Red Dolan, of course. He's escaped."

"What?"

"It happened last week," she continued. "I learned from a source that a couple of guards were bribed and that he and several of his men were spirited outside the prison after dark."

"This not good."

"Yes, Tonto, but we can't worry about Dolan now."

"But there's more." Laura pulled her reporter's notebook from her bag and searched through some notes. "Yes, here it is. I learned that there seems to be a bigger force behind Dolan that is really pulling the strings. According to my source, it is a group known as... the Black Arrow or some such silly name.

"Apparently, this band of outlaws is the real cause of all the crime that's been happening out West. I believe they're planning something in Memphis but just what and when I..."

"Kemo Sabay!"

"STOP, Miss Devlin."

Laura looked puzzled. "Why, what's the matter? Don't

you want to know what I've uncovered?"

The Ranger seemed anxious. "The information that you have collected, have you written it up, yet?"

"No, of course not. The story's not complete."

"Then, that's the way it must stay for now."

Laura backed away from the Ranger. "Why, I'm a reporter, sir. It's my job to uncover the facts. Besides, this is a big story, probably the biggest."

"Laura," the Lone Ranger said, softly as he moved closer. "It's because I care about your welfare that I'm asking you not to print any of this for the time being."

She looked deep into his eyes. "But if it can put an end to all the lawlessness..." She stopped. "You know something, don't you?"

He couldn't hide the truth from her and quickly realized that if he was to have her complete cooperation, he would simply have to trust her with some of the information he knew, but just how much he wasn't sure.

"Something's going to happen in Memphis, isn't it?" Her instincts and his eyes told her she was right. "I thought so."

"Laura, to share anything more with you would just be irresponsible for me in light of my pledge."

She continued to stare into his eyes. "It must involve a pretty powerful official for you to feel so strongly."

She tried to coax more from him but, to his credit, the Ranger kept silent. This only served her purpose more. She looked again, "Who could be so important that... the President! He's speaking in Memphis next Tuesday. That's who it is, isn't it?"

"Girl plenty smart, Kemo Sabay."

"It's bigger than I thought. This is going to be the story of the decade." Quickly, she began to pack her notes to leave.

"Laura," the Ranger pressed. "You can't get involved. These men are killers. They'll stop at nothing to achieve their end. If you get in their way, well, they wouldn't hesitate to..."

"Hesitate to do what? Kill me?" she said defiantly. Casually, she stepped closer to the Ranger. Then, in the blink of an eye, she pulled a small colt from her handbag. "I can take care of myself."

He held her shoulders gently. "Please, Laura, now that you know, I'm asking you not to get involved in this."

"And what will you do?"

"I'll be happy to give you a full accounting as soon as it's all over."

"I want to be there when you stop them from killing the President."

"NO!" he answered firmly.

"Then I want to know all the details, now. "

"Why do you need to know everything, now?

"I want the story to be as complete as possible so we can run it in Wednesday's edition. We'll scoop the majors and I want my by–line to be right out there for them all to see."

The masked man hesitated, "I want your word that you will not interfere or be anywhere near Memphis."

She turned and sat down alongside him. "I want to know everything—from the time you got involved to now." She turned to a fresh page in her notebook. "And don't skip the part about your meeting with the President, either."

The masked man looked astonished. "How did you know about that?"

As she pulled out a pencil, she just smiled. "I didn't... until now."

The Lone Ranger sat down and began summarizing everything that had happened. He covered the part about Dolan and his gang. He even retraced his earlier involvement with the outlaw.

Laura took notes on everything. But her questions didn't stop there. She continued to ask about other things in his past, things he had not shared with anyone.

(It was somewhere during this part of his story that I began to fade. When I saw Tonto yawn, I knew I wasn't the only one suffering through another one of his windy "sidebars." Fortunately, he got back on track. Unfortunately, that's when he caught me.)

"What are you doing, Jim?"

Hidden behind a rock with a concealed earpiece, I had my Watchman tuned to the News. The news was over but Letterman was on and... "Wait," I said, "this is good. Dave's gonna do the thing with the bear."

"The bear suit guy?" *Tonto asked leaning closer.* "I don't think a quick break'll hurt, Kemo Sabay. I still have some tea by the fire."

I set the screen up on a rock. Tonto and I crowded closer just as Dave was getting started.

"We caught it on a good night, Jim," *the Indian winked.* "I've only caught this bit once before."

"Really, I think I've seen 'em all."

Cheers from the audience echo through the cave as I turn up the volume.

"Look," I said. "Dave's gonna recap. Here's the one where the guy in the bear suit tried to hail a cab and... YESSS! We found out, he could do that. Then, he played: can a guy in a bear suit... get a hug from a stranger?"

More replay and... More cheers.

"Piece of cake."

Tonto nodded. "That's the one I saw. Wonder what Dave's gonna try this time to juice up the excitement and dramatic tension?"

The answer to our questions flashed across the screen in big titles: Can a Guy in a Bear Suit... get a hug *from a cab driver?*

"Hey, Kemo Sabay, check it out!"

But the masked man just sat near the fire with his back to us.

Tonto waved him off.

"What's his problem?"

"Ahhh, he's pouting."

I looked over at him. "What, are you sure?"

Tonto grabbed my shoulder. "Hey, the bear's back out on Broadway, now."

I turned back to the screen just as a remote camera in front of the building slowly zoomed in on the guy in the bear suit trying to get a cab.

Just then, some guy in a business suit steps in front of our bear and tries to snag his cab.

Tonto was outraged. "What the... HEY, pal! We're not playin', Can a Guy in a Business Suit! Get that guy..."

Our bear pushes the business guy out of the way.

"All right, he's got the cab," I said. "He's askin' the cabby. Uhh, oh, the cabby's not buyin' it. Oh, c'mon, buddy, it's just a bear!"

Jeers from the audience.

Tonto points to the side of the screen. "Look, there's another cab across the street."

Crossing Broadway, our bear disappears from the camera's view.

"Where's the guy in the bear suit, now?" a voice asked.

Tonto and I turned around to find the Ranger looking over our shoulders. "Well," he shrugged, "as long as we're watching."

By this time Dave was sparring with his producer to get a camera back on the action.

Tonto jumped to his feet. "C'mon, Morty! You're the producer. Do something!"

Suddenly, they cut to another camera angle and...

"YESSSSSS!" the Ranger cheered.

Then, with a big, musical flourish, our bear gets his hug from the cabby. That's when it hit me.

"WAIT A MINUTE! I just got it. You're in love with Laura Devlin! That's what this is all about."

For the first time I caught the Ranger completely off guard.

"You're blushing! I don't believe this. The Lone Ranger's in love AND he's blushing!"

Tonto just smiled.

"Now, we're gettin' somewhere. This is gettin' good. Okay, let's continue.)

It was late Tuesday afternoon in Memphis when Tonto and I arrived at the President's train. With Tonto waiting nearby, I carefully approached the last car. A sentry on duty thought he heard something and walked to the rear entrance of the car just as the President's secretary opened the door.

"Sentry?"

The guard snapped to attention. "Yes, sir."

"At ease, soldier." The secretary handed him a sealed note. "Take this message to Major Conklin, immediately."

"But sir, I'm not to leave my post until my relief shows

up."

"It's not a problem, soldier. The President is due to leave to make his speech shortly."

"Begging your pardon, sir, but regulations clearly state that..."

The secretary smiled. "I will take complete responsibility, corporal. It's important the Major get this message as soon as possible."

"Yes, sir!" The sentry saluted and was gone.

Instantly, the Lone Ranger stepped from the shadows onto the rear platform. "Good evening, mister secretary."

"Lone Ranger! You startled me."

"I must see the President, immediately."

"He's having some pictures taken at the moment but I'm sure he'll see you. Wait here." A moment later, he ushered the Ranger inside.

As soon as the masked man entered, a photographer brushed by him poised with camera equipment. "Just one more, mister President."

"That will be all, for now, Miss Devlin."

"Laura!" the Ranger said.

The young reporter got up from the chair and tried to pretend she wasn't as uncomfortable as she was.

"You know this man, Miss Devlin?"

"Laura, I thought you agreed..."

"My paper sent me on assignment to do a story on the President's speech and..."

But the Lone Ranger realized he had more important matters at hand. "May we be alone, sir. What I have to tell you is of the utmost urgency. "

"Of course. You'll have to excuse me, Miss Devlin. But

this is official business."

"Just one more, sir," the cameraman begged as he eyed the image of the President in his viewfinder and held his flash bar high.

Just then, the Ranger glimpsed a man at an open window of the car. "Mister President, LOOK OUT!" Instantly, the masked man pushed the Chief Executive out of the path of the assassin's gun. Shots were fired. The Ranger drew his gun and fired back just as the camera's flash bar exploded.

"The President's been shot!" a voice screamed.

At once, soldiers rushed into the car from all sides with the secretary in the lead. "I don't believe it," he gasped looking at the masked man's gun drawn over the slumped figure of the President. "Sentries, arrest that man. Arrest the Lone Ranger!"

"WAIT! There was a man at the window," the masked man said.

"Impossible!" the secretary said, looking around. "Arrest him!"

"What are you talking about?" Laura shouted.

"Sentries, get her out of here!"

Two men quickly grabbed the reporter and rushed her out just as more shots were heard from outside the train. In the confusion, the Ranger slipped out the rear and into the night.

"After him, men! After the Lone Ranger!"

The next day, a story and photos appeared in the Kansas City Sentinel of the masked man's attempt to kill the President. For the first time in his distinguished career, the Lone Ranger was connected to a gang of outlaws.

(But it was worse than that," the masked man added.

"Worse! It gets worse?"

"I had miscalculated the extent to which the Legion was organized and the level of their commitment, Jim.")

Tonto was in town for supplies. Later, that evening, the Lone Ranger thought he heard him approach but before he could utter a word, he felt a heavy gun butt against his head.

When he came to, his eyes were covered and his hands and feet were securely tied, and he was hanging over a saddle. He wasn't sure how long they rode. It could have been a few hours or days. At one point, they seemed to be slowly climbing a hill. The air grew cold and thin. He didn't remember how many times he blacked out.

The next time the Ranger awoke he seemed to be in some kind of a cave. He could hear a large group of men, at least a hundred, maybe more. After some adjusting he was able to peek through a part of his blindfold. That's when he noticed two large fires at the far end of the cave. Between them, he saw a man on a platform. But his face was covered by a large mask. The Lone Ranger noticed that the two fires cast a shadow, a flickering shadow in the shape of a black arrow.

The Ranger was drawn to the powerful voice coming from the man giving a speech to the others. Moving closer to listen, the leader spoke with power and authority.

"...our organization is growing stronger by the month. We've got brains and money. The law is scattered. They never know where or when we'll strike. Stagecoach robberies. Bank swindles. Whatever it takes. We'll tear the stars and stripes off every flag pole west of the Mississippi. The West shall be ours! The Legion of the Black Arrow will live forever!"

A band of about three–hundred cheered, wildly.

The leader paused a moment to reflect angrily. "The

President of the United States still lives. But by this time next week, our Santa Fe group led by Red Dolan will have solved this problem once and for all. The rest of you will report to your group leaders for your assignments. That's all."

As the outlaws began to disperse, four men entered the section of cave where the Ranger was being held. "C'mon, mister. Someone wants to talk to you."

With his hands still tightly bound, the Lone Ranger was led to another corner of the great cavern. Along the way he could hear the rumble of a river that flowed nearby. Suddenly, he was brought face to face with the leader.

"So, this is the Lone Ranger." He took several steps closer then tore the bandana from the Ranger's eyes. "You don't look so tough, mister."

He kept his temper in check. He knew that whatever he said or did would be closely watched.

"Relax, mister, you were brought here for a reason. Take a look at this." He held up the front page of a newspaper. "Take a good look."

The headlines and pictures told how the President was nearly struck down by none other than the Lone Ranger.

"It's a lie, of course," the Ranger said, cooly.

"True enough, but you and I know that most people will believe it. By now this story and picture are in every newspaper in towns from coast to coast. Your reputation as a man of justice is finished." He laughed.

They all laughed.

(These evil guys do this a lot.)

"You might be right," the Lone Ranger grimaced. "You said you had a purpose in bringing me here."

The leader slapped the Ranger on the back. "As I said, your reputation is finished but your knowledge and skills can still be put to good use... by us!" The leader walked in a circle around the masked man as he continued. "I'm giving you a choice, mister. Join our cause and live to share in our glory."

"And if I don't?"

They all laughed, again. "You die. It's that simple. Look around and you'll recognize many men in our enterprise whom you have put behind bars. If your answer is 'no', I can assure you they will take great delight in seeing that your death is slow and painful." He stepped closer with a more earnest whisper. "Join us and together we can rule an empire the likes of which the world has never seen."

The Ranger was about to speak but held back.

"It's midnight now. You've got till dawn to make up your mind." The leader started to walk away, then paused. "It's useless to escape, of course. There's only one way out and that's closely guarded."

The masked man was returned to the other corner of the cave. His captors untied his hands and gave him something to eat. A couple of the gang members acted more friendly, but he was watched closely, just the same.

At that moment, Laura Devlin sat alone in studied silence staring at her typewriter. Things couldn't be much worse, she thought. The President almost shot. The Lone Ranger, the prime suspect. Her own editor jumping on the story in spite of her version of the events.

"Face it, Laura," she could still hear him say. "You're just too close to this one to really know what happened!"

She wondered how much she would be responsible for if and when the Lone Ranger was caught or killed. And how much longer she would keep silent.

Hours later, after they were asleep, the Ranger carefully studied the cave. The entrance was no good. Like the leader said, it was securely guarded. And he couldn't hold them all off without arousing the others. Then, he examined the small river that stretched the length of the cave before disappearing into a wall on the other side.

As dawn came, he quietly made his way toward the river. Suddenly, one of the gang heard his footsteps. "Hey, the masked man's tryin' to escape!"

The Ranger sprinted for the river as shots were fired. He felt a burning sensation in his left side as he hit the water.

"Ya got 'im, Smokey!"

The leader scrambled to the river's edge. "What happened?"

"The Lone Ranger, boss. I shot him trying to escape."

The leader scanned the river with a lantern straining to see any sign of the Lone Ranger.

"Looky there!" Smokey said, pointing. "His body is drifting past that rock."

The leader smiled. "He's done for, boys."

Meanwhile, after the Ranger's disappearance, Tonto had successfully tracked him to the Black Arrow cave. After a few days of careful observation, he discovered his masked friend on the banks of the river on the other side of the mountain. His escape can only be called miraculous. After Tonto nursed what turned out to be a flesh wound, he told the Indian what he had learned. "We've got to get to the President, Tonto."

"That's very risky, Kemo Sabay. There are posters all over the country offering a sizable reward."

"It's a risk we'll have to take."

The next day, the two headed east. Checking several sources, the Lone Ranger learned that the President's train was once again in Kansas City. Arriving at dusk, he and Tonto studied the train yard from a safe distance.

"The train has a lot more guards than before."

"Yes, Tonto. Since that last attack they're not taking any chances. But I've got to get down there and try to talk to the President, myself. You make camp here and wait for my return."

An hour went by when Tonto recognized the soft footsteps of his friend. "Tonto, I couldn't meet with the President. He's just too carefully guarded. We'll have to wait."

"I don't think it's safe to stay here." The Indian pointed along the ridgeline. "Look there. I've had my eyes on those two for sometime now."

"Do you think they are part of the Black Arrow?"

"I'm not sure."

"Let's not stay to find out."

Quickly, the masked man and Indian packed their things and saddled up.

("Tonto was right in more ways than one, Jim. Those men on the ridge were members of the Black Arrow. But down below, something worse was taking place."

"Worse, still?")

As the Lone Ranger and Tonto prepared to ride out, a soldier quickly approached another man on foot.

"What is it, Biggs?"

"It's them, sir," the soldier pointed. "The Lone Ranger and his Indian friend. They're against the horizon, now." Biggs raised his rifle. "I can still pick 'em off."

"Don't shoot! You'd miss at this distance. Besides it

would rouse everyone. The President might wonder why I'm out here." The secretary watched as the other two men on the ridge followed at a safe distance behind the masked man and Indian. "So, the Lone Ranger escaped the cave. That fool, Nesbitt. I told him it was useless to try and recruit the Lone Ranger."

"What do you want me to do, sir?"

"You're to ride to Santa Fe at once. Give this message to our contact there." The secretary watched as the masked man and Indian disappeared in the distance. "He doesn't know it yet, but the Lone Ranger is riding right into the biggest mistake of his life."

("So, the real leader of the Black Arrow is the President's own secretary, huh?"

"Yes, Jim, but I'm afraid it was worse than that."

"Jeez, Louise! How can it get any worse?")

The look on his face was grim. For once the justice fighter's great strength and courage, his daring and resourcefulness were taxed to the utmost in fighting this dreaded Legion of the Black Arrow.

Convinced that Dolan and his gang were planning something outside the town of Santa Fe, the Lone Ranger and Tonto rode like the wind. Not only did they have to try and thwart the mighty Legion whose strength grew daily, but the masked man had to clear himself of the terrible crime for which he was framed.

As they approached the outskirts of Santa Fe late one afternoon, a fierce lightning storm struck causing them to take temporary shelter under a rocky outcrop.

"The sheriff here, doesn't know you, Kemo Sabay."

"I'll have to rely on his sense of honesty to help us."

"Maybe the Black Arrow isn't here. I haven't seen any sign of those two men from the ridge for several days now."

The Indian pointed to some railroad tracks nearby. "Railroad tracks lead to town. Maybe they have taken the train."

"They couldn't do that, Tonto. This section of track is not open yet. "Hmm," the Ranger thought. "I wonder if the railroad has anything to do with Dolan's plans?" Just then, the Ranger glimpsed something tucked back against the rocks.

Tonto's eyes widened when the masked man pulled out a long bow and two black arrows.

The two continued into town and were careful to approach the rear of the jail without anyone observing them. As they got near a window, Tonto was the first to notice Sheriff Hank Hackett speaking with someone else. "Kemo Sabay, the girl in the sheriff's office it's... Laura Devlin!"

"Good." The Lone Ranger knocked loudly. "Maybe she can help us with the sheriff."

"Uh, oh! She just left through the front."

They heard a horse quickly gallop away from the front just as the sheriff opened the door. "The Lone Ranger and Tonto?"

The masked man didn't pull his guns but remained ready, just in case.

"Tarnation, you're wanted clear across the territory, masked man."

"For a crime I was trying to stop, Sheriff."

"I thought the whole thing sounded fishy," Hackett said as he welcomed them inside. "I remember what you done for Pete Barker in Powderhorn, last year. Far as I'm concerned you're a square shooter with me. But what brings you to Santa Fe?"

"Red Dolan and his gang."

"Dolan! Thought he was in prison."

"He escaped a few weeks ago. Have you noticed any strangers in town lately, Sheriff?"

"What's he look like?"

"He's big and powerful with dark eyes and a keen mind."

"Now that you mention it, a big fella come through here a few days ago. Looked like a card sharp. Said he was an inspector of some kind, engineerin' or somethin'. What's he up to?"

"Treason."

"Plottin' against the government? Say, I wonder if this has anythin' to do with the President comin' to Santa Fe for the big ribbon–cuttin'."

"What ribbon cutting?" the Ranger asked.

"Why, for the new bridge 'cross Black Jack Canyon. President's train supposed to be the first one over."

"What?"

"Governor's men were in here yesterday settin' things up, masked man."

"That explains it, Tonto. Dolan and his men are planning to do something to the bridge. I'm sure of it. Where is Dolan now, Sheriff?"

"Well, like I wuz sayin' a man fittin' that description come through here askin' directions to the bridge. Afraid I told him how to get there, too."

The Ranger started to leave. "That's where we're heading, Tonto."

Hackett grabbed his arm. "Hold on. It wouldn't be smart to go out there alone, at night. There's a thousand places where they can bushwhack you from. Why don't you wait 'till I can round up a posse in the morning?"

"I don't want to lose any time, Sheriff, but thanks for the

warning."

"Kemo Sabay, we don't know how many men Dolan has. We might just need a little help in rounding them all up."

"I agree masked man," the sheriff said. "Why don't me and the boys plan on meetin' you at the foot of Eagle's Point, tomorrow morning? You can't miss it. It's where the top of the canyon sticks out to a point. Here, I'll draw you a map."

("Wait a second. I thought you said it got worse?"

"I was just coming to that, Jim.")

At that moment, a lone rider was rapidly approaching the entrance to Black Jack Canyon. A lookout carefully trained his rifle on the figure and readied to squeeze the trigger...

(Just then, the masked man gave me a look that told me more than I was prepared to know. "No, it can't be! Nooooo!")

End Part I

EPISODE TEN

Justice Wears a Mask

This time it was the Ranger who took the bathroom break and since we're headin' into the home stretch with this epic, maybe it wouldn't be a bad idea if we all took one. Go ahead. I'll wait.

While we're waiting, I'll do a quick recap for the benefit of the *Adventure Deficit Disordered* –

After a close call involving the front end of a train, the Lone Ranger captured Red Dolan and his gang. But as he's led away, the outlaw promises a crime wave the likes of which the country has never seen, and one more thing: "I'LL KILL YOU, LONE RANGER, IF IT'S THE LAST THING I DO!"

Frustrated at every turn to stem the lawlessness, the masked rider of the plains is summoned to meet with the President. However, outside the city where the meeting is to occur, the Lone Ranger rescues Laura Devlin, a reporter for the Kansas City Sentinel, who has been covering the crime spree throughout the West.

Later, informed by the President of the existence of a seemingly unstoppable force known only as the Legion of the Black Arrow, the Chief Executive gives the Ranger his special assignment: "Find out what you can of this conspiracy and help formulate a plan to defeat them. The future of our country depends on it."

Despite several leads, the Lone Ranger and Tonto's attempts continue to be hampered at every turn. Somehow, information about their plans was getting back to the Legion.

About this time, Tonto learns of a plot to kill the President in Memphis. That evening, they are surprised at their campsite by Laura Devlin, who brings news that Red Dolan has escaped. And one more thing: "Apparently, this Legion is planning something in Memphis."

Concerned that her knowledge puts her own life in jeopardy, the masked man pleads with her not to follow the story to Memphis. She relents, but only if he promises to fill her in on all the details, like right now! He does, *(Biiig mistake, in my opinion,)* along with a mini–series covering his life. But that's not the big news: "WAIT A MINUTE! You're in love with Laura Devlin!"

(This whole thing's sounding like Melrose Place.)

In Memphis, the Lone Ranger meets the President only to discover him finishing an interview and photo op with Laura Devlin. The good news is that the Ranger prevents the President from being shot. The bad news is that he's framed for the attempt. That's when, Worse Part Number One happens: the Ranger is kidnapped by the Legion and given a choice, "Join us or die!"

After a miraculous escape through an underground river, the Ranger is found by Tonto and, together, they ride to try and square things with the President. That's when we come to Worse Part Number Two: the President's secretary is in cahoots with the Black Arrow!

(Did I say, Melrose Place? Change that to Dallas.)

Unable to meet with the President and having learned that Red Dolan and his men are planning something big outside Santa Fe, the Lone Ranger and Tonto hit the trail. Arriving at Sheriff Hackett's office, Tonto spots Laura Devlin inside but when the masked man knocks at the door she quickly disappears. The sheriff informs the Ranger of a man matching Dolan's description who was out to inspect the bridge. Hackett agrees to help the masked man by gathering up a posse in the morning. They arrange to meet at Eagle's Point, a spot just outside of Black Jack Canyon where Dolan and his men are suspected of hiding.

Which brings us to Worse Part Number Three and the exciting conclusion.

~

At that moment, a lone rider was rapidly approaching the entrance to Black Jack Canyon. A lookout carefully trained his rifle on the figure and readied to squeeze the trigger when his companion recognized who it was.

"Hold it, Burly! It's only Laura."

("No, it can't be. Not Laura Devlin?")

The reporter quickly dismounted and ran over to Red Dolan. "Quick, put out that fire!"

"You've been riding hard."

"I had to take the long way around. He'll be using the main trail and I didn't want to take any chances of him catching up to me."

"He's come, then?"

"He may even be in the canyon as we speak."

"Well, out with it. Is that all you have to tell me?"

"I doubled back carefully and overheard that Hackett will round up a posse in the morning. But the masked man and Indian were continuing on tonight. Tomorrow, they'll all meet at the foot of Eagle's Point."

"Eagle's Point. Hmm," Dolan said, rubbing his chin. "Perfect. There's a cave about half way up the cliff. With a buffalo gun we'll be able to finish him off once and for all. Then we can proceed with our plans for the bridge." The outlaw stepped closer. "You know, Laura, you've been very useful to the cause." He grabbed her and tried to press her closer until she slapped him away. He lunged at her again until something caught his attention. "Sneak gun, huh?"

"I find it comes in handy when I'm dealing with varmints like you, Dolan."

"Say, what is this? First you come out here and tip us off and..."

"And that's ALL I'm doing. I agreed to supply information about the Lone Ranger in exchange for source material for my stories. That deal is complete." She hesitated a moment when she saw the look in the outlaw's eyes. "...until I report back to the leader, of course. And I don't think he'd like it much, if he were to hear that a valuable resource, such as myself, was taken advantage of by the likes of you, Dolan." She pressed the gun to his chest.

The outlaw backed off. "All right! You can put the gun away. You win."

Laura knew that an outlaw like Dolan was always unpredictable. So, she kept her eyes trained on him as she walked back to her horse and prepared to ride out.

"Where are you headin'?" Dolan shouted.

With the reins firmly in her hands, she shot him a hard look. "You just worry about your part of the plan, Dolan." With that, she rode out the same way she came in.

Meanwhile, on a train heading west, the President was going over the schedule with his secretary.

"The Governor will introduce you at noon, sir, so it's

important that we arrive on time."

"Tell me, Thomas, why is a ribbon–cutting for a bridge so important for me to attend?"

"Governor Ashworth wields a great deal of influence with western delegates. His support will be vital to your re–election campaign, sir."

The President's attention never lingered long over the obligations of politics. He relied on his secretary for such things. "Any word from the Lone Ranger?"

"No, sir," the aide said. "We've had no further contact with him since he and his confederates made that attempt on your life in Memphis."

"I can't believe he had anything to do with that!"

"We can't afford to believe otherwise, mister President. Besides, if he's innocent of any involvement, why hasn't he stepped forward to clear himself?"

The Chief Executive sighed. "I wish there were more we could do."

"I have a feeling the entire matter will be settled soon."

"I pray that you are right. For the sake of the country."

Later that night, Laura Devlin rode slowly back to town. She was thinking about the deal she had struck with the man who said he would help her become the best reporter in the West. The man who later turned out to be the leader of the Black Arrow. But that was *after* she had already succeeded with several news stories, stories whose information came directly from the man's contacts. If only she'd known she was unwittingly helping the Black Arrow. That was her first mistake. Her second was continuing her deception with the Lone Ranger. By now she had developed certain feelings for him and she felt he had some for her. But what could she do now?

She reined up her horse when she caught sight of a low campfire burning up ahead. She was taking a chance. What if it wasn't the Lone Ranger and Tonto? What if it was members of the sheriff's posse who got an early start? Or more of Dolan's men? With these questions flashing before her, she rode directly into the camp.

The masked man and Indian greeted the young reporter with skeptical glances. In quick order she found herself leveling about everything, including her activities on the President's train. "Don't you see," she pleaded. "I had to go. My editor had this interview scheduled without my knowledge before you and I talked."

"What about that photo?"

"Jimmy just happened to get off a lucky shot. The editor saw the film before I did and the momentum took over from there. My version of the story didn't come out like that, masked man. You've got to believe me!"

"What were you doing at the sheriff's office tonight and why did you run out when we arrived?"

Now, she was scared. She wanted to tell the Ranger everything, but not like this. She didn't want him thinking she was part of this Black Arrow conspiracy. She didn't want him hating her. "I was sent ahead to check information with Sheriff Hackett."

"Why did you leave so quickly, when Tonto and I arrived."

"I... I panicked."

"Panicked?" the Ranger said. "You don't seem to panic when it comes to covering your story."

"Oh, hang the story," she groaned. "I'm here with you, now, aren't I? I want to help. And there's more."

As she sat down beside him she began to explain and own up to her involvement with the Legion, how it grew from innocent ambition to a corruptible tool for the group's purposes. As he continued to listen, the Ranger's confidence in the young woman began to return, somewhat. She told of the man who had helped her with her stories, about Red Dolan and his gang's plan for both the masked man and the bridge. "I'll take my punishment, Lone Ranger, whatever that may be. I just want things to be settled between us."

Immediately, the Lone Ranger and Tonto began discussing plans for tomorrow.

"You're not going to be directly involved, are you?" Laura interrupted. "I told you, Dolan will kill you tomorrow if you go out there!"

"Tonto and I have a mission to fulfill. It's our duty."

The young reporter couldn't believe what she was hearing. Knowingly going into a death trap was suicide to her. "Oh, why do you persist in this, this 'holy' mission of yours when every man's hand is against you? Even the President thinks you're one of these outlaws!"

"That's because someone has clouded him from the truth."

"What could be worth risking certain death from either the Black Arrow or the law?"

"Do you really care to know?"

"Yes," she said, sincerely.

When it came to what he stood for, no one was as sure as the Ranger.

(Uh, oh, here comes another speech.)

"Many who settled this country were men and women of uncommon fortitude, Laura."

(Yup, there's the choir music.)

"They handed down to us a great legacy. It is a legacy in which citizens have the right to live as free people in a land where there is true equality of opportunity. It is our duty to be unceasingly vigilant and prepared at all times to fight those who dare to challenge our way of life.

"We have a great nation and with the will, the heart, and the courage we can make it even greater. This is our legacy, Laura. It is the legacy of every American."

(Fade choir.)

"But, aren't you afraid?" she asked him.

"My father once told me that courage, true courage is the ability to see things through, no matter what. It is standing up for one's principles, even if you must stand alone."

"You're not alone, Kemo Sabay."

The Lone Ranger smiled. "You're right, Tonto." He could still see concern in her eyes. "Yes," he conceded, "I am afraid, Laura, but I cannot let that prevent me from doing what I know needs to be done. Do you understand, now?"

She just stared into his eyes. "I think I do." Nothing else seemed to matter, for the moment. Right now, she felt more safe than she had in a long time. That's when she leaned closer to him. His eyes met hers and softly, gently, they kissed.

("NO WAY!!"

Tonto shot me a look. "Way!")

The next morning, Laura awoke to find Tonto in the process of breaking camp. "Tonto, where's the masked man?"

"He left to scout Eagle's Point."

"Eagle's Point?" Quickly, her mind raced through last night. "But he doesn't know which direction Dolan will attack from." She jumped on her horse before Tonto could turn around and rode off toward Eagle's Point.

"WAIT!" the Indian shouted.

At that moment, Sheriff Hackett held up his hand to halt a line of possemen. "Whoa! All right, men, Eagle's Point is just 'round the bend, so stay sharp."

"You know, Hank, if we'd have cleared out this canyon like I told you before, we wouldn't be faced with roundin' up a bunch of two–bit coyotes, now."

"Yeah, well, it's different this time, Barney. I told you, these men are part of a group that wants to take over the entire West. The gang out here is headed up by Red Dolan."

"DOLAN!" one of them shouted. "I didn't know we were going up against Dolan and his gang when you said you needed help in roundin' up some outlaws. We could get killed!"

"Relax, Eddie, the Lone Ranger's out here, too," Hackett continued. "He knows Dolan and he's been out here scoutin' things ahead of us."

Eddie nervously looked around. "Where's the masked man, now?"

"We're set to meet him and Tonto at the foot of Eagle's Point," Hackett said, waving them forward. Now, let's git goin'."

Meanwhile, Red Dolan stood near the top of a rocky outcrop scanning the horizon through a spyglass as another henchman approached.

"You got those charges planted, Chet?" Dolan asked.

"Everything's set. We've got twenty minutes from the time the fuses are lit."

"Good. By the time that bridge blows, we'll be safely on the other side of that ridge. And with the country in complete chaos, our leader will be able to step in easily.

Now, there's only one more thing to take care of."

"What's that, Red?"

"The Lone Ranger."

"Any sign of the masked man or Injun?"

"Not yet."

"I thought you said he was supposed to meet the sheriff at the foot of the cliff."

Dolan smiled as he continued his surveillance. "He's smart. That's open ground around the foot of that cliff. He'll keep under cover until... wait, I see something."

In the clearing, Hackett and his posse reined to a halt. Eddie moved forward and started looking around. "Thought you said the masked man'd meet us here, Hank?"

Hackett just shook his head. "That's why I'm sheriff and you're not, Eddie. He's not going to take a chance and step out in the open by himself." Hackett turned to the others. "Keep your eyes peeled and your guns ready, men. I don't trust anything that moves 'round here." Hackett maneuvered carefully through a patch of thick brush. "Lone Ranger, you out here? Lone Ranger!"

"Over here, Sheriff, behind this clump of brush. I'm glad to see you and your men."

"What do you want us to do, mister?"

"I think we'll have to fan out and..."

Suddenly, Laura Devlin, riding hard, pulled up around the Point. She jumped off her horse and ran over to the others. "Masked man... MASKED MAN. WHERE ARE YOU!"

In the urgency of the moment, the Ranger stepped into the open. "Laura, what are you doing, here?"

Out of breath, she continued. "I couldn't wait! I had to warn you. The attack, it'll be coming from..." she started to point just as Tonto pulled up alongside the others.

Suddenly, the Indian noticed a reflection coming from the cave on the other side of the canyon. "Kemo Sabay, LOOK OUT!"

Laura stepped in front of the Ranger just as one great rifle shot exploded. She gasped and collapsed into his arms.

"Laura!" The Ranger pulled her down and into the brush as the others scattered for cover.

"Looky, Sheriff," Eddie pointed. "A man's comin' outta that cave on the other side of the canyon. And he's carryin' a rifle."

"That's the sniper. OPEN FIRE, MEN!" Hackett shouted.

The Ranger bent closer to Laura's face.

"I... forgot to tell you," she whispered, "...about the cave."

"Don't try to talk, now." The Ranger pressed a bandana to her wound as he turned to Tonto.

The Indian leaned closer to examine the wound. "It looks bad, Kemo Sabay."

"The bridge," Laura coughed. "... must stop... Dolan."

"Get this girl outta the line of fire," Hackett ordered.

As soon as she was moved the posse attacked the wall of the canyon with a volley of shots.

Suddenly, the group watched as Burly Davis fell from his rocky perch.

"GOT 'IM!"

"Good work, Dusty!"

"Wait a second," another said. "What's that over there?"

"Where?" the Ranger said, grabbing a pair of binoculars.

"Someone's climbin' up the bridge."

Through the glasses, the masked man could see Red Dolan and one of his henchmen carefully working their way up the support structure of the bridge. "Dolan's lighting a fuse."

"Draw a bead on him, men!"

"It's no good, Sheriff. He's out of range at this distance."

"Let's mount up and get 'im, then!" Hackett said. But as soon as the group headed into the open, they were immediately met with a barrage of gunfire now coming from the ridge above the cave. "TAKE COVER!" Hackett warned as he and the Lone Ranger jumped behind a boulder. "Must be Dolan's men."

"Yes, and they've got good positioning on us."

"SPREAD OUT AND STAY DOWN, MEN!" Hackett yelled. When he turned back, the masked man was gone.

With one swift move, the Lone Ranger mounted Silver and headed off toward the bridge.

"Tarnation! GIVE THE MASKED MAN COVER, BOYS!"

At that same moment, a train's whistle could be heard in the distance.

"Great Scott," Hackett said. "The President's train!"

"I've got to help him!"

"Don't try it, Tonto. You'll never make it through all that fire!"

But before the sheriff could finish, the Indian leaped on Scout's back and rode out after his friend.

"Dagnab it all! "COVER 'EM BOTH, MEN!"

As soon as the Lone Ranger reached the bridge he jumped from Silver and made his way quickly to the foot of the structure. With his guns drawn, he looked around for Dolan but stopped when he glimpsed Chet ready to light a fuse on the other side.

"DROP THAT MATCH. YOU'RE COVERED!"

The henchman appeared willing to follow the Ranger's instructions when he suddenly turned and lit the fuse. He pulled his gun and was ready to fire on the masked man when he lost his footing and fell.

Just then, the Ranger heard another whistle blast. "No time to lose!" The masked man holstered his guns and began to climb.

Hearing the commotion, Dolan returned to the bridge and spotted the masked man making his way toward the first charge. The outlaw pulled his gun, when...

A silver bullet from Tonto's gun smashed Dolan's gun causing the forty–four to fly out of the outlaw's hand. Tonto jumped from his horse as he reached the foot of the bridge.

Instantly, the outlaw turned and began to climb after the masked man.

It didn't take the Lone Ranger long to reach the location of the first charge. He yanked the fuse from the keg of powder and watched as it dropped harmlessly to the ground below.

With the train's whistle blasting again, the masked man now spotted Dolan moving up after him. But there wasn't time to think about that. He had to get to the second charge and the fastest route seemed to be to climb the remaining distance to the top, traverse the tracks, then head down the other side.

Tonto watched from below, trying desperately to think of a way to help.

On top of the bridge the masked man could clearly see the train on the horizon. He started to sprint down the tracks when a hand suddenly reached up and tripped him. One of his guns slipped from its holster and fell through the rails to the ground below.

Using his powerful arms, Red Dolan hoisted himself onto the top of the bridge. The masked man carefully got to his feet and turned with his other gun drawn. Instantly, Dolan kicked it from his hand. It landed several feet from them both, stopping just short of falling between the rails. The dark eyes of the outlaw glared at his masked nemesis. "This time, there is no escape, mister."

With the train approaching, the two men began a fist fight to end all fist fights, a duel to the death. The masked man charged but the outlaw was ready. Because of Dolan's sheer size and strength, the Ranger's blows seemed to lack their usual force. Dolan, on the other hand, was tough and strong from years of hard living. And he used everything he could. He kicked and gouged. He clawed and bit.

But the masked man wasn't through. Not by a long shot. Where he could not match Dolan for power, he more than equaled him in quickness and positioning. He hammered away at the side of the outlaw's massive chest. At one point, one of Dolan's ribs cracked. Then the two men locked and went down. The Lone Ranger's head struck a rail.

He was half stunned when Dolan clamped his powerful hands around the masked man's throat. "Now, I'm going to choke the life out of you!" His grip grew tighter and tighter. "Won't... have to... put up with you... any longer."

With the train whistle blasting in his ear, the Lone Ranger's fighting heart would not give up. He mustered his strength for a final, mighty effort and managed to wrench free and strike a hard blow to the outlaw's chin.

Now, it was Dolan's turn to be stunned. The outlaw reeled backwards, then fell to his hands and knees.

The Ranger didn't wait for the big man to recover. He moved forward ready to finish the fight. That's when Dolan saw his last chance. The masked man's gun rested on the wooden tie directly in front of him. The outlaw picked it up and quickly whirled on the justice fighter.

Out of breath, and nearly beaten, Red Dolan grinned at the final irony as he slowly stood and faced his enemy. For once, things had turned in his favor. The two men heard the train's whistle once more but Dolan never took his eyes off the Ranger who remained frozen. "Now, I'm going to kill you, mister. And with your own gun! Imagine," the outlaw laughed, "the Lone Ranger killed with one of his own silver bullets. Don't you think that's funny?"

The Ranger remained silent. If he was going to die he wasn't going to give the outlaw any additional satisfaction.

Red Dolan pulled the hammer back on the gleaming, pearl–handled Colt and held it in a direct line with the masked man's head. "Say goodbye, Lone Ranger!" The outlaw slowly squeezed the trigger and the shot echoed across the canyon.

The Ranger's head twisted horribly from the concussion of the slug as he collapsed to his knees. But a strange expression came over Dolan's face when the gun fired. He tried to laugh but had trouble breathing. That's when something else caught his attention—a red stain on his chest that began to grow. He never felt the gun slide from his hand but it didn't matter because he was too busy trying to stretch and reach something behind him—a black arrow. Dolan saw Tonto standing below, an empty bow in his hands. A dark haze swirled before the outlaw's eyes as he slipped from the edge of the bridge.

The piercing sound of the train's whistle helped clear the Lone Ranger's head as he slowly got to his feet. The impact of Tonto's arrow had moved Dolan's hand just enough to cause the silver bullet to crease the side of the masked man's head. He signaled to Tonto that he was alright, but when he looked down he could see the spark from the fuse working it's way closer to the second powder charge.

The train was now within two minutes of the bridge. The masked man knew he couldn't reach the final charge in time as he had originally planned. However, a piece of rope left behind from the construction crew presented a possible, yet risky, solution. Securing the rope to a rail that cantilevered over the side of the bridge, he climbed down and swung out reaching for the fuse. His first attempt left him many feet short. Pulling back, he pushed off for a second try... closer, closer... "TONTO, I CAN'T REACH IT!" he shouted. For once the Ranger was at the absolute limit of his abilities.

At the base of the bridge, Tonto waited no longer. He positioned the last arrow in his bow, pulling back on the string with every ounce of strength he had. He took precious time in careful aim. He knew he'd only have one chance. His sharp eyes tracked the progress of the fuse. He calculated the remaining distance.

The Lone Ranger watched the burning fuse and clenched his fists tighter around the rope for one more attempt. He pulled himself back, as far back as he could. With the train's whistle screaming in his ears, he let go, swung out into space and...

Tonto held his breath, released his last arrow and...

The Ranger was within inches of reaching the fuse when a black arrow flew past his hands and struck the fuse. He watched as the fiery spark reached the arrow's tip, sputtered and... snuffed itself out.

The roar of the President's train as it powered over the bridge only a few feet above the Ranger shook the structure like an earthquake as it passed.

("Wheeeeeeeewwwwwwwwwwwwwwwwwwwww!")

Only after the train rounded the bend and the silence

returned to the canyon, did the Lone Ranger loosen his grip and begin the climb back down.

After rejoining Hackett and his men, there was only one thought on the Lone Ranger's mind. "Laura?"

Hackett just shook his head.

The Ranger turned away from the others and sighed heavily.

(If there's one thing in life more deadly than fallin' in love with the Cartrights, it's fallin' in love with the masked man.)

Just then, the Ranger noticed something. Along the ridgeline, above the cave, he saw soldiers swarming over the remaining members of the Black Arrow. "Did you call in the cavalry, Sheriff?"

"Figured it couldn't hurt to have a few of the boys from Fort Benson help us out, masked man."

"Good thinking, Sheriff."

(Wait a second. That's it? 'My babe's dead, oh well!' The Ranger needs to vent, expose, exfoliate ... something, or he's gonna have some real fear–of–intimacy problems.)

Hackett signaled to one of his men who rode forward with a man tied to the saddle of his horse. "And we got another little surprise for you, masked man."

The Ranger smiled when he recognized Thomas, the President's secretary.

"We found him watchin' the doin's on that ridge over there with a couple of other polecats from that Black Arrow gang."

Late that afternoon, the President exchanged warm handshakes with the Lone Ranger and Tonto as two military aides entered his private car. He handed a small envelope to the masked man.

"Thank you, mister President," the Ranger said. "Your words mean a lot to Tonto and myself."

"Excuse me, sir," one of the aides interrupted. "The engineer is ready to head back to Washington."

"Very well, Major Parker."

"Tonto and I will be going, mister President."

"Thank you again, Lone Ranger and thank you for the special gift." The Chief Executive's hand closed around something the masked man had given him.

"Adios," the Ranger said.

The President watched as the two justice fighters left the private car before turning to his aides. "Gentlemen, there goes a great man."

The younger officer looked puzzled. "Excuse me, sir?"

"He's an example for all of us, Captain Holland. He's someone we can all strive to emulate, who seeks justice and truth, fights for law and order and who's not afraid to speak out for what's right and fair no matter what the personal cost."

"I don't understand, sir," Parker asked. "How can one masked cowboy and an Indian be all of those things?"

"That's because he's not a cowboy in a mask," the President said, firmly. "And the Indian he rides with is every bit his equal in quality and courage."

Parker bowed respectfully. "I'm sorry, mister President. I meant no disrespect. It's just that I've never heard you talk about anyone like this before."

"That's because there's never been another pair like them, Major." The President stared out the window of the train as he watched the Lone Ranger and Tonto ride to the top of a ridge. The riders paused, for a moment, framed by the sunset. "By God, I wish there were more like him... like them both."

Holland followed the President's glance. "Where's he heading off to in such a hurry? People would pay to listen to what he has to say. He could speak on the very principles you mentioned, sir."

"Forget it, Captain. That man is a doer not a talker."

Parker stepped closer. "I've heard rumors that he's a man with a rather unpleasant past."

The President spoke softly as he stared out the window. "A long time ago he was part of a special breed." He broke off his reverie as he fingered the Texas Ranger badge in his hand. Only two other people knew the Ranger's secret. The President knew, more than anyone else, how important it was that it remain that way. "I'll tell you one thing, Major. If everyone acted as that masked man does, there'd be no crime."

The President watched, wistfully, as the two riders disappeared over the ridge, then turned to his aides with finality. "It's not important who he *was*, gentlemen. It's more important who he *is*. He's the... Lone Ranger."

~

I sat there for a time with my mouth open. I just couldn't think of anything else to say. "What an adventure! And I thought that train thing at the beginning was something... then your escape from the Black Arrow cave... that fight on the bridge... those amazing arrow shots!"

Tonto smiled. "So, Jim, I suppose the value in this story is rather obvious."

"Are you kidding? Even Superman would have trouble coming up with the courage necessary to do all that and he had all that super power stuff workin' for him! Hey," I said, leaning closer. "Whaddya think? In a fair fight, could the masked man take the caped crusader?"

Tonto just rolled his eyes. "The kind of courage the Ranger is referring to, Jim, is not necessarily the physical kind."

"Oh. Yeah. Right. It was something he mentioned to Sheriff Hackett."

"No," Tonto said.

I flipped through my notes. "One of his meetings with the President?"

They both looked amazed at all the notes I had collected but Tonto shook his head again and started to say something when I held up my hand.

"Wait, don't tell me. Red Dolan? No. The leader of the Black Arrow?"

"There's only one major character, left," the Indian said. He waited for me to catch up. "Remember when Laura confessed her involvement with the Black Arrow?"

"Yeah." I looked in the notes, again.

"Second campfire scene."

I started flipping forwards.

"Part two."

I stopped when I came to a big notation. "You mean the 'kiss' scene?"

"There are two kinds of courage, Jim," the Ranger began. "Physical courage is when you risk personal injury. Moral courage is..."

"'...the ability to see things through, no matter what,'" I said. "Had it under the 'kiss' scene."

"It should be the 'moral courage' scene," Tonto said.

The Ranger continued. "It refers to the inner strength necessary to resist any obstacles or compelling forces and do what needs to be done, what *should* be done in spite of personal consequences."

"In spite of personal consequences, huh? So, then I guess that means you'd have to be pretty fearless?"

"No. Courage is not the absence of fear, Jim. It's committing yourself to act *in spite* of the fear."

"Like getting rid of the Black Arrow. Hmm," I thought. "I guess it takes plenty of moral courage to live up to your principles, to do what you know should be done even in the face of those all those people against you."

Tonto nodded.

"And that Black Arrow gang even offered you a spot on their team," I said.

The masked man and Indian exchanged looks.

"That was pretty much a 'no–brainer,' Jim," Tonto said. "But escaping from the cave and figuring out how to deal with the Black Arrow in spite of all the things that were going on took persistence. And that's part of courage, too."

"Yeah, how did you do that, anyway?"

The Ranger gave me another one of those "square" looks of his. "A person of character holds to his principles no matter what, Jim. He knows that giving in will erode the best he is, the best he can be. I made a promise to the President to find the Black Arrow and help defeat them. I had a duty to do whatever it took to keep my promise."

I was busy writing this last part down, when I noticed he and Tonto were starting to pack up their things, all the stuff in the cave.

"Our time here is just about finished, Jim. Tonto and I will be heading out in the morning."

I started to say something, but held up. I was just getting used to them and their stories.

Tonto began rustling up some dinner, when he looked over. "Got anything for dessert?"

"As a matter of fact, I've got one more package of..."

"Don't take this the wrong way, Jim, but I'm a little burned out on the cheesecake thing."

I dumped out everything in my pack and sifted through what was left: some hardtack... blecch, and... oh, YEAH... my emergency stash of...

"Hey, are those *Tootsie Rolls?*" Tonto asked. "I haven't had a Tootsie Roll since... But you probably want to keep those for the ride back tomorrow."

"No. That's okay."

His eyes lit up. "Are you sure?"

"I've got something else for tomorrow," I said tossing 'em over. Then I started thinking about what savory dish Tonto might whip up for our last meal together. Maybe a nice cornish hen like he talked about the other night or perhaps one of those tasty low–fat risottos the Ranger mentioned.

"Here we go," he said, pulling out several cans from his supplies. "Beans and franks."

I tried to force a smile.

"Good thing we got a great dessert to look forward to."

Tonto started working on the dinner as the masked man continued putting his things in order. I kept busy packing my own stuff. But I couldn't shake the feeling I had. I didn't want it to end. Not yet, anyway.

MY NOTES:

- The Lone Ranger is morally **Courageous**.
- Moral courage is the inner strength to overcome obstacles or compelling forces to do what should be done, no matter the personal consequences.
- It is standing up for what you believe.

After dinner, I looked through my notebook and the values we had covered—the things that mattered most to him and Tonto: Honesty, Fairness, Caring, Respect, Loyalty, Tolerance, Duty and Courage. I glanced over at my Watchman as the news was ending. Do I know everything I need to know in order to be, what the Ranger called, a person of character—someone who lived from his principles? And how can I use these values when it comes to making the right decisions?

EPISODE ELEVEN

The Lone Ranger Unplugged

Close–up on the United States Attorney General: "This man cannot, I repeat, canNOT go around and arrest whomever he wants at gunpoint in the name of justice. This is *not* how we do things in this country."

Voice–over: "Charges from the nation's top law enforcement officer and a prime–time response from the accused."

Close–up on the Lone Ranger: "I have always tried, to the best of my ability, to live by the laws of this land in order that men and women may live and work in a country that offers liberty and justice for all."

Voice–over: "Tonight, what's the truth? We'll be joined by Republican Senator Angelo and the Lone Ranger along with his steadfast Indian companion, Tonto."

"This is *Nightbeat*. Reporting from Washington, Ned Newsman."

NED: They say he's a vigilante. They say he's been playing by his own rules far too long and that if he's allowed to continue, he will turn the war on crime into a blood bath, pitting neighbor against neighbor. Tonight, the danger of a showdown in the U.S. But first, some background.

The Lone Ranger has been revered in western heritage as upholding the rights and privileges of the underdog, the downtrodden. He's been the standard bearer of a set of principles that has made the United States one of the strongest countries in the free world.

"With liberty and justice for all" is not just a slogan for this man but a way of life. He has actively sought out and arrested criminals through his own remarkable blend of deduction and shrewdness.

These along with his astonishing skill with horse, rope, and when the occasion warranted, gunplay, have truly made him legendary in the early western United States. But 60 years later, times have most certainly changed. And along with the complexities of a modern society, criminals have rights of their own that cannot be ignored.

So the questions arise: is the Lone Ranger's kind of justice really necessary anymore? Do his actions condone a kind of vigilanteism? And if he's allowed to go unchecked, will he be sending the *wrong* kind of message to youngsters?

In the Senate today no less a figure than Pete Angelo led an attack against the Ranger. In a scathing speech on the floor of the Senate, Angelo criticized what he called "blatant vigilanteism" as dangerous to the core of this nation's standards. It was a riveting indictment against the kind of law practiced by some people in this country under the guise of justice. Here is a brief portion of that speech.

Cut to: *Senator Angelo on the floor of the Senate.*

ANGELO: We have a man today who continues to serve what he calls justice. We have a man who, with shameless disregard for the very Constitution he holds dear, bursts into people's homes and businesses, pulls out a high caliber handgun, and makes a citizen's arrest for what HE believes to be criminal wrong–doing. Sometimes, a scuffle occurs resulting in the poor victim of his contempt being shot. And he does this over and over again, without regard to the rights and privileges accorded ALL men... at least according to MY copy of the Constitution. And what has the current administration done about it? Nothing.

My friends, this incident may be a small bump in the road of justice but it speaks mountains about 'Me–Generation' public ethics present in this administration. This is not just a case of blatant vigilanteism. It's about the arrogance of power!

Cut to: *Ned at his desk.*

NED: Joining us now are Senator Angelo, the Lone Ranger and Tonto. Mr. Ranger, we'll get to you and Tonto in a moment. First, I want to be clear about just what Senator Angelo is charging. Senator, you gave a powerful speech today in which you not only indicted the Ranger's actions, but went a step further and laid this at the feet of the present administration. Did you hear the statement made by the Attorney General this afternoon, sir?

ANGELO: Yes, I did, Ned and all I can say is, that's just what you'd expect to hear.

NED: How so, Senator?

ANGELO: Come on, Ned. The Lone Ranger and Tonto have been getting away with this sort of thing for a long time, now. Only AFTER this issue was brought out by myself and...

NED: ...just a minute, Senator...

ANGELO: ...AND MY fellow Senators, did the administration say anything at all about it!

NED: In all due fairness, Senator, the Lone Ranger has been performing these actions through several administrations, Republican as well as Democrat. So, to place it at the feet of the current administration sounds a little partisan, don't you think, sir?

ANGELO: No, and I'll tell you why. This administration has repeatedly said over and over about the need for a strong law enforcement policy. Throughout his campaign, the President said that he was going to focus, "like a laser beam" on law and order. And then he goes right around and lets this... this... Lone *Deranger*, I call him, walk around with a gun and do whatever he pleases. He's got to be stopped. It's just that simple.

NED: But don't his results count for anything, Senator?

ANGELO: Results? You want to talk about results? The man enters a bank through the back door in the middle of a transaction between the bank president and a customer. Shots are fired and he and Tonto end up dragging both the customer AND the bank's president to jail before they're even accused of anything. I mean, where's the sense in that, Ned? Come on.

NED: But later, Senator, the Lone Ranger did provide evidence that the bank president had embezzled thousands of dollars from customers' accounts.

ANGELO: Fine. Great! Work within the system. That's all I'm saying. I mean, this bank president... Hargrave, I think his name is, now has a right to privacy suit pending because this *Deranger* came in and just took the bank's records. No court order. No warrant. He just broke in and took what he wanted.

NED: When we come back, the Lone Ranger and Tonto respond.

Cut to: *Snappy commercial for Hanes underwear then,*

back to Ned.

NED: One of the great pillars of American justice, the
          Lone Ranger, is facing a crisis. In the light of
          charges brought against him for misconduct there
          is a growing public outcry that his activities be
          curtailed once and for all. On the other hand, there
          is a sizable group in this country that advocates the
          use of firearms and in taking the law into their own
          hands, when necessary. Mr. Ranger, comment?

RANGER: Yes. First of all, Ned, let me start by saying that
          Tonto and I hold dear the principles upon which
          this great country of ours was founded. It has been
          our long–standing mission to help rid the country
          of the kind of criminal that takes advantage of the
          rights of decent, honest citizens. Our job is to do no
          more or no less than to make things equitable for
          all.

NED: That's fine, sir. While I applaud your ideals I
          cannot help but wonder if your methods are a little
          outdated. Why not the obvious? Why not just get a
          badge and work within the system as Senator
          Angelo suggests?

RANGER: Ned, I made a pledge many years ago to the people
          of this country to help fight for the rights of the
          oppressed wherever injustice operated. As part of
          that pledge, I maintain my anonymity for the
          purpose of not allowing anyone or anything to
          attach itself to my deeds, in order that my purpose
          be seen as nothing less than pure.

NED: But isn't that just a nice way of rationalizing
          taking the law into your own hands, sir? More
          importantly, what kind of example does that give
          youngsters?

RANGER: Let me be clear, here, Ned. I never go beyond the
          bounds of fair play. In most cases, I work with a
          local sheriff. Wherever we go, Tonto and I always

try to teach youngsters the difference between right and wrong by practicing right thinking, and right action ourselves.

NED: All right. Let's take a look at that for a moment. What would you say are the necessary requirements of a justice fighter?

RANGER: Well, I would say that, first, it requires having both the mental reasoning and compassionate understanding for the law, as it applies to all. It requires the skill and cunning to be able to, not only discern who the wrong–doer is, but to devise and implement a plan that will lead to his or her successful capture.

TONTO: I'd like to jump in here, Ned, if I may.

NED: You may say anything you like, Tonto.

TONTO: I think it's important to know, that the characteristics my friend speaks of, are, in his case, highly developed. By that I mean, he's been doing this for some one–hundred years, now. So, that they have become almost instinctual. But at the same time, the Ranger is scrupulously fair with everyone.

NED: How so?

TONTO: He will always make a plausible argument in favor of a suspected crook if substantial evidence is lacking.

NED: Have you ever known him to make a mistake?

TONTO: Sure I have. He's not perfect. But again, this is why we take the kind of time that we do to be as sure as possible and when we make a mistake, we go back and fix it.

NED: What kind of checks and balances do you use, Mr. Ranger, to be, as Tonto says, "...sure as possible."

RANGER: Well, we're very good at overhearing a lot of conversations by doors and windows.

TONTO: And the crooks are very good at giving themselves
           and their plans away, Ned.

RANGER: Sometimes, a member of a gang will implicate his
           boss through confession.

TONTO: Sometimes, the Ranger and I will happen upon a
           crime already in progress.

NED: What about cases where none of that information is
           available to either of you?

RANGER: In such cases we are usually summoned by a
           governor or sheriff who already suspects someone
           or a gang but can't seem to catch them in the act.

TONTO: That's where we come in, Ned. The Ranger and I
           can infiltrate the gang, listen for information or
           create a plan that will reveal the crooks so that we
           can catch them in the act.

NED: When we come back, Senator Angelo and the Lone
           Ranger face off.

*Cut to Graphic:***Lone Ranger Opinion Poll**

> *57% say Lone Ranger is guilty of misconduct.*
>
> *41% say No.*
>
> *2% have no opinion*
>
> *Margin of Error: +/- 3%*

Go to commercial, then, back to Ned.

NED: Joining us once again are Senator Angelo, the Lone
           Ranger and Tonto. Senator, why don't you ask the
           first question.

ANGELO: Well, the first question I have, Ned, is this: does
           this man know the difference between right and
           wrong?

RANGER: (*chuckles, slightly*) I like to think that I do,
           Senator.

ANGELO: Great! What is it?

RANGER: Right is defined as what is good, proper or just.

Right conduct is action that conforms with a set of standards or principles set down by society and applied equally to all.

ANGELO: And which set of standards do you follow, Mr. Ranger?

RANGER: Tonto and I have always followed those standards as set down in the Bill of Rights and the Constitution.

ANGELO: And where does it say in those documents that it's okay to sneak into the rear of a bank, pull out a high–caliber handgun and...

TONTO: Hold on there, Senator. We didn't sneak into that bank. We walked in and...

ANGELO: (*interrupting*) ...give me a break, Tonto! You both went in through the back door, pulled your guns, shots were fired ...

TONTO: (*interrupting*) ...ONE shot was fired, Senator.

ANGELO: (*interrupting*) ...Come on, I read the transcripts.

TONTO: (*interrupting*) ...I fired that shot, Senator, if you'll permit me to interrupt with the truth, here, because the Black Hood was about to...

ANGELO: (*shouting over him*) ...TRUTH! YOU WOULDN'T KNOW THE TRUTH IF IT WALKED INTO YOUR TEPEE AND CRAPPED!

Why can't you both just admit that you exceeded your authority, and stop all of these guerrilla tactics that you and the *Deranger* have used against the rights of others?

(*silence*)

Well? . . . I'm waiting for an answer.

TONTO: Bite Me.

NED: Gentlemen, please!

ANGELO: That's okay, Ned. I just want to know something,

mister Ranger. Upon who's authority do you act?

RANGER: Upon the authority of the Governors of several states...

ANGELO: Uh–huh.

RANGER: ...and the President of the United States.

ANGELO: The President of the United States.

RANGER: Yes, Senator.

ANGELO: You've got this in writing?

RANGER: Here in my pocket. (*He pulls out an old, folded piece of paper and hands it to Angelo.*)

As you can read, Senator, it clearly states that, "the bearer of this letter, the Lone Ranger, is to be given every due consideration and complete cooperation on behalf of the United States Government."

Signed, Ulysses Simpson Grant, President of the United States, dated, 1875.

ANGELO: (*Laughs*) And you expect the validity of that paper to hold up in court today? You're dreamin'!

NED: Let's take another break.

*Cut to Graphic:***Lone Ranger Opinion Poll**

Do you support or oppose the Ranger's Actions?

95% Support

4% Oppose

1% no opinion

Commercial, then back to Ned.

NED: We're back. Mr. Ranger you wished to comment.

RANGER: Yes, Ned. My purpose in coming tonight was not to argue with Senator Angelo, but rather to help shed some light on some of the reasons why Tonto and I act as we do in order that we may put criminals behind bars.

NED: And what are those reasons, sir?

RANGER: The reasons cut to the core of what I believe is a problem still present in society today. It is one of education, involvement and personal responsibility by parents, teachers, all of us!

All of us need to get more involved in an effort to teach our young people, by our own example, the kinds of traits we want them to go forward with into the world.

If we want them to be honest, we must practice honesty ourselves in our homes and businesses.

If we want them to be respectful and caring, we must embody those traits in the most practical things we do every day.

Senator Angelo speaks about the rights of people. And I believe in those rights, Ned. But I also believe that there is a corresponding responsibility. If we want the right of free speech, we must not speak carelessly about another. The right to bear arms carries with it the responsibility of using them in a trustworthy manner.

ANGELO: We have another right in this country, Mr. Ranger. It's called DUE PROCESS! Ever heard of it?

RANGER: I have, Senator. And I very much respect its principle. And it is the universal principle behind all laws that I most carefully regard.

ANGELO: Oh, so, you'll obey some laws and not others?

RANGER: I didn't say that. But I do believe that some laws need to be challenged when they unintentionally go against the principle of fair play for individuals or groups.

ANGELO: And who determines which laws are good and which need to be challenged, Mr. Ranger? I've got a copy of the Constitution, right here. Why don't you just point out which ones you'll obey and which ones you won't?

NED: Gentlemen, gentlemen. Tonto, you wished to add
            something.

TONTO: Yes, Ned. I just wanted to say that the Senator
            places a great deal of importance on paper. The
            white people seem to think paper has some
            mysterious power to help them in the world. My
            people need no such writings. Words that speak
            truth sink deep into our hearts. The Indian never
            forgets them. On the other hand, if the white man
            loses his papers, he is helpless. Now, you tell us,
            Senator, that the paper the white Chief signed may
            no longer be valid in your courts. What about the
            court of the Great Mystery? What about *Wakan
            Tanka*?

NED: Senator, comment?

ANGELO: Ned, I haven't the foggiest idea what this Indian is
            talking about. I can only tell you that if the court
            accepts it, that's good enough for me.

~

From behind, I heard the Ranger chuckle as he watched
me writing up this last little scenario. "All right," he
said. "Since you seem so interested, let's talk about what
makes up a proper code of conduct."

I grabbed my notebook and waited while he finished
packing his stuff. Silhouetted against an extraordinary full
moon, I sat and watched him. He truly *was* a legendary
champion of justice. And it wasn't because he was well
known. Only a few knew who he really was. So, it wasn't
the fame. And it wasn't for his skill with six–gun, rope and
horse. Several times, he told me of others who were faster
on the draw and he swears that he's never seen anyone the
equal to Bill Cody for ropin' and ridin'. No, he was
legendary for doing the right thing by people. That's why he

was legendary.

The Ranger walked over from the other side of the cave and sat down next to what was left of the campfire.

"So," I began, "what *is* a proper code of conduct or ethics, as we call it?

He gave some careful thought to the question before he spoke. "For centuries, Jim, many great people have tried to come up with one clear thought. And I don't pretend to speak any more authoritatively than any of them. I can only tell you what it means to me."

I listened closely. As far as I was concerned, this was the crunch part of the whole thing, the reason we started talking in the first place, and I wanted to get it straight.

"Ethics," he said, "is not about what we say. It's about what we do. It's a code of conduct based on certain universal, moral duties and obligations that indicate how one *should* behave. It deals with the ability to distinguish good from evil, right from wrong and what is proper from what is improper."

"So, how are the eight values involved?

"Those eight values represent my core set of beliefs that guide and direct my choices and actions." He took his time and spoke carefully, allowing me to get it all down. "Values are the tools we use in making decisions. What we build, in the process, is our own character. And it is our character, Jim, that ultimately determines the course of our lives."

"But aren't freedom and happiness things of value, too?" I said.

"They can be, if you regard them as such. But the values I am referring to are those we have talked about: honesty, fairness, caring, respect, loyalty, tolerance, duty and courage. It is these core values that I find essential in guiding all my decisions."

"So, how does it all work? What do *you* consider when making an ethical decision?"

"Actually, there are three ideas I use to help guide my decisions. The first is this, 'what you do not want done to yourself, do not do to others.'"

"Isn't that something from the Bible?" I asked.

"Many teachings have similar doctrines, Jim. Actually, the teacher Confucius said this several hundred years earlier. It means that a person of character takes into account all those affected by his decision. If you would not like to be lied to, don't lie to another."

"Treat others the way you wish to be treated," I said.

"The problem with this idea alone, is that it does not take into consideration possible competing interests of those involved. It doesn't make clear the rights of an individual versus the rights of a community of people. An obligation to moral excellence requires us to consider others *besides* ourselves."

"What's the second idea?"

"'Act only that maxim through which you can at the same time will that it should become a universal law.'"

"Huh?"

He smiled. "According to the German philosopher Immanuel Kant, each of us has an absolute *duty* to do what is right; to do only those acts which you are willing to allow to become universal standards of behavior for everyone, including yourself."

"A universal standard. Well, that makes sense."

"However, the difficulty with this thought is that it offers no flexibility when a person is faced with a choice between two ethical values. Under Kant's code, one can never lie or deceive to achieve a 'greater good,' such as saving an innocent life from outlaws or sparing the feelings of a friend from an honest opinion."

"Good point. And the third idea?"

"The third idea puts forth that proper conduct is to be judged based on the outcome or consequences of the action. Looking at the possible outcome allows a person of character to evaluate competing ethical values in terms of likely results."

"Like my situation with John at the hospital," I said.

"Yes. Unfortunately, that's a good example of how this line of thinking, when used alone, can be misused through rationalization to establish an 'end–justifies–the–means' mentality. Such a position tends to place expediency over principle."

Now I was confused. "If all these ideas have shortcomings that can interfere with making the most ethical choices, what do you do?"

"I consider all three," he said. "Let's use the situation with your friend at the hospital, as an example.

"First, all decisions must take into account and reflect a concern for the interests and well–being of all people likely to be affected by your actions. Who were all the people likely to be affected in your decision?"

"Well, the hospital, John, maybe his wife, I guess his daughter, Becky."

"Were you not affected by your decision?"

"Yeah, I guess so."

"Second step: ethical decisions place the core values of honesty, fairness, caring, respect, loyalty, tolerance, and duty above all other values."

"Well now, this is where the problem starts," I said. "I wanted to be honest, but in all loyalty to my friend, John, and caring about his condition..." I paused to think this over. "Well, don't all those other values overrule being honest to the hospital?"

"Let's see by looking at the third step: whenever it becomes plainly necessary to oppose one core value in order to honor another, a person of character should do the thing that will produce the greatest balance of good in the long run. In this step, there are some things to look at closely.

"First, make sure you have *all* the facts. Be careful to separate facts from assumptions, or opinions and predictions that might lead to rationalizations. Examine the consequences of your potential action. Consider the long run versus the short run of your actions. Try to come up with at least three ethical options. How does your hospital dilemma look to you now?"

"Well, I never had a chance to think things through, entirely. I felt like I was on the spot for an answer. And I assumed that if I told them John didn't have insurance, he'd immediately be sent to another hospital. At least, that's what I heard happened to another guy."

"Did you have first–hand knowledge of John's condition to make that decision?" the Ranger asked.

"Well, no, not really. I was kind of caught up in the emotion of the moment. Thinking about it, now, I guess I should have waited to see what the doctors were planning on doing. Most emergency rooms stabilize a patient before they ever consider moving him to another hospital."

"What about the consequences of your actions?"

"Well, I never would have guessed the consequence concerning Becky, that she would lie to help a friend. I guess I could have gone into the next room to fill out the form, instead of lying in front of her."

"Was that your only alternative?" he asked.

It didn't take me long to see how I had justified myself into making a decision out of expediency. The more I started thinking about this the more I realized that there *were* other choices. "I could have explained the situation to the hospital. They probably would have taken John's best interest to heart before transferring him to another hospital, if they did that at all. I could have made more of an effort to reach John's wife and discuss the matter with her or held off until she arrived to make the decision herself."

(Lightbulb!) "I guess there were lots of things I could have done."

"Many times, Jim, we can trap ourselves into thinking that an action we choose as necessary, is right. Or that good intentions make it right."

(Uh, oh—he's giving me another one of those "square" look things again.)

"When making an important decision, look at the alternatives. Consider the impact on all people likely to be affected. Determine who is likely to be helped or harmed. Remember that your core values take precedence over all other values. If two core values conflict, choose that value that will result in the greatest good in the long run."

After carefully writing all this down, I studied on it for a moment. "You know something?"

"What's that?" he said.

"I think I am beginning to understand now. If I only had this information before, I would have done things much differently."

The Ranger returned to his packing.

(Lightbulb #2!) "Hey, didn't you tell me earlier that I might have a different perspective on things after we talked?"

He gave me another one of those "knowing" smile things.

"I really do and . . ." *(Lightbulb #3!)* "I even thought of what I should do next."

"What is that, Jim?"

"Well, several things, actually, but first off, I need to sit down with Becky, and her Mom and Dad and tell her what I did wrong. After all, responsible people better themselves when they see a chance to correct their mistakes." I said.

"You're learning," he smiled. "Never forget, Jim, that a person of strong moral character is *committed* to doing the right thing. Through his commitment, he understands and recognizes that we all rely on one another and that the cost of doing anything less upsets the balance of us all. The fact is, almost everything we have which is worth having we owe to the help, support or encouragement of others."

"But what about the person who must compromise their principles in order to feed their family?" I asked.

"I wonder if such a person would feel comfortable in explaining to his family exactly *why* he had to compromise? Sometimes, it takes a great deal of fortitude to follow the truth of your conscience. A person of character will, to the best of his ability, tell the truth to others because he, himself, wants the truth in return. All people want and need the truth. Because, by his example, he inevitably does something to either increase or decrease the amount of truthfulness in the world. That's why we must demonstrate these values in the most practical things everyday. And by our doing, be an example to others, especially to youngsters.

"What we need to do in character–training is not to attempt to create a lot of separate qualities such as honesty, fairness and caring as if they were unrelated tricks taught to a dog. Rather, to see the value of all these qualities as the expression of a single spirit.

"As teachers we are obligated to awaken this spirit within others, to strengthen it where it needs strengthening, to encourage it, so that it may grow and to render it as a responsible, intelligent resource that we can all share and trust in."

I looked at my watch. It was almost one–thirty in the morning. The masked man smiled as he looked over at Tonto who was lightly snoring. He nodded a good night and moved back into the cave.

Crawling into my sleeping bag, I laid back looking up at the sky.

~

NED: We have only just begun to get into a lively discussion when our time has run out. Lone Ranger would you consider coming back next week to continue the discussion? Would you like that, Tonto? (*Tonto leans closer to the Ranger to discuss.*)

TONTO: Thanks, Ned, but the Ranger and I will have to take a pass on that.

RANGER: (*chuckles*) Tonto is kidding. Of course, Ned, we would be happy to come back, schedule permitting, to continue the discussion.

NED: My thanks to Senator Angelo, the Lone Ranger and Tonto... and to Jim, the source of tonight's moral dialog. That's our report for tonight. I'm Ned Newsman and this has been... Nightbeat.

~

The next morning I watched as they both packed up the rest of their gear. Then the Lone Ranger walked over to me, removed his glove and extended his hand. "So long, Jim."

"So long," I said, shaking his hand firmly. "I got quite a lot out of our campfire chats."

"So have I."

"Here," I said, handing him a slip of paper.

"What's this?"

"Just an idea on updating that 'signature' line of yours. Try it out, if you're interested."

"Thanks, Jim," he said as he tucked it into his shirt pocket.

"How can I ever thank you for everything?"

"You can thank me by showing others what it means to live by a code of conduct that helps, supports and encourages all of us. Oliver Wendell Holmes said that to do right was to be 'faithful to the light within.' If you strive to do that, you cannot go wrong." Then, he turned and leaped onto Silver.

Tonto extended his hand. "You can thank me with that Watchman of yours, Jim."

"Do you really have time? I mean, out on the trail and all?"

"Truth is," he said leaning closer. "I really miss watching *Dr. Quinn, Medicine Woman*."

"Have you got any final words for me?"

He thought for a moment. "Always speak straight, Jim, so that your words may go as sunlight into the hearts of others."

I looked him in the eyes as I handed him the TV. "Will we ever meet again?"

He mounted Scout in one swift move. "Good friends will *always* meet again, somewhere."

"Adios, Jim," the Lone Ranger smiled.

"Take care, *Kemo Sabay*," Tonto added.

"Me?" I said, pointing to myself.

The Indian nodded back with a smile.

Then the white horse called Silver and the paint horse Tonto called Scout, whirled and raced away. I stood and watched them disappear into the distance... wondering. Then, as if in response to my thought, the Lone Ranger's voice carried through the night, as he shouted in the distance. "Hi–Yo Silver, Away–y–y–y!"

EPISODE TWELVE

The Benediction

"So," she said, crisply. "Where's the epiphany?"

"Epipha–what?"

"The revelation, brilliant insight. You know... where's the beef?"

I cradled the phone under my left ear as I hastily scribbled notes.

"You're asking the reader to wade through a lot before you get to the punchline and the punchlines themselves don't quite stand up to the wait..."

As she droned on, it was all beginning to blend together with the stack of rejection letters staring back at me on the corner of my desk.

"After careful consideration, I'm afraid that it's not something I could get behind... generate enough enthusiasm for... too heavy on horse–opera, too light on insights, too cute, longwinded. Besides, I didn't find the wisdom of the Lone Ranger to be all that illuminating."

I sat silently staring at the computer screen, my head filled with nothing but questions and doubt. What do I do? How do I convince them of the value of his message?......... what would the Lone Ranger do?

"...don't give up."

I glanced over my shoulder and there he was. He sat down next to my desk, pulled some reading glasses from his shirt pocket and began looking at the computer screen. "Nice job, Jim." He scrolled up. "Looks like you've been quite faithful to the things we discussed." He chuckled when he came to one line. "I like your humor, too. But why stop here?"

"I'm not stopping. I'm stuck!" I said, pointing to the letters. How am I supposed to get your message out to people if everyone tells me 'no'?"

"You'll find a way," he said walking around the room noticing the accumulation of notes, half open books, boxes and CD's piled all over. "I'm beginning to see why you travel with so many things on the trail." Then he turned to leave. "I've got to go."

"Wait. What about some help?"

"With what?"

"How am I going to get a publisher interested in this stuff? How do I get them to believe?"

He turned around slowly. "What do *you* believe, Jim?"

"What do *I* believe?" I said.

I thought about it for a moment longer then looked at him squarely. "I believe in being *honest*; in telling the truth as I know it. I believe that being truthful builds trust with others and that we all want and need that in our lives.

"I believe in *fairness* and the importance of being open, reasonable and equitable with others in all matters.

"I believe in being *caring* and compassionate of others; that seeing ourselves in another creates an awareness and an understanding that we are all here to help, support and encourage one another.

"I believe it's important to *respect* all things: man,

woman, animal and earth; that genuine respect not only means being courteous and polite but respecting the rights and decisions of others as well.

"I believe that *loyalty* is the most important test of character; that to be loyal means being faithful to commitments and obligations, but most importantly, to principle.

"I believe in demonstrating *tolerance* toward others; in having a fair and open–minded attitude toward anyone who may be different.

"I believe in doing your *duty*; in seeing what needs to be done and doing it; in being answerable for my actions and correcting any mistakes I may make because responsible people pull together and make all they do worthy of pride.

"I believe in the *moral courage* necessary to stand up for what I believe and overcoming... *(uh, oh, there's that lightbulb, again)*... any obstacles or compelling forces that stand in the way of what should be done." I smiled at him. "I guess this publishing issue is one of those 'obstacle' things, huh?"

"You'll find a way," he smiled.

I made a quick note of this on my computer. When I turned around he had disappeared. "Wait... what do you mean, I'll find a way?" I opened the door and moved down the hall in the darkness. But it was too late. He was gone.

"..........you found me, didn't you?"

He's back!

"Tonto told me of a movie he once saw. In this story, a young farmer was convinced he had to plow under a portion of his crop to build a baseball field. In spite of many obstacles, he found a way to build that field."

"Yes," I said, "but he had a voice telling him what to do."

"But the voice didn't tell him *how* to do it. I've given you everything I believe in; everything I stand for. People *will* listen, Jim." He started to leave, again.

"Look," I said, "in that movie, Kevin Costner didn't do it by himself. He had James Earl Jones to help him."

"...you'll find a way.."

Standing in the darkness of the living room, I flipped on a light and the room was empty. "All right, now just HOLD IT, masked man!"

.........No answer.

"I need a little more help than that."

..............No answer.

"Just tell me WHO I should send it to. How about that?"

..................No answer.

"I'M NOT KEVIN COSTNER!"

"Of course you're not Kevin Costner. You're some doofas shouting at three o'clock in the morning!"

I turned to find my wife standing in the hallway staring at me.

"Go back to bed." I opened the slider and walked out onto the balcony. I looked out over the empty stretch of desert shimmering under a full moon. Just then, I glimpsed a tall figure dressed in white walking into the distance. He turned and waved to me. I waved back.

"Who are you waving to?"

"No one... just the Lone Ranger."

"Honey, I know this book thing is important to you but get a grip... it's just a story."

I continued to watch as the masked man disappeared behind some mesquite. "Silver must be on the other side of that clump o' trees."

She pretended to play along. "So, what's he doing here,

checking out his percentage of the royalties?"

"Percentage? You mean, like a reward or somethin'?" I laughed. "Wouldn't be of much use to him." Just then, I caught sight of him astride that magnificent, snow white stallion as they headed out toward the horizon. "You see, honey, his job is seeing that justice is done, that ALL people are treated fair and square, and that the West continues to grow and prosper on the same principles that founded this country of ours. That's his reward."

I glanced back inside. She had fallen asleep on the couch. I stared out into the night. "Yup, he's ridin' out now, to join Tonto, headin' for somewhere else, where there's trouble... where justice is needed." I turned to go back inside. "I wonder if... naaaa!"

That's when I heard a hearty cry ring out into the night, "Hi–Yo Silver...

...the Ranger has left the building!"

THE LONE RANGER'S CODE OF THE WEST

The Lone Ranger is **Honest**–
>   Honesty is being truthful, sincere and straightforward.

The Lone Ranger is **Fair**–
>   Fairness is being open–minded and committed to the
>   equitable treatment of all.

The Lone Ranger is **Caring**–
>   Caring is showing kindness, generosity and
>   compassion toward others.

The Lone Ranger is **Respectful**–
>   Respect means not taking advantage of others as
>   well as being polite and courteous.

The Lone Ranger is **Loyal**–
>   Loyalty means a faithfulness to commitments and
>   obligations to family, friends, community
>   and country but most importantly, to principle.

The Lone Ranger is **Tolerant**–
>   Tolerance is the ability to accept differences and not
>   judge people harshly *because* they are different.

The Lone Ranger does his **Duty**–
>   Doing your duty means being responsible and
>   accountable
>   for your actions. It means earnest thought before action.

The Lone Ranger is **Morally Courageous**–
>   Moral courage is the inner strength to overcome obstacles
>   or compelling forces to do what *should* be done, no matter
>   the personal consequences.

WHAT WOULD THE LONE RANGER DO?
(Character–Based Decision Making†)

1. The Lone Ranger considers the interests and well–being of
   all likely to be affected by his actions.
2. He makes decisions characterized by the core ethical
   values of honesty, fairness, caring, respect, loyalty,
   tolerance, duty and the moral courage to do what needs to
   be done.
3. If it is clearly necessary to choose one ethical value over
   another, the Lone Ranger will do the thing that he
   sincerely believes to be best for society in the long run.

†Adapted and used with permission from the Josephson Institute.

ABOUT THE AUTHOR

Jim Lichtman is an ethics specialist whose experience has taken him from television post–production to creating and writing successful advertising.

In 1990 Mr. Lichtman and management specialist Dr. James Melton cowrote a training series designed to enhance individual responsibility, communication and team performance. The series has been adopted into the business curriculum of corporations and higher–education institutions all over the world.

A graduate of the Josephson Institute of Ethics, Mr. Lichtman's seminar, "Values, Ethics and The Lone Ranger" is gaining widespread popularity for its uniquely entertaining and pragmatic approach to ethics.

When not working, Jim can usually be found mountain–biking long forgotten back trails around Palm Desert, California. *(But you'll never get him to reveal the location of Red Rock Canyon. So, don't even Think about it.)*